"*You* don't frighten m̶... " vowed in an even softer v̶...

Pushing himself up on one elbow, he stared down at her for an endless moment, searching her face. Then muttering a low oath, he lowered his head to capture her mouth possessively.

A feeling of triumph filled Skye. She had *finally* broken through his resistance. His kiss was hard and compelling, his mouth hot and tasting of need. For all that he strove to bury his emotions, Hawkhurst was the most passionate man she knew. His raw intensity set her senses whirling. She strained toward him, her breasts seeking closer contact with his naked chest.

In response, he cradled her face with his hands to give his tongue better access and kissed her deeply, ravenously, as if he couldn't get enough of her taste. At his savage-tender assault, desire flooded Skye in a mad rush . . . but then suddenly he drew back and dragged in a shuddering breath.

Disappointment surged through her, but only fleetingly. Grasping the hem of her shift, Hawkhurst pulled the garment over her head, practically ripping it in his urgency.

She had riled the beast enough, apparently. Or perhaps he was merely reclaiming control, Skye conceded. Perhaps he was tired of letting her hold the upper hand and this was his means of reprisal for prodding and teasing him.

If so, it was extremely effective. At his dangerous look, the pulsing quickened between her legs.

"You are wrong, darling," he said silkily. "You haven't begun to ache yet."

By Nicole Jordan

Legendary Lovers
Princess Charming
Lover Be Mine
Secrets of Seduction

The Courtship Wars
To Pleasure a Lady
To Bed a Beauty
To Seduce a Bride
To Romance a Charming Rogue
To Tame a Dangerous Lord
To Desire a Wicked Duke

Paradise Series
Master of Temptation
Lord of Seduction
Wicked Fantasy
Fever Dreams

Notorious Series
The Seduction
The Passion
Desire
Ecstasy
The Prince of Pleasure

Other Novels
The Lover
The Warrior
Touch Me with Fire

Secrets of Seduction

A Legendary Lovers Novel

NICOLE JORDAN

BALLANTINE BOOKS • NEW YORK

Secrets of Seduction is a work of fiction. Names, characters, places, and incidents are the products of the author's imagination or are used fictitiously. Any resemblance to actual events, locales, or persons, living or dead, is entirely coincidental.

A Ballantine Books Mass Market Original

Copyright © 2014 by Anne Bushyhead
Excerpt from *The Art of Taming a Rake* by Nicole Jordan copyright © 2014 by Anne Bushyhead

Published in the United States by Ballantine Books, an imprint of Random House, a division of Random House LLC, a Penguin Random House Company, New York.

BALLANTINE and the HOUSE colophon are registered trademarks of Random House LLC.

This book contains an excerpt from the forthcoming book *The Art of Taming a Rake* by Nicole Jordan. This excerpt has been set for this edition only and may not reflect the final content of the forthcoming edition.

ISBN 978-0-345-52531-4
eBook ISBN 978-0-345-52532-1

Cover design: Lynn Andreozzi
Cover illustration: Alan Ayers

Printed in the United States of America

www.ballantinebooks.com

9 8 7 6 5 4 3 2 1

Ballantine Books mass market edition: May 2014

For Jay, for always.

Secrets of
Seduction

Chapter One

East Sussex, England, September 1816

She had never before pursued a man, but in matters of the heart, sometimes a lady needed to take fate into her own hands.

In the gathering dusk, Lady Skye Wilde peered through her carriage window at the hulking mansion shrouded in fog and drizzling rain. Built two centuries before, Hawkhurst Castle was an enormous edifice of gold-hued stone, complete with turrets. Once magnificent, it looked forsaken now, although faint lights shone in a lower-story window, giving Skye hope that her mission would not be in vain.

The Earl of Hawkhurst needed a bride, and she intended to interview for the position.

In truth, she'd been plotting this moment all summer long, ever since learning of Lord Hawkhurst's intention to marry again. Now that the moment was at hand, an army of butterflies was waging battle in her stomach.

Skye was keenly aware her entire future could depend on this first meeting.

Before she lost her nerve, she pulled her cloak hood over her fair hair and stepped down from her carriage into the rain. No doubt it was idiotic to purposely get caught in a storm, yet the brewing tempest played well into her scheme to plant herself on the earl's front doorstep. A downpour increased the odds that he would take pity on her and provide her shelter, perhaps even allow her to stay the night.

An ominous flash of lightning in the near distance warned Skye that she had little time before the worst weather hit. Even so, she hesitated to approach the sweeping stone steps that led up to the massive front door.

She had encountered the earl only once, yet Hawkhurst—known as Hawk to his intimates—was the kind of man no woman ever forgot . . . or any girl, either. When she was thirteen, she'd fallen head over heels for him and had been heartbroken to learn he was already wed. Then, shortly afterward, he'd suffered the most terrible of tragedies, losing his beloved wife and very young son to a fire here at his family seat.

From her vantage point, Skye couldn't see the charred remains of the burned rooms. The fire must have started in another wing—

A second bolt of lightning, this one much closer, was followed swiftly by a crash of thunder that startled the already fractious carriage horses. Glancing behind her, Skye called out an order to her coachman to drive the team around to the stables and seek refuge.

"My lady, I dislike leaving you here alone!" he shouted back over the growing bluster of wind and rain.

She appreciated the concern of her loyal servants—two grooms and a coachman—who were more like bodyguards than lackeys. Her brother Quinn insisted they accompany her for protection on her travels, even though she was now three-and-twenty. Skye usually suffered her strapping attendants with good grace, since they allowed her a measure of independence that most unattached young ladies lacked. But now they were decidedly in the way.

"I won't come to harm!" Skye insisted. "Lord Hawkhurst is a close friend of my aunt. He will not turn me away in a storm."

At least I trust not, she added to herself. Hawkhurst was known as a great lover of horses and a master horseman. In all likelihood, he would not evict frightened animals from his estate, even if he might want to refuse their human owners.

"If you are certain, my lady—"

Another crack of thunder cut off his sentence.

"Yes, go quickly please, Josiah!"

Just then the heavens opened up, and the drizzle became a torrent of driving rain.

The two grooms hastily climbed onto their rear perch, and the carriage drove off. Skye sprinted for the stone staircase and wondered if she had underestimated the storm's danger. Her cloak hood barely protected her face as big, stinging drops pelted her tender skin. Quelling a gasp at the cold impact, she ran almost blindly up the steps. By the time she reached the top landing, she was thoroughly drenched.

Between the gloom and the buffeting rain, she could

barely make out that the knocker had been removed from the door. She rapped with her knuckles for several long minutes, then pounded with the heel of her hand.

No one answered.

Although half-expecting the door to be locked, she tried admitting herself. The knob turned freely, so she pushed open the door. An instant later it abruptly swung wide, pulling her forward. Skye stumbled over the threshold and would have pitched face-first onto the floor if not for a pair of strong arms saving her.

Skye did gasp then. Held against a broad chest and a very male body, she looked up, her heart pounding. In the enormous entrance hall, the flame of a single wall sconce cast flickering shadows over her savior's visage.

It was the lord of the manor himself, Morgan Blake, the sixth Earl of Hawkhurst.

Skye caught her breath anew at his stunning masculine beauty: High forehead, chiseled cheekbones, aristocratic nose, sensual lips. And his most striking features: winged black brows above dark-fringed, storm-gray eyes.

He looked more rugged than she remembered, perhaps because of his tousled, overlong raven hair and the stubble roughening his strong jaw. His face held more character as well, and lines of pain that hadn't been present before. Of course, he was ten years older now, and at four-and-thirty he had seen far more of the dark side of life.

Those penetrating eyes still had the same spellbinding effect on her, however. When her gaze locked with his, heat streaked through Skye, stark and raw, like a bolt of lightning.

He might have felt the same electric flash of fire, for he reached up with one hand and pushed back the hood of her cloak to reveal her pale gold hair. Frowning, he touched her face, as if wondering if she were real.

It was a moment of enchantment she could never have anticipated.

Her heart still in her throat, Skye parted her lips but remained mute as she returned his searching stare. Then Lord Hawkhurst seemed to realize he was holding her. Appearing reluctant to let her go, he helped right her balance and released her.

Disappointment swamped Skye. Being held in his arms was as breathtaking as she'd dreamed it would be, and she had not wanted his embrace to end. This intimate manner of meeting was unplanned but much better than she could have hoped for . . . until she suddenly spied the weapon in his other hand.

He wielded a deadly looking dagger and seemed prepared to use it on her.

Skye swallowed hard before realizing his weapon was the sort of knife used for paring quill pens.

"My l-lord," she managed to say with relative calm. "You needn't defend yourself from me. I am not a thief or assassin. Had I been, I would not have knocked on your front door."

"If not a thief, then who are you?" he asked in a voice that was commanding and pleasantly deep.

"I am Skye Wilde, the niece of your close friend Lady Isabella Wilde."

His brows drew together sharply. "Did Bella send you here?"

"Yes . . . I mean, no."

"Which is it?" He sounded impatient.

"Actually, she did not send me. I came on my own, all the way from London—" Skye stopped herself. When she was nervous, she became breathless and spoke too rapidly. "Forgive me, my lord. I chatter on when dangerous gentlemen glare at me and threaten me with knives."

His expression softened a measure as he lowered the blade to his side. "Are you daft, setting out in a storm?"

She hid a smile at his accusation, since she'd just been wondering the same thing. "When I left home this afternoon, it was not storming. And I don't believe I am daft, merely desperate. May I please come in before you ring a peal over my head? Afterward you may scold me as much as you like."

Hawkhurst made a soft sound of disapproval in his throat, something like a growl, but stepped back to allow her entrance. As she moved past him, he glanced out at the darkening courtyard below, which was nearly obscured by rain. "Where is your carriage?"

"I took the liberty of sending it around to your stables. My horses and grooms needed shelter. I felt certain you would want my horses safe. Perhaps you should shut the door," Skye added sweetly. "Rain is gusting in and flooding your marble floor."

He stared at her again for a moment, as if not crediting her boldness. Then, curtly acting on her suggestion, he closed the door and blocked out the storm before turning to face her.

The hall was quieter now, although still echoing dully from sheets of rain lashing the manor.

Skye smiled up at Lord Hawkhurst. "I do beg your pardon, my lord. We got off on the wrong foot. May we start afresh? I am Lady Skye Wilde, and I am happy to meet you at last. Have you not heard of me?"

"Yes, I have heard of you." He did not look pleased by the fact.

"I thought Aunt Bella might have mentioned me. You and I are practically family."

He gave her another frowning glance, this one rife with skepticism. "How did you arrive at that conclusion?"

"Well . . . we are not related by blood, but my aunt has known you for ten years. You and she are such good friends, I feel as if I know you myself. And you are acquainted with my elder brother, Quinn Wilde, the Earl of Traherne. I was never officially introduced to you, but I saw you once a long time ago, when you and your wife attended a ball at our home, Tallis Court in Kent. I was the girl hanging over the banister, watching the dancers below."

Even in the dim light, she could see recognition dawn in Hawkhurst's eyes.

"I am flattered that you remember me," Skye said honestly. "Except for a brief moment, you paid no attention to me that evening."

"I feared you might be in need of rescue."

Skye felt her cheeks warm at the reminder. She'd been watching the glittering company with her cousin Katharine from the gallery above the ballroom. When the devastatingly handsome Lord Hawkhurst had looked up at her and smiled, her heart had instantly melted. Stricken with awe, she'd nearly tumbled over the railing. The earl had leapt closer, prepared to catch her and break her fall if necessary. Fortunately—or unfortunately, Skye had thought at the time—her cousin's quick action in grasping her skirts had saved her from disaster.

Uncomfortable awareness flooded Skye. This was twice now that she had almost fallen at his feet. How embarrassing to appear so awkward with a nobleman she wanted earnestly to impress.

"I am not usually so clumsy, I promise you."

He did not seem interested in prolonging their discussion. "What brings you here in the midst of a storm, Lady Skye?"

His abruptness was rather unmannerly, but given her unexpected arrival, she could forgive him.

"My aunt wrote me a letter of introduction and explained my purpose to you. . . ." Fishing in her reticule, Skye pulled out a folded letter that was a bit worse for wear and presented it to him. "Please, will you read this?"

Hawkhurst broke the wax seal but barely glanced at the contents, perhaps because it was difficult to read in the scant light. When he made to move closer to the wall sconce, Skye spoke up. "Is there a fire where I may warm myself?"

He hesitated before finally replying. "There is one in my study. Follow me."

When he strode off across the entrance hall, she hurried to keep up with him and found herself eying his tall, athletic form with admiration. He was dressed informally—white linen shirt, buff breeches, and riding boots—and the way his clothing clung to his broad shoulders, lean hips, well-formed buttocks, and muscular thighs emphasized his stark masculinity. It was brazen to admit, Skye knew, but the intense physical attraction she felt for Hawkhurst now was much less pure than when she was a mere girl.

She was also brazen to call at his nearly deserted country estate when no one suitable was present to act as chaperone. Yet to attain her heart's desire, she needed to be bold and daring. She would not let the risk of scandal deter her. Courting scandal in their amorous affairs was a Wilde family legacy, and she was a Wilde, through and through.

When they entered a dark corridor, Skye glanced inside the rooms they passed. The fact that the elegant manor was damp and musty from disuse was no wonder, considering that it had been shut up for more than ten years. But the furniture was still shrouded in holland covers.

"I expected you to have servants to answer your front door," she commented to the earl's back.

"The elderly man who acts as caretaker is hard of hearing and didn't heed your pounding."

"But I understood you arrived here a full week ago. I thought by now you would have tried to set the castle to rights."

Only after another pause did he answer her probing remark. "I haven't yet arranged for a full-time staff. Some women from the village came today to begin cleaning, but with the storm approaching, I sent them home before it grew too dark."

"That was kind of you."

Hawkhurst made another low sound of dismissal in his throat and kept walking.

"I am grateful that you opened your door to me," Skye pressed, "although you frightened me out of my wits, brandishing that knife at my throat."

"You did not look particularly frightened."

She had not been—but then she knew the sort of man she was dealing with. "I suppose you have an excuse for your extreme reaction. You can't help yourself. You were trained to be suspicious. You have been a spy for the Foreign Office for many years. You joined while still attending university, did you not?"

Hawkhurst halted in his tracks and glanced back at her. "Who told you that?"

"My aunt, of course. She also warned me that you were a determined recluse. But you could be a trifle more welcoming, for her sake if nothing else."

His eyebrow shot up at her impertinence. Hawkhurst regarded her for several more heartbeats, obviously reassessing her.

He must finally have realized that she was attempting to lighten the mood, for her complaint won her the barest hint of a smile. "You break into my home and then take *me* to task?"

"I did not *break* in," she pointed out genially. "You admitted me."

"Much to my regret."

Just then the darkness in the corridor was broken by another lightning flash. When he continued on his way, Skye followed in his footsteps.

Upon arriving at his study, he allowed her to precede him. To her relief, this room at least looked habitable. A fire was crackling in the hearth and a low-burning lamp rested on a massive desk.

"You may sit there by the fire," he said, pointing to a leather wing chair that was angled before the hearth.

His invitation seemed slightly grudging, but Skye did not take offense. "Do you mind if I remove my cloak first? I am chilled to the bone." Her discomfort was not a lie. Her cloak was soaked through and her gown was damp at the bodice and sodden at the hem.

Hawkhurst murmured something under his breath that sounded much like, "It serves you right," but he stepped closer to aid her.

When he reached out to lift the cloak from her shoulders, Skye's own breath suddenly turned ragged at his close proximity. After she handed over the garment, revealing an elegantly tailored traveling dress of forest green kerseymere beneath, his gaze dropped to her breasts.

Instinctively she went still as his marvelous eyes traveled over her body in dispassionate appraisal. She was well aware of her physical attributes and that her feminine countenance and figure appealed to most men. Usually she had suitors falling at *her* feet, declaring themselves in love with her. Yet she had no clue what Hawkhurst was thinking or feeling.

There was no question about her body's reaction to *him,* however. She was not sexually experienced, but the intense fascination she felt for him was most certainly sexual, her desire that of a grown woman, not merely the love-struck awe of a young girl. But what he did to her insides was more remarkable. His mere nearness filled her with fluttery excitement and sweet yearning—a response she had never felt with any man but him.

She had no difficulty picturing Hawkhurst as her husband now, just as she'd done numerous times in her romantic dreams these past few months. If he were her husband, though, she could have removed her gown instead of standing there shivering in her clammy one. If he were her husband, she could have undressed down to her shift and moved into his arms. Indeed, she could have bared her entire chilled body to him and shared his warmth. . . .

The alluring image dissolved when he took her dripping cloak and spread it near the hearth to dry, then went to his desk without another word.

As she removed her wet gloves, Skye could tell Hawkhurst was clearly displeased to have her in his home. She ought to be intimidated by his surly manner; any normal young lady would be. But few gentlemen had the power to shake her, perhaps because she was accustomed to handling the strong-willed men in her family.

She usually was able to bend them to her own will with sweet reason. She suspected in this case, though, it would take a good deal more than reason to sway the earl. Indeed, the sheer size of her task daunted her. But if Lord Hawkhurst was looking for a wife, it might as well be her, Skye judged. At the very least, she wanted to see if they were a compatible match. And regardless of her romantic hopes, she needed a hero just now, and he was a genuine hero.

Skye drew a steadying breath to bolster her courage. She had contrived to land on his doorstep, and now she had to capitalize on the opportunity she had created for herself.

"Will you please read my aunt's letter, my lord?" she asked.

Obligingly, he turned up the flame on the desk lamp, then held the letter nearer the light. It was then that Skye really saw the burn scars marring the back of his hands.

A sudden lump formed in her throat. Hawkhurst was still the most beautiful man she had ever seen, but also the most deeply scarred. Not just on the outside but on the inside, if her information was correct. After all, he had crawled through fire to save his wife and young son, futilely as it happened. With his life shattered, he'd exiled himself to a distant Mediterranean island and spent the past decade engaged in dangerous deeds, not caring whether he lived or died.

Skye's heart went out to him. Perhaps that organ was too tender, but as the youngest Wilde cousin of the current generation, she was known for being the sensitive one, in addition to being the most mischievous.

Mentally chiding herself for staring at the earl's scarred hands, she busied herself spreading her gloves on the hearth. Then she settled into the wing chair and began to remove the pins from her chignon, since her damp hair would dry more quickly if down.

For a short while as he read, the silence in the study was broken only by rain spitting against the windowpanes and the occasional snap of a log in the hearth fire.

When Hawkhurst absently reached for a snifter that was almost empty, Skye noticed the crystal decanter half-filled with what appeared to be brandy. Evidently he had been drinking, which partially explained his morose mood.

It was not surprising that he would be sitting alone here and brooding. She would have brooded also if she'd had to face the ghosts of her dead family, as he doubtless had upon his arrival at the castle after a decade of being absent.

In fact, it was his castle that had made Skye wonder if the earl might be her ideal match. According to her cousin Kate's matchmaking theory, the five Wilde cousins—Ashton, Quinn, Jack, Katharine, and Skye—could find true love by mirroring legendary lovers in history and literature.

Skye hoped that her romance would follow a French fairy tale written nearly a century ago, where a beautiful young lady had been delivered to a beast whose lair was a palace.

Of course, Lord Hawkhurst was not a beast in the literal sense, but a scarred recluse somewhat fit the role. And this gloomy mansion could be a beast's lair, Skye thought with a shiver.

Just then Hawkhurst looked up from the letter. His gaze narrowed on her as she combed her fingers through her tangled tresses. Then he said rather brusquely, "Lady Isabella's missive falls far short of the explanation you promised. She says only that you have a request to make of me. So what do you want, Lady Skye?"

Skye hesitated, knowing she had to choose her words carefully. Naturally she could not tell him her true reason for being there for fear he would think she was stalking him. Her purpose had to remain her secret for now. Therefore, she would employ an entirely different excuse to ensure her chance to pursue the earl.

"I need you to find someone for me."

"Who?"

"My uncle's long lost love."

Hawkhurst appeared dubious. "Why the devil do you think I could help?"

"Because you are an expert at solving puzzles and finding missing people. Two years ago when Lady

Isabella was abducted by a Berber sheikh and carried off to the mountains near Algiers, you found her and rescued her, to her immense gratitude."

When the earl was silent, Skye offered absently, "I will pay very generously."

That was obviously the wrong approach, for he shook his head. "My services are not for hire."

"Then do it as a favor for my aunt."

That argument did not appear to sway him, either.

At his reticence, Skye gave a soft huff of exasperation. "You are a hero, Lord Hawkhurst. You should want to help me."

Her claim brought a flash of genuine amusement to his features. "I am no hero."

"You are indeed. And you belong to a secret league of heroes called the Guardians of the Sword. In fact, you are the league's most renowned member."

His expression suddenly became enigmatic, but his tone revealed his displeasure that so much had been disclosed about him. "I expected more discretion from Bella."

"You ought not blame her. I was quite persistent."

That was certainly true. She had quizzed her aunt at great length about every facet of the earl's past. Isabella had a long relationship with the Guardians, having first encountered them many years ago through her first husband, a Spanish nobleman. And after knowing Hawkhurst for the past ten years, she thought of herself much as an older sister to him and yearned for his happiness.

"But don't fear," Skye added quickly. "She told me little more than the name of your alliance of spies and that it exists as a clandestine branch of the British Foreign Office. I know, however, that you have a long list of commendable qualities. You are honorable, supremely clever, and a leader of men. Before the tragedy struck, you were a devoted husband and father. And since then, you have risked your life countless times over and saved numerous lives."

His answer was gruff, almost harsh. "That still does not make me suitable for your task."

Skye eyed Hawkhurst in frustration. She was not about to admit failure, not when she felt such great urgency to act. His spy career might still be shrouded in secrecy, but her aunt had been completely frank about his unromantic affairs. Hawkhurst soon intended to wed the great-niece of his superior and mentor—a cold marriage of convenience strictly for political purposes.

He had not begun his courtship yet; he was merely readying his house to receive a new bride. But given his plans, Skye had little time to discover if she and Hawkhurst were a match and, if so, to somehow prevent his betrothal and marriage to another woman.

She was never one to turn away from a challenge, though.

Tamping down her frustration, she offered the earl her most winning smile. "Just hear me out, my lord. *Please*. It is the least you can do, given your friendship with my aunt."

Leaning back in his chair, he folded his arms over his chest. "Very well. You have five minutes."

Chapter Two

Waiting for her response, Hawk watched Lady Skye, unwillingly entranced. Even wet and bedraggled, she was lovely. Her face was fine-boned and classical; her hair a shade of champagne silk; her wide eyes the vivid blue of a cloudless summer's day, a reflection of her uncommon name.

Contrarily, she didn't reply to his decree at once, merely leaned closer to the hearth to dry her damp tresses. The firelight behind her rimmed her ivory profile and shimmered through the curtain of her hair as she used her fingers like a comb.

Her movements were unconsciously sensual and made Hawk swear an oath under his breath. Granted, he'd gone too long without female companionship to satisfy his carnal needs, but why this particular female roused such a powerful ache in him, he couldn't say.

The impact had begun the moment he opened his front door to her. Lady Skye caught him completely off guard, a feat even his worst foes rarely managed. And when she'd fallen into his arms, his baser instincts had taken control, instantly hardening his loins.

It was his body's unwanted reaction, in addition to learning her identity, that had made his tone gruffer than normal.

She was still affecting him painfully now. If he were to conjure up a sexual fantasy, Lady Skye Wilde would fit the role exquisitely: lithe figure, ripe breasts, feminine grace, enticing warmth. Not overly tall, she looked somewhat delicate, like fine crystal, but he suspected her fragility was an illusion.

She was definitely a novelty, though, intruding into his bleak, nearly deserted house at this late hour and insisting he give her a hearing. Bold, yet charming as the devil . . . or a siren. For a brief moment he'd even wondered if she was part of an enemy scheme. In his profession, it wasn't unusual to employ beautiful sirens to gain vital secrets.

Yet he did recall encountering Lady Skye a decade before. The enchanting girl was clearly a grown woman now, with her damp gown molding her elegant curves. She smelled of fresh rain and roses, a scent that wreaked havoc on his senses. And that smile of hers . . . That smile could slay dragons—or render a man witless.

Doubtless he was suffering the effects of too much brandy, but this was still the most aroused he'd been in years.

Hawk stirred uncomfortably in his desk chair, knowing he damn well needed to hold his lust in check. For one thing, Lady Skye was Isabella's niece by marriage. For another, she was an unaccompanied female in his household. No honorable man would take advantage of her vulnerability, even if she *had* willfully orchestrated this compromising situation herself.

He had best be rid of her, just as soon as he heard the cursory details of her proposition—which admittedly had surprised him as much as her unexpected arrival.

Hawk shook his head to reduce the alcoholic haze and repeated his warning of a time limit, prodding her to get on with her explanation.

"I am not certain five minutes will be enough," she replied easily. "It is a long story."

"Then you had best begin."

She did not seem at all intimidated by his abrupt manner. Indeed, just the opposite; her blue gaze seemed understanding and sympathetic as she launched into her tale.

"You may know that Isabella's late third husband, Lord Henry Wilde, was the younger brother of my uncle Lord Cornelius."

Hawk nodded, aware that the vivacious, half-Spanish widow had wed three times, the last to a British nobleman's son. Bella was now in her midforties, but her beauty and charm were still turning male heads. "Go on."

"Well, Lord Cornelius is only a distant relation to my branch of the Wilde family, but my brother Quinn and I think of him as our true uncle. He took over our legal guardianship when I was ten, along with that of my three Wilde cousins after all our parents perished when their ship sank at sea."

Somewhat surprisingly to Hawk, she quickly glossed over her loss to focus on her uncle.

"At the time, Uncle Cornelius was a literary scholar of some note but gave up his bookish life to devote himself to raising five unruly children. He is over sixty now and a dedicated bachelor. Even though he is the dearest man imaginable, I have always thought him rather dull and a Wilde only by name. For generations our family earned a reputation for our passionate romances, but Uncle never followed suit—or so I thought until last spring, when I was helping to organize his library. I found a packet of letters hidden there. They were written some twenty-five years ago—his correspondence with a young lady from a nearby district. Imagine my surprise to discover that my staid, elderly uncle had experienced a tragic love affair when he was a young man."

Lady Skye glanced at Hawk expectantly. No doubt she was counting on his natural curiosity to win her more time. When he gave her no encouragement, she went on doggedly.

"When I questioned Uncle about his thwarted romance, he admitted that his true love had died. Apparently, she'd been forced into an unhappy marriage to a baron, and after giving birth to a daughter, she became so despondent, she flung herself into a river and drowned. Her death left Uncle Cornelius heartbroken and is the reason he never married. Except that . . . only recently I learned she didn't die after all. In fact, I was able to obtain proof that her drowning was a ruse."

"I suppose you mean to tell me what happened to her," Hawk said without enthusiasm.

Lady Skye smiled a bit triumphantly for dragging a response from him. "I admit I was so intrigued by the letters that I decided to investigate my uncle's secret past further. His correspondence held several clues. The midwife who delivered the baby daughter also served as the go-between for Uncle Cornelius and the lady, and her name was mentioned frequently when arranging their rendezvous. The letters were franked from a village near Beauvoir, the family seat of the Marquises of Beaufort, where Uncle Cornelius grew up—and where he raised the five of us Wilde cousins. Beauvoir is not far from my home, Tallis Court. Two months ago, I went to the village to question the midwife. She is very old now and quite forgetful, but I managed to coax the story from her."

Hawk hid a wry smile. Even on so short an acquaintance with Lady Skye, he could well imagine her ability to cajole secrets from her unwitting targets.

"I was shocked by the tale she told me," Skye confessed. "The lady's noble husband was beating her so badly, she feared for her life. To escape the abuse, she thought she had no choice but to stage her death with the midwife's help. Once her daughter was born, she secretly fled to Ireland to live with sympathetic kin."

"It is not so easy to fake a drowning," Hawk remarked. "Her body would have been easily identified."

"But it was not immediately found and was presumed to have washed away. Months later, when coincidentally a corpse was uncovered many miles downstream, it was thought to be the lady's. So there was no further reason to search for her." Lady Skye pursed her lips. "I don't know for certain, but I think she may still be alive, living in Ireland."

"And you wish to find her."

"Yes. If it is at all possible, I would dearly love to reunite my uncle and his true love. But, actually, my goal is more complicated than that."

Hawk raised an eyebrow. "How so?"

Her charming smile flashed again. "I thought you would never ask. I believe the baby daughter was actually my uncle's child and not the baron's."

"What makes you think so?"

"First, the timing of her birth. She was born barely nine months after the lady's marriage. But there are other indications—certain of the daughter's mannerisms and features. The set of her eyes bears an uncanny resemblance to my uncle's, for instance. Her hair color also is similar, although his has turned silver by now."

"You have met the daughter?"

"Yes. When I realized she was living in London, I searched her out. She is near my same age but has already accomplished a great deal in her life. She is a botanical scholar and a gifted artist, with an expertise on roses. When I read a scientific paper by her, I was surprised to find her writings have a literary bent like Uncle's. Of course, I could not tell her the real reason for my interest in her work."

Hawk was impressed by Lady Skye's attention to detail, but still skeptical of her conclusion. "If the lady was carrying Cornelius's child, why wouldn't she have told him?"

"Because she was married to a wealthy, powerful nobleman and feared his retribution. According to the midwife, she would not go to Cornelius for help, for she couldn't bear for him to be hurt. She despaired of leaving her newborn daughter behind also, but the possible consequences would have been worse. Making her infidelity public would have caused an enormous scandal, and the baron's violence against her would likely have intensified. And he might have taken his revenge on the child or, at the least, disowned her. Yet if she took the baby, she feared he would never stop looking for her. If she simply died, her daughter would have the possibility of a good life."

"It sounds tediously melodramatic," Hawk drawled.

"Indeed," Lady Skye agreed. "But a scandal could still result if I go charging off, announcing my theory to the world. The baron remarried a year later, and if his first wife was still alive at the time, he would have committed bigamy. He is now gone, but his son inherited the barony, and there could be a question of his legitimacy. So you see if I am to investigate further, why I must tread carefully?"

Hawk did see the impediments Lady Skye faced, but she didn't seem to expect a reply from him as she continued.

"Furthermore, until I know if the lady is alive, I don't want to tell my uncle and raise his hopes. If she is not, there may be no reason to dredge up the painful past. Yet I cannot simply drop the matter or ignore my conscience. Uncle doesn't know he might have a daughter. If it is true, he should know about her. And she should likewise know about him. As I said, he has been like a father to me, and he deserves every happiness."

"Why haven't you asked your brother or cousins for help?" Hawk asked.

"Because they are fully occupied at present. Quinn is something of a genius who occasionally dabbles in science, and he has disappeared from London, I presume to work on his latest invention, although he sometimes acts contrarily just to thwart me. My cousins Ashton and Jack both recently married. I don't wish to intrude on their privacy with their new brides, particularly when a search might take them out of the country. Only Aunt Isabella and my cousin Katharine know about Uncle Cornelius's woeful past, and they are both eager to remedy his heartbreak if possible."

"So you've been plotting all these months to reunite the long-separated lovers?"

She flashed him a brilliant smile. "Yes—but I have gone as far as I can on my own, which is why I need *you*, my lord. Someone with your particular skills will have a much better chance than I of locating a fugitive wife after all these years. The midwife could only recall the first name of the lady's relation in Ireland, not the surname or the county she fled to. I understand that you know Ireland fairly well, since you often purchase horses there."

"Ireland is a large country," he parried.

"But since you are a master spy, surely you can find her. And the trail is not entirely cold. Along with the letters I found a miniature portrait of the lady, commissioned by my uncle. Her daughter is her spitting image, except for the eyes and hair, so you would have a likeness to go on. I have the miniature here in my reticule, if you care to see it."

Hawk deliberately ignored her offer. "Even if I were inclined to help you, I haven't the time just now."

Lady Skye nodded sagely. "My aunt told me why you returned to England. You are preparing to make a marriage of convenience."

"Is there nothing Bella kept to herself?" Hawk murmured, his tone halfway between exasperation and annoyance.

"I told you, you should not blame her," she replied amiably. "I had to worm the information about your secret organization out of her." Her smile was rueful, almost apologetic, and completely charming. "When I am determined, I usually get my way."

Hawk made a scoffing sound, which Lady Skye ignored in turn. "Aunt Isabella is very fond of you, Lord Hawkhurst, and believes you will help me, in part because she says you enjoy a good mystery as much as a challenge."

Hawk glanced down at the letter on his desk. Bella had indeed predicted that he would relish the challenge and said he would be doing her an immense favor if he were to help her niece.

Amazingly enough, he was actually tempted to agree, and not simply for the enjoyment of testing his skills. He wanted an excuse to delay his courtship. He had no desire to ever marry again, especially to a shy young lady barely out of the schoolroom. Yet he ardently wanted to ensure the league's future, as well as to fulfill an obligation to Sir Gawain Olwen, the aging leader of the Guardians who hoped to retire shortly.

There was no one Hawk esteemed more. The baronet had not only revived the clandestine league to its original purpose and steered it with a steady hand in the decades-long fight against French domination, he'd become mentor, guide, and fatherly role model to numerous members over the years, particularly Hawk.

Sir Gawain had been his salvation when he was mired in grief, giving him a reason to live by bringing him into the order and training him to be one of its most effective agents. He would have gone half-mad otherwise.

It irked Hawk that Isabella had disclosed so much about his private affairs to Lady Skye. The Guardians' secrets were not his to share. He'd sworn an oath of allegiance many years ago. Nor could he reveal the real reason he'd chosen to court this particular young lady—because he needed a bride of Guardian lineage in order to take over leadership, as required by the charter. Headquartered on the Isle of Cyrene off the southern coast of Spain, the Guardians of the Sword was centuries old.

Sir Gawain's great-niece was a blood descendant of one of the original founders, but while she fit the necessary lineage requirements, she was only nineteen and a quiet, gentle girl who seemed afraid of her own shadow and tended to swoon at the slightest provocation. Wedding her was purely a cold-blooded proposition. But to carry on the work of the Guardians, he was willing to sacrifice for the good of the organization. Hawk would be named Sir Gawain's successor and would lead in his wife's name and those of his future children, if any.

Therefore, he'd decided to wed the girl, despite his personal disinclinations. Moreover, he had already set events in motion, Hawk reminded himself as he reached for his glass and took a swallow of brandy. He had a path to follow for the immediate future, and it didn't involve haring off to Ireland, chasing after someone else's fugitive lover who may or may not still be alive.

"I'm afraid I cannot help you. I can't spare the time."

Skye did not seem distressed by his answer. "I thought that might be the case. I suppose you must effect repairs to your house in order to welcome a new bride and offer her a worthy home."

Hawk's gaze narrowed on her, but he shrugged. "I cannot bring a bride to a mausoleum."

"No, certainly not." She hesitated before saying softly, "Your return to Hawkhurst Castle cannot have been easy for you."

No, indeed. Hawk took another long, burning swallow of brandy. Facing his desolate, long-shuttered house had been far harder than he'd anticipated. He'd thought time had dulled his pain, but since his arrival, there had been long spells when grief gripped him as fiercely as ever.

Even though he had avoided the family wing altogether, especially the nursery where the fire had started, he couldn't escape the unbearable memories. In fact, that afternoon he'd been drinking to drown out his dark reflections. . . .

At his grim silence, Lady Skye reverted back to the topic of overseeing repairs. "What arrangements have you made for rebuilding the castle thus far?"

It was a benign subject, so Hawk was willing to reply. "I've engaged an architect who has commissioned workmen to demolish the burnt rooms and restore the damaged wing. Construction is to start at week's end."

"From the brief glimpse I had, there is a great deal of other work to be done as well. You will need to hire a full-time staff and clean away ten years of dirt, then inventory the contents of the house. . . . What of the rest of the estate?"

He couldn't see the reason for her leading questions but saw no harm in answering. "The stables and tenant farms are in much better condition than the house. I have grooms to look after the horses and a steward who takes good care of the land."

He would never jeopardize the countless lives and livelihoods that depended on his land. It was only the house he'd let go to ruin.

Lady Skye started to ask yet another question but Hawk interrupted her. "It isn't just the house repairs that will occupy my time. I will soon be engaged in a courtship."

"Of course, you must woo your bride. I have not met Miss Olwen yet as she is not out in society. I understand she lives a retired life in the country."

Lady Skye was nothing if not persistent, Hawk acknowledged with more than a tinge of exasperation. But if she thought he would allow her to quiz him about his prospective bride, she could think again.

When his gaze narrowed on her in disapproval, she went back to drying her pale hair and seemed content to let silence fall between them again.

Watching her over his glass, he couldn't help comparing her with Sir Gawain's niece, Amelia Olwen. Lady Skye Wilde was most definitely not shy and retiring. Instead, she was a vibrantly sensual woman. Sitting there bathed in the soft glow of firelight, she was having a profound effect on his senses.

It had been a very long time since he had shared this room with a beautiful woman, Hawk was aware. But her entrancing loveliness was weaving a spell over him.

Or perhaps he was dreaming the entire unusual episode. If so, it was the most pleasant dream he'd had in a long while.

He wasn't imagining the fierce attraction between

them, though. When he met her gaze again, a charged silence suddenly enveloped them.

He wanted this woman, and she wanted him, too.

He could easily envision taking Lady Skye to his bed. Hell, he could imagine taking her right there in his study: Slowly removing her damp clothing. Easing her down on the carpet before the hearth fire. Spreading her silken hair around her face. Parting her thighs and slowly plunging inside her. . . . He had a suspicion her passion would match his own—

Hawk grimaced, annoyed at himself for dwelling on forbidden images and increasing the already painful ache in his loins. He had definitely been without a woman for too long.

On the other hand, making her the object of his sexual fantasies was a good way to divert his mind from the dark memories that haunted his house. . . .

Cutting off that line of thought, Hawk drained the last of his glass and gave his final, curt answer. "I understand your desire to help your uncle, Lady Skye, but, regretfully, I must decline."

He expected a protest or more argument, but she merely smiled and said pleasantly, "We can discuss it further again in the morning, my lord."

Chapter Three

Skye was unsurprised when the earl's eyes narrowed. "In the morning?" he repeated.

"Yes. I have hopes you will allow me to stay the night."

"That isn't possible."

Skye pointedly glanced at the now-dark windows being pelted by rain. "There is a storm raging outside. You wouldn't send me out in this dreadful weather, would you?"

He ignored her perfectly reasonable question. "You are not staying here tonight."

Skye wasn't deterred by his adamancy. She had vowed to help her uncle and she wouldn't give up. More important, she wouldn't abandon her pursuit of Lord Hawkhurst when she had barely begun.

She put on her most expressive face and softened her tone to a plea. "My lord . . . I have traveled a long distance to speak to you. My grooms and coachman are wet and cold and hungry. Surely you will give us shelter for one night?" When he remained silent, Skye added for good measure, "If you make us leave now, my horses could be hurt."

She could see him wavering and persisted in laying out more arguments. "I suspect you are too much of a gentleman to expel us."

Her claim elicited a curt response from Hawkhurst. "I am too much of a gentleman not to expel you. You cannot sleep here alone, overnight, in a deserted bachelor's abode."

"What is the harm? You are a dear friend of my aunt. It isn't so shocking that I would seek refuge in your home until the storm passes. Besides, no one will even know I am here."

"The servants will gossip."

"You said you have very few servants employed here, and mine are completely loyal to me."

"I have few servants employed in the *house,* but I brought half a dozen grooms from my home on the Isle of Cyrene."

"Why so many?" Skye asked curiously.

"Because I breed horses. Purchasing blood stock in conjunction with this trip is an efficient use of my time and keeps me occupied."

And is a way to distract yourself while repairs are under way, Skye thought to herself, feeling another keen pang of sympathy for him. "My aunt tells me you possess a superb stable, and you said the buildings are in better condition than the house. Would you have room for my coachman and two grooms?"

"Yes, my stable hands have their own quarters behind the barns, and there is ample room for visiting servants, but the issue is not space but your reputation."

"I am not worried about that."

She was almost certain any potential damage to her reputation could be contained. Her advantages of breeding, family, fortune, and high-ranking connections would largely shield her from society's condemnation if word got out about her brazen actions. And risking scandal was well worth the chance of finding her soul mate in Lord Hawkhurst.

As for her family, her aunt and cousin Kate whole-heartedly supported her plan to pursue the earl but hadn't accompanied her because she needed privacy to conduct her evaluation.

Wisely, she hadn't told the rest of her family. Since she was female and the youngest Wilde, her brother and uncle and male cousins were overly protective. And she had only prevaricated a little when she'd claimed her brother was too occupied to help her. Quinn had indeed made himself scarce recently, but less out of contrariness than to avoid Kate's matchmaking schemes.

Quinn outright laughed at the notion of legendary lovers. Skye, on the other hand, had embraced the possibility, even one as far-fetched as a fairy tale about a beast who was not truly a beast and the beauty who freed him from an evil spell. Her cynical brother didn't understand her deep-seated desire to find her own true love. Quinn often accused her of being too idealistic, of constantly dreaming of what could be, and he wasn't mistaken.

"Please, my lord," Skye tried once more. "You may send me away tomorrow, once the storm subsides."

Thankfully, the earl's reluctance gave way to reason. "Very well. But you will leave first thing in the morning, storm or no storm."

Skye hid her vast relief. "Thank you. You are very generous."

"No doubt I will regret it," he muttered.

Before he could change his mind, Skye rose and went to the hearth to don her damp cloak.

"What are you doing?"

"I need to tell my servants we are staying and to make certain they have food and beds for the night."

"I am not letting you go out to the stables."

"Then perhaps your caretaker could go for me?"

Hawkhurst frowned. "I told you, he is elderly. He's so frail, he might be blown away by the wind. I will go myself."

It was another sign of his uniqueness, a nobleman volunteering to perform menial tasks in place of his elderly servant.

"That is kind of you to spare him," Skye replied. "But I should go. I am already half soaked."

"Did you bring a valise with a change of clothing?"

"Yes, but I can sleep in my shift if need be."

For a moment his gray gaze drifted lower over her body, as if he were imagining her in her shift. "There is no need. I will fetch your valise."

"I don't want to put you to so much trouble. If you have some extra dry clothing for me to wear, I could make do."

Hawkhurst hesitated, then shook his head and stood abruptly. "No, I have nothing for you to wear."

The gruff note had returned to roughen his voice. He took up the lamp on the desk and moved toward the door.

"Do you mind if I find something to eat in the kitchens?" Skye asked.

"I have no cook to prepare a meal for you."

"That is no matter. I'm sure I can manage on my own."

He looked skeptical but shrugged. "I will show you to the kitchens."

Quickly gathering the rest of her things, Skye followed him from the study and attempted to fall into step beside him. She had to hurry to match his long stride as he moved along the corridor.

He was at least a head taller than she, with a commanding demeanor that shouted nobility and a powerful, athletic build that made her feel intensely feminine and protected. His authoritative presence was rather comforting when the lamplight cast dancing shadows all around them. Hawkhurst Castle was more elegant manor than keep or fortress, but so dark and gloomy, she could easily believe it haunted by the ghosts of his late family.

Because the estate was entailed, it could not have been sold, but with his wealth, Hawkhurst had the means to purchase another home for his new bride—which made it all the more admirable that he had returned to face his past.

A shiver ran down Skye's spine at the thought of ghosts, and she moved a little closer to Hawkhurst. When her arm accidently brushed his, she felt that fiery jolt of awareness again. Her startled glance upward at his strong profile caught a muscle flexing in his jaw, as if he, too, had felt the heat.

He led her down a flight of stairs, deep into the bowels of the castle. When they finally reached the kitchens, which comprised several large rooms, Skye was relieved to see a fire going in both the hearth and the cookstove.

Hawkhurst indicated the door to the pantry and spoke tersely. "I will leave the lamp with you." Then he flung a cloak around his broad shoulders and left by way of a rear entrance.

Before the door shut behind him, Skye could hear the rain drumming against the pavement outside. She regretted making him brave the storm for her sake, but she hoped to repay him by preparing some hot tea and a meal for him.

Skye rummaged in the pantry awhile, then busied herself putting a kettle on the stove and slicing some bread and cheese to toast over the fire, then paring apples.

She also lit two more lamps to chase away the shadows. It was a bit unnerving to think of staying at the castle overnight. She did not like sleeping in unfamiliar places, for strange beds usually brought on disturbing dreams about the deaths in her own family—her parents' and those of her cousins in the same tragic shipwreck. But she was determined to make her own destiny and not let her future be tossed around like a rag doll by fickle fate.

Thus far her plan was on course, Skye reflected as she speared a thick piece of bread on a knife to hold over the fire. Indeed, her first encounter with Hawkhurst had left her feeling absurdly hopeful and that she could move on to her next step—rapidly improve their acquaintance. Regardless of whether their relationship could be based on a fairy tale, in order to decide if they would make a good match, she had to know Lord Hawkhurst much better.

Yet he had countless secrets he was unwilling or unable to share. And even though she much preferred honesty to subterfuge, she had to keep her legendary lovers theory secret for now. She would constantly have to pretend disinterest and hide the yearning inside her, for Hawkhurst would surely evict her if he knew of her romantic interest in him.

It would be odd playing the aggressor, Skye knew. She had been pursued by countless gentlemen but had never been the pursuer herself. Thankfully, she had priceless advice to rely upon. Aunt Bella had wed three husbands and knew how to win a man if it came to that.

Skye was melting a wedge of cheese when a soft footfall sounded behind her. The earl's sudden appearance from out of nowhere made her jump, and she barely managed to bite back a cry.

"I did not hear you come in," she murmured weakly, raising her hand to her throat.

"I returned through another entrance. Your servants are settled in," he said as he hung his drenched cloak on a wall peg, "and I set your valise by the rear stairway."

"Thank you, my lord," she said earnestly.

"I see you have made yourself at home," he added, glancing around at her preparations. She had laden a tray with china and cutlery and set tea steeping in a pot.

She flashed him a rueful smile. "I might seem like a damsel in distress at the moment, but I detest being helpless."

His expression turned wry. "I would guess that you are rarely helpless. But it is unusual for a lady to know her way around a kitchen."

"My cousin Jack is frequently hungry. Growing up, I often kept him company in the kitchens in the middle of the night, so it seemed wise to learn to cook at least simple things." Skye gestured at the teapot and plates of toasted bread and cheese. "I wasn't certain if anyone would prepare your supper, so I made enough for both of us. Will you join me?"

"I am not hungry."

She hesitated, wondering how much to press. She wanted to ply him with food and warmth, but she doubted he would allow it unless she disguised her intent. "Then will you please stay with me for a while? I would rather not eat alone."

Lord Hawkhurst gave her a long look, as if questioning her motives. But he shrugged and murmured, "Very well," much to Skye's gratification.

"Will you take the tea into the servants' dining room and bring the tray back to me? I want the cheese to melt a little more."

When he did as she asked, she piled the rest of their meal on the tray and let him carry it to the long dining table while she lit another lamp. Skye served the food, then waited until they were settled before commenting in a conversational tone, "I thought you would be glad I am staying overnight. If nothing else I will provide you company."

"I am in no mood for company."

"It is no wonder, shut in like this in this gloomy castle. It cannot be enjoyable living here practically by yourself. But some hot food and tea should improve your mood greatly."

His reply was another wordless utterance of disagreement.

"You tend to growl a great deal, don't you?" Skye asked.

"What do you mean, 'growl'?"

"That low, grumbling sound of displeasure you make. It makes you seem excessively grumpy."

Hawkhurst raised an eyebrow at her frankness.

"Fortunately I have had ample practice dealing with grumpy men. Especially Jack when he is starving or in his cups."

She gestured at the earl's untouched plate. He had taken a drink of tea but hadn't touched the food. "This cheese with a bit of apple is quite delicious, my lord. Won't you try a bite?"

"I don't need you to feed me, Lady Skye. In fact, I can prepare my own meals if need be."

Skye nodded sagely. "You must have learned as a spy."

His brows narrowed on her again. "What is this obsession of yours with my career?"

She kept her expression innocent. "I cannot help but be curious."

"Your curiosity will have to remain unsatisfied."

"I understand completely. Aunt Isabella said all your secrets must remain shrouded in mystery."

He gave something like a snort. "She has already revealed far too much. I intend to throttle her when I next see her."

"You need to forgive her, my lord. Moreover, I hope you will forgive me for wanting to cheer you up. It is long force of habit, dealing with my brother and cousins. And I know from their experience, vast quantities of brandy won't settle well in an empty stomach. You can drink more if you eat something first. So if you wish to drown your sorrows, you would do best to take at least a few bites."

Hawkhurst stared at her for a long moment. She thought he might growl at her again, but he smiled unwillingly, as if he was amused in spite of himself. With his knife, he cut a piece of softened cheese and laid it on a piece of toast, then chewed quickly. "There, are you satisfied?"

"It is a start."

Her desire to comfort him was only natural, Skye reflected. She wasn't imagining the lines of sadness etched into his handsome face. Once more she noticed the burn scars on his hands. The sight deeply stirred her compassion. By all accounts the Earl of Hawkhurst had lived a fairy-tale existence until fate had intervened so cruelly to shatter his life.

In truth, they had that much in common at least. Fate had taken her beloved parents from her. But she'd had her brother and cousins and uncle to help alleviate her grief. He had to be lonely, living in near solitude in this enormous house, dwelling on his tragic memories—a situation she could help rectify if she was allowed to stay.

Her fair hair and delicate features made her appear angelic, but she was far from an angel. Her sense of mischievousness had gotten her into trouble more times than she could count. A dose of mischievousness might be precisely what Hawkhurst needed to enliven his dour life, although tonight was likely not the most appropriate time.

Still, she could attempt to put him at ease and coax him to lower his guard with her. Her best approach might be to ask him about his breeding stables, Skye decided. "Aunt Isabella says you raise magnificent horses—that you have crossed Thoroughbreds with Barbs for stamina and speed."

"Yes. This past week I purchased two broodmares and a stallion."

"I should like to see them. I am very fond of horses myself."

His gray gaze found hers across the table. "You won't have time. You will be leaving early in the morning."

"You know, I don't *have* to leave. If you are concerned about propriety, I could ask Aunt Isabella to come here to act as my chaperone."

Hawkhurst shot down her suggestion with a curt word. "No."

"There could be some major advantages to having us both here for a time," Skye continued, still hoping to convince him to let her stay. "A great deal more work needs to be done on your house beyond construction and repairs. If you want to impress your new bride, you could use a woman's touch."

Silence was his only reply, although he did swallow a slice of apple.

Skye pressed on. "You said you have only an aging caretaker and some women from the village to cook and clean for you. At the very least, I could aid you in hiring a full-time housekeeper and other household servants. For that matter, I could ask my cousin Katharine to hire staff from an employment agency in London."

Hawkhurst drained his teacup. "Has anyone ever told you that you are excessively meddlesome?"

"Oh, yes. It is one of my many failings." She offered him a self-deprecating smile as she poured him another cup. "But I truly wish to offer my help. It is only fair if I can repay you in some small measure for aiding me in my search."

His gaze turned thoughtful. "There is no need for my involvement in your search. I know someone in London who may be able to help you locate your uncle's former lover."

Skye felt a twinge of unease. She didn't want help from anyone else. "But I want you, my lord. I prefer to keep Uncle Cornelius's story as private as possible. By all reports, Lady Isabella is almost like an older sister to you. She will be terribly disappointed to learn you are not the gentleman she believes you to be. Will you honestly let her down so cruelly?"

His mouth curved at her question. "What are you about? Playing on my guilt?"

"But of course." She was prepared to use whatever leverage she had to persuade him. "How else am I to convince you?"

He chuckled, a low, reluctant sound. His laughter sounded rusty from disuse, as if he was long out of practice, which no doubt he was. "There is no way you will ever convince me, Lady Skye."

"I know you feel that way now. My unexpected arrival surprised you. But I believe—at least I sincerely hope—that when you've had time to consider, you may change your mind. I assure you, *I* am not giving up."

Hawkhurst shook his head in evident disbelief at her persistence.

"Just think on it, my lord," Skye added. "It will be far more discreet if I stay here at the castle. I inquired thoroughly. The village of Hawkhurst has no inn, and the nearest posting house where I could find lodgings is on the London–Hastings Road in Robertsbridge, over a half dozen miles away. It will cause less gossip if I remain here rather than travel back and forth all that distance each day in order to see you. There you go again, making that growling sound," she pointed out, although she smiled sweetly to take the sting from her observation.

Skye was not as sanguine as she tried to appear, however, and Lord Hawkhurst remained stubbornly unyielding as they finished their meal in relative silence. When they carried the remainders to the kitchen, his orders were curt.

"Leave the dishes for the day servants to wash. I will show you to your room now."

He was clearly impatient to be rid of her, but Skye bit her tongue. Although it was far too early to retire to bed, she could hardly complain. At least she had brought a novel with her to read and could entertain herself until she was sleepy. Remaining awake would be better anyway, since she would have less chance to dream unsettling dreams.

Hawkhurst turned out all but one of the lamps and carried it with him as he left the kitchens. Once again Skye hurried to keep up with him.

He picked up her valise by the back servants' staircase, then escorted her up two flights of stairs, explaining as he showed her to her room: "The family wing was damaged and is boarded up now, so I sleep in the guest wing. My bedchamber is down the hall from this one."

Opening the door, he preceded her inside the dark room, where he set down her valise. "You can see that we are unprepared for guests." Dusty holland covers swathed the furniture, and the air was cold and damp.

"If you will light a lamp, I will build a fire."

"I can make do without a fire," Skye offered. "I don't want to be any trouble."

"We are long past that point," he said dryly. "Give me a moment and I will fetch some logs for you from my rooms. There should be clean linens and blankets in that cupboard there if you care to make up the bed. And at the end of the corridor is a housekeeper's pantry, where you will find towels and fresh water so you can fill a pitcher for washing."

"Thank you. I am certain I can manage."

The moment he left, Skye found herself wishing he could have stayed. A flash of lightning lit up the bed-chamber with a bright glare, and was soon followed by another clap of thunder. The storm seemed just as ferocious as before. It would not be easy, sleeping there in the strange bedchamber in the eerie house. At least Lord Hawkhurst would be nearby if her dreams grew too terrifying.

Chiding herself for her missishness, Skye distracted herself by pulling the holland covers off the bed and folding them neatly, then sorting through the linens and pillows in the cupboard. She was glad when Lord Hawkhurst returned, however, with an armful of logs.

Depositing his burden beside the hearth, he knelt to begin building a fire. It still astounded her that a no-bleman of his caliber was willing to perform such menial tasks for her sake. Most aristocrats wouldn't deign to dirty their hands with servants' work.

When he glanced over his shoulder at her, he seemed rather surprised as well that she was capable of making up her own bed. He used a tinderbox to light the fire, and by the time she finished her task, flames had started to lick the logs.

He watched his handiwork for a moment, while Skye found herself watching *him*. Firelight poured over him, highlighting the sculpted bones of his face. Carved in simple planes, it contained a stark beauty that held no trace of prettiness but was striking all the same.

Feeling enchanted, Skye held her breath. The spell remained as he rose to his feet and brushed his hands against his breeches.

"Thank you, my lord," she murmured, unconsciously moving toward him.

"Is there anything more you need tonight?" he asked.

I need you, was her unbidden thought. "No. You have done more than enough."

Realizing her voice had instinctively turned husky, Skye cleared her throat and halted a few steps from him. "I am sincerely grateful."

"Then I will leave you now."

For a moment, however, he remained unmoving as he stared down at her. The dark fringe of his lashes defined eyes that had turned to silver—a look that was spellbinding.

In response, Skye went totally still. Butterflies had suddenly returned to riot her stomach—a nervous agitation that had nothing to do with anxiety about the storm or fear of bad dreams. Rather, it was intense sexual awareness.

Being alone with Lord Hawkhurst in the bedchamber, with the golden glow of firelight highlighting his masculine beauty, sent pinpricks of lightning rippling over her skin to penetrate deep inside her.

It was amazing what this man did to her, how easily his nearness made her forget all about her alien surroundings. She had been kissed before by ardent suitors, passionately and at great length. But not one of them had ever affected her the way a simple look from Hawkhurst did.

She was not a complete novice about carnal relations, either. She had learned enough from her aunt about the arts of seduction to know theoretically what happened between a man and a woman during lovemaking. And she was prepared for resistance from Lord Hawkhurst to even her simplest advances.

Yet she wasn't at all prepared for his impact on her. He made her pulse race and her body burn. Sensual images flashed in her mind, begetting a myriad of emotions . . . pleasure, heat, anticipation.

Skye took another step closer, drawn toward him like a helpless moth to a beckoning flame.

When his gaze dropped to her mouth, her own lips parted but no sound emerged. She could picture herself kissing him, embracing him. She could envision sharing this bedchamber with him, this bed . . . how it would feel if they undressed each other and lay side by side . . . bare, warm skin touching. . . .

She thought he might be sharing the same fantasies, for his hand started to lift, as if he might reach up and touch her face. But, just as quickly, the moment ended.

The delectable images abruptly faded when Hawkhurst stepped back and crossed to the door without another word. Turning back to her briefly, he sketched her a slight bow and let himself out.

Skye exhaled slowly, mingled disappointment and relief rushing through her. In the span of one more heartbeat, she would have walked straight into his arms. And all her careful plans would likely have been shattered.

This would never do, she warned herself. She had to conquer her intense attraction for Hawkhurst, for one false move could get her instantly banished from his castle.

With a grimace of disgust at her lack of self-control, Skye spun around and marched toward her valise so she could change out of her still-damp gown and prepare for bed, quite alone.

Chapter Four

Hawk shut his guest's bedchamber door with unintended force. Tearing himself away from Lady Skye had been supremely difficult when she was looking at him with desire written all over her beautiful features. The huskiness of her voice, the soft yearning in her wide blue eyes, told him clearly that he could have her if he'd wished to.

Actually, he did wish to, rather urgently. She was pure temptation. It was absurd, how fiercely she aroused him. When he'd locked gazes with her, sheer lust had blazed through him. He'd forced himself to leave before acting on his primal urges.

Hawk swore another low oath to himself.

It was even more absurd how a delicate-looking beauty had put him on the defensive so effortlessly. He couldn't believe her audacity, barging into his castle, making herself at home, wrangling an invitation to stay for the night, threatening to complain to her aunt about his ungentlemanly behavior. It was a low blow, using Bella as leverage.

And then she'd accused him of being a recluse and a grump. No one until Lady Skye had dared confront him on his moroseness. He hadn't always had a taciturn nature, Hawk reflected grimly; it had only developed so over time.

However, his surliness tonight when she'd asked if he had any dry clothing for her to wear was because she'd touched a still-aching wound inside him.

Perhaps he could have unearthed some of his late wife's gowns, but that would have seemed like a betrayal of Elizabeth. Fortunately avoiding comparisons of the two women was fairly easy since they were not much alike in figure or appearance. Elizabeth had been more solidly built with dark hair and more vivid coloring.

Not pale and delicate and sensual like Lady Skye.

Not annoyingly persistent or refreshingly bold, either.

Despite Hawk's determination to remain unmoved by her arguments, Lady Skye had amused him and even made him laugh for the first time since leaving Cyrene for England three weeks ago. Conversing with her, sparring with her, had provided a welcome distraction from his depressing though elegant monstrosity of a house.

Especially on a night like this. The storm had dredged up too many excruciating memories, for this was much like the night his wife and son had died.

By then, he'd been working for the British Foreign Office for four years and married to Elizabeth for three. The hour was late and he was returning home from business in London when he'd ridden through the estate gates to see an eerie glow in the night sky. The fire had begun in the nursery and trapped Elizabeth and two year-old Lucas, Hawk later learned. A drenching rain had eventually extinguished the flames and spared the rest of the house, but he'd arrived much too late to help his family.

His failure to save them had changed him forever. He had survived when he hadn't wanted to.

In fact, his grief and guilt were what had sent him to Cyrene in the first place. When Sir Gawain offered him membership in the elite league, exiling himself to a Mediterranean island nearly a thousand miles away had seemed a fitting punishment.

Instead, the Guardians had given him a fresh purpose. For the past decade, they had filled a huge hole in his life when he'd desperately needed it. And now, to return the favor, he'd come home to Hawkhurst Castle to court Sir Gawain's niece.

He hadn't slept much since his arrival. In truth, he'd deliberately remained awake each night for as long as possible, making himself utterly exhausted so that he could eventually close his eyes without haunting images preying on him, relying on copious amounts of fine liquor to help keep the ghosts at bay.

Lady Skye was right. Too much brandy with too little food was not good for his temper. But drinking was better than prowling the halls of his empty house and remembering the love and laughter that had once filled it.

He was bone-tired now, Hawk realized. Even so, he had no desire to risk temptation by retiring to his bedchamber just down the hall from his unwanted guest.

Hardening his jaw, Hawk turned toward the back staircase. He had every intention of resisting Lady Skye, no matter how irresistible she was. He would send her on her way first thing in the morning, before his effort to remain impersonal and aloof failed spectacularly.

Meanwhile, he would return to his study and continue making heavy inroads into his store of expensive vintage brandy.

By the time he made his way upstairs again four hours later, the storm had died down and an uneasy quiet had descended over the house. Wearily Hawk entered his bedchamber and shed his clothing. He was about to don a nightshirt when he heard a muffled cry from outside his room.

Wondering if he was imagining ghosts, he opened his door and let his gaze sweep the dark corridor as he listened intently. When the cry of distress echoed more loudly this time, he realized it had to be coming from Lady Skye's room. A vague sense of apprehension filling him, he quickly pulled on a dressing gown and went to investigate.

Her chamber was dimly lit by the hearth fire's burning embers, but he could see her lying in bed, whimpering, evidently in the throes of a nightmare. In her thrashing, she had flung off the covers, and her nightdress had ridden up to midthigh, exposing pale, slender limbs.

Hawk hesitated on the threshold, reluctant to be drawn in. Then she cried out again and he felt an unwanted softening inside him.

He shut the door quietly behind him and moved closer, his protective instincts stronger than his need to guard himself. He understood the terror of nightmares, having dealt with his own for many years.

The dampness on her cheeks told him she'd been crying in her sleep. Tears still welled beneath her closed eyelids as he gazed down at her.

Wanting to console her, Hawk gingerly sat beside her on the bed and touched her shoulder gently. She came awake with a violent start, her entire body shaking. Spying him, she gasped, then pushed herself up and lunged at him, wrapping her arms around his neck and holding on for dear life.

Reflexively, Hawk slid his arms about her, even before a wrenching sob escaped her.

"Please . . . hold me . . ." she pleaded hoarsely.

Hawk eased onto the bed more fully and held her as she'd asked, murmuring soothing sounds the way he had once done for his young son. Lady Skye clung tightly, shivering. Pressing her face into the curve of his neck, she tried to get even closer, as if she might burrow into him. Hawk responded by gently stroking her hair, her arm, her slender back. . . .

Her body continued trembling, though. Seeking his warmth, she pushed aside the lapels of his dressing gown and rested her cheek against his bare chest. "Please . . . don't leave me. . . ."

At the fear engulfing her, Hawk felt a sharp ache near his heart. Determined to keep her warm and safe, to hold the terrors at bay, he brushed her cheek with his fingers, wiping away the tears. All the while he murmured to her in a quiet, crooning tone, gentling her as he would a terrified young mare, sprinkling kisses upon her temple, her hair. . . . Before he realized it, he was breathing deeply of her fragrance, taking it inside him.

Her delectable scent penetrated his brandied haze,

awakening his other senses to full primal life. Suddenly sexual awareness hit Hawk like a blow. Very little separated their bare bodies—her cambric nightdress, his brocade dressing gown. He hadn't sashed his robe tightly enough, either. His manhood stirred, while desire, heavy and urgent, tightened his body.

Hawk bit back a groan. Embracing her like this was severely testing his fortitude. What he'd meant to be a comforting embrace had turned unexpectedly heated. Every part of his body vibrated with the tension she had created, and in another moment, he'd grown fully aroused.

He suspected Skye felt a similar desire, for she went very still. Beneath his fingers, he could feel the rapidly beating pulse in her throat. Then her hand curled around his nape and moved lower, beneath the collar of his robe. When she drew a shallow breath, he knew she was feeling the burn scars on his back, the ridges of puckered flesh caused when a smoldering beam had crashed down upon him.

Faintly, her hand stroked the back of his neck, and she pressed her lips to his chest, as if consoling *him*.

"I am so sorry," she whispered.

Her face was damp with fresh tears, he realized. She was crying over him. Hawk froze. He didn't want her pity. Catching her wrist, he drew her fingers away from his damaged flesh, unwilling to bear her efforts at solace.

Unfortunately, she raised her face to him.

Temptation beckoned anew. Huge sapphire eyes, ripe rosy lips, flawless ivory skin. Hawk locked his jaw, fighting her allure, but he had no defense against her tear-filled eyes.

Bending his head, he kissed a path along her cheek-bone to her soft lips. She tensed at first, as if startled, yet the quiver of her mouth under his kiss told him she felt the same intense attraction. When he deepened the pressure, her resistance melted. Rather than pushing him away, Lady Skye responded with fervor, leaning into him as if hungry for his mouth, for his touch.

When she opened to his penetrating tongue, heat seared him. Heat he didn't want. Possessiveness he *shouldn't* want.

He almost left her right then. Buffeted by the emotional jolt of her kiss, Hawk badly wanted to pull away. But instead, his hand slid down her body, caressing, stroking. He'd been too long without a woman, without a soft feminine touch, and every nerve and fiber in his being was clamoring for her softness.

When his palm skimmed along her bare thigh, a rasping murmur that had nothing to do with protest sounded deep in her throat. And when his hand rose again to cup the ripe swell of her breast, she arched into his touch.

She was as eager for him as he was for her, Hawk knew without a doubt.

His lips moving on her flushed face, he laid her back against the pillows and pulled down the bodice of her nightdress, then drew back to drink in the sight of her.

He'd imagined how she would look in the golden glow of firelight. Ivory, velvet-smooth skin. Firm, lush breasts. Rosy-tipped nipples. Luscious, inviting warmth.

Hawk drew a long, labored breath. No sane man could resist her beauty, and arguably there were times when he was not wholly sane—like now, when his head was reeling much less from the liquor that had loosened his self-imposed inhibitions than the powerful shock to his senses.

Craving her warmth, he reached for her. Her eyes closed this time while her back arched again, her creamy breasts trembling, peaking, filling his hands.

Lowering his head, Hawk kissed one exquisite crest. When Skye whimpered softly, he remembered the rough stubble on his jaw and wondered if he had hurt her. But when he began to suck on her nipple, her sigh of pleasure told him he was mistaken.

He intensified his ministrations, his lips closing more firmly on her breast, his tongue coaxing the taut bud to greater arousal.

She was straining against him now. Her fingers curled in his hair, pulling his mouth closer, as if begging him not to stop.

He had no intention of stopping. All he cared about just then was touching her, exploring her. His blood was pounding violently, but as he stretched out beside her, he willed himself to patience, knowing he had to see to her pleasure first.

Reaching beneath the hem of her nightdress, he grazed the curls at the apex of her thighs, then lightly cupped the rise of her woman's mound, molding it.

She gave a soft gasp, but when he parted her silken folds, her thighs opened wider, unconsciously giving him better access. He ran a finger along her quivering flesh, teasing the small nub of her sex, rolling it back and forth, caressing with his circling thumb. She shivered with delight. Then he eased a finger inside her, finding a hot slick moistness and causing her to moan.

Not relenting, Hawk probed deeper, using his thumb to rub and tease. A sob of pleasure escaped her. A heartbeat later she shuddered, her hips twisting and writhing as he stroked her to passion.

It was not long before he brought her to climax. Gripping his shoulders, she came against his hand in a rush of sensation. Hawk draped his arm around her, holding her still when she jerked against him. When it was over, she lay there unmoving, limp and sated, rapture on her exquisite face.

Eventually her eyelids fluttered open and she stared at him in wonder. She seemed stunned, dazed . . . perhaps because she had never climaxed before?

Hawk was pondering that intriguing question when she swallowed and spoke hoarsely. "Don't leave me. . . ."

His heart melted at her pleading whisper. "I won't. I want you too much."

He wasn't about to leave now. She was lush and wet and in a state of sweet sexual arousal, and his manhood was hard and near to bursting. The thought of how she would feel when he plunged inside her made his pain even worse.

"I want you, too," she murmured almost shyly. Reaching out, she brushed his loins in a tentative exploration.

Her delicate touch made Hawk inhale, partly in surprise. Given her genteel upbringing, combined with her appearance of fragility, he would have presumed her to be an innocent. But any doubts about her experience faded when she curled her fingers around his shaft. Hawk nearly groaned.

In truth he was gratified by the bold way she fondled his body. She seemed to have forgotten all about her nightmares, and modesty as well. It was as if the caressing darkness had cast away *her* inhibitions.

In response, Hawk crushed the last of his own resistance. Sitting up, he yanked off his dressing gown and then eased her nightdress from her body.

He hesitated a moment then, staring at her tempting form. Firm, proud breasts, slender waist, elegantly curving hips, sweet thighs, the nest of pale curls shielding her cleft.

She was slick and swollen, her pink flesh glistening in the firelight. His cock swelled in response. He wanted to remain tender, gentle, but it was damned difficult when all he could think about was losing himself inside her delectable warmth.

When she sought to pull him closer, he moved over her, easing his thighs between hers, settling his weight. Fitting himself snugly between her thighs, he let her feel the thick length of his erection.

He was breathing more rapidly now, surrounded by her scent, her taste, her texture. Yet strangely, she seemed more calm. She gazed back at him steadily, her face flushed with desire. He could see that she wanted him, would welcome him as her lover.

She was the epitome of an erotic male fantasy, offering herself to him this way.

Without further delay, he mounted her, probing her entrance with the head of his shaft, parting the tender, swollen lips of her femininity. Her cleft was slick with her moisture, reducing the friction as his cock eased in. She was tighter than he expected, though. Through his carnal haze, he noticed the slight grimace on her beautiful features.

He slid inside her as carefully as possible, and when

he was finally sheathed, he held himself still, letting her body grow accustomed to the thickness and length of him.

She was biting her lip, but then she moved her hips slightly, as if testing the fit. When she managed a soft smile, it was all he could do to control his triumph. Lowering his head, he pressed light kisses on the fullness of her mouth as he began to move inside her.

When he felt her inner muscles clenching around his throbbing shaft, he ached to increase the rhythm. Instead, he captured her luscious mouth more fully, kissing her urgently, plunging his tongue inside the way he wanted to do to her body.

The wildness running through him built rapidly and his desire rose to a fever pitch. He needed her, he needed this, with a kind of desperation he'd never felt before.

She seemed to have the same need, for her slender legs and arms wrapped around him tightly.

Hawk knew he should go slowly, should strive for finesse, but the tight, glorious fit was driving him mad. It had been too long and he was too far gone. He burned for her, burned with the primitive need to claim her.

His mouth devouring hers, he thrust harder inside her. In return, she clung to him, her nails scoring his back as passion flared white-hot between them.

Then his whole body ignited with consuming heat. Hawk went rigid an instant before all his pent-up passion exploded. His climax blasting through him over and over, he found his own fierce, shuddering release.

In the aftermath, he collapsed upon her and buried his face in her lustrous silken hair, his breath coming harshly in the quiet chamber. The pleasure he'd had with her had been shattering, Hawk realized as he breathed deeply of her sweet, clean fragrance that was tinged with the potent musk of sex.

She hadn't climaxed a second time, though. Vowing to do better, he eased his weight to one side and would have rolled off her, but she wouldn't let him go.

Her arms were still wrapped around him, her fingers drifting lightly over his back. She was stroking his scars again, Hawk knew, yet he couldn't bring himself to object.

He exhaled in a weary sigh.

Lady Skye Wilde. A paradox if he'd ever met one. A passionate, sensual creature one minute. A tender, ministering angel the next. She radiated sympathy and compassion as she cradled him to her breast, holding him, comforting him with her hot, sweet body.

Oddly, he cherished the comfort. Even more oddly, Hawk felt a sense of peace for the first time in a long, long while.

Peace and exhaustion. Lethargy sank over him, making all his bones feel heavy—not surprising since the explosive passion had drained him of all energy. The countless sleepless nights had taken a toll also, as had the spirits he'd drunk throughout the evening.

Whatever the reason for his release, he was finally able to let go of the pain and dark memories.

Giving in to exhaustion, Hawk fell asleep holding her, deeply, amazingly content.

Chapter Five

Rays of morning sunshine slipped beneath the window curtains into her bedchamber, allowing Skye ample light to study the earl's slumbering form. He had slept peacefully through the night, as had she. Wrapped in his warmth, she hadn't wanted to move.

At dawn she'd risen to wash herself, don her nightdress, and stir the fire to remove the chill from the air. Now she was sitting on the bed beside her lover with her legs drawn up, her chin resting on her knees as she watched him.

Her lover. The term filled her with delight. So did her memories of his incredible lovemaking.

Aunt Isabella had warned her what to expect, but knowing the physical principles was not the same as participating. The actual experience had exceeded her wildest fantasies. It had been like drowning in sweet fire.

Yes, there had been pain at first, but the discomfort had quickly faded. She felt different now, Skye decided, taking stock of new sensations assailing her: The unfamiliar delicacy of her body. The unaccustomed ache between her thighs. The sensitivity of her breasts. The tenderness of her mouth.

The stubble shadowing Hawkhurst's jaw had scraped her skin, resulting in whisker burn, yet she didn't mind. How could she when he'd given her the most blissful pleasure of her life?

Simply looking at him gave her pleasure. He lay on his side facing her, the covers drawn up to his waist, exposing his bare torso. He was dark and sinfully handsome, with his high cheekbones and chiseled jawline. His magnificent face, she now knew, was matched by a magnificent body. Strong, graceful, long-limbed. She was frankly awed by the heat and steel beneath his smooth flesh.

Not all his flesh was smooth, however. The sight of his scars in the growing light of day made her ache with sorrow. It appalled her that such a beautiful work of art should be so disfigured.

His back had suffered the worst damage. His shoulders in particular were covered with puckered burn weals that were thick and hard. Oddly enough, he had other scars, too, perhaps the results of his dangerous profession. One was rounded, as if made by a bullet. Two more were long slashes, possibly from a knife or sword blade. But those were insignificant compared to the burns.

She could only imagine the physical pain he'd suffered from the castle fire, even discounting his emotional pain. The thought brought tears to Skye's eyes. Foolishly, she wanted to press her lips against his ravaged skin and take away the hurt.

She would have to hide her sadness and sorrow

from Lord Hawkhurst, though, for he wouldn't want her pity. He wasn't the sort of man who invited pity. Even in sleep, he was arresting, powerful.

She hadn't meant to go so far as to lose her virginity to him last night, however. She'd flung herself against him, true, clinging so tightly she'd nearly choked him, but her motives had been entirely innocent at first. And then his consoling warmth had seeped into her bones, driving away the chilling fear of her nightmare. She could feel her trembling subside as he expertly molded his lips to fit hers. With his masterful arms holding her and his tender kisses kindling her senses, he'd inflamed her to aching arousal. . . .

Apparently she had done the same to him, Skye reflected, her gaze lingering on his bare, smoothly muscled chest. It was no wonder that Hawkhurst had reacted as he had, considering the brazen way she had explored and fondled him. Yet there had been an intensity in his embrace, almost a desperation, as if he needed her more than his next breath.

The same need had filled her. A hunger so strong that she felt dazed. She had longed to be part of him.

She couldn't regret becoming a woman in his arms. In truth, she was amazed by how right their joining had felt—as if she'd never lived until he'd touched her, kissed her, melded with her.

She couldn't help wondering if their consummation was a sign that they were meant to be together. She could picture this man as her husband, and waking next to him each morning. Indeed, the past night could have been their wedding night, Skye thought dreamily. But regardless of whether Lord Hawkhurst was her life's mate, she would never be able to look at him again without remembering the feel of him moving inside her.

Fresh pleasure flooded her as she remembered his hardness inside her, his urgent thrusts as he took her.

The quivery feelings in her midsection persisted as Hawkhurst finally stirred awake. When he first spied her, a faint smile of greeting touched his mouth, while his gray eyes held unmistakable warmth. He reached out to touch her bare toes that were peeking from beneath the hem of her nightdress—to see if she was real, she supposed.

At the intimate contact, Skye felt her stomach turn fluttery again, but then a frown claimed his mouth.

Raising his head, Hawkhurst glanced around the bedchamber before returning his gaze to her. He must have recalled where he was and whom he was with, for those fathomless gray eyes leveled on her with an intensity that unsettled her.

Skye felt a flush stain her cheeks. She could no longer ignore the fact that she was still dressed in her night-clothes, alone with a naked man in her bed. A splen-didly naked man who had plumbed the secrets of her body the night before.

The stomach-tightening awareness of his maleness made her feel shy and uncertain. She wanted to appear casual and sophisticated, but she was in way over her head, Skye silently admitted. How did one behave after a blazing night of passion with a new lover? With a *first* lover?

Suddenly she wished she had fled before the earl had awakened. But that would have been cowardly. She would just have to brave it out.

"I decided to let you sleep," she explained in a rush.

"You were so weary that I didn't have the heart to wake you, and I thought it best if I didn't go wandering around your house and startling the servants with my presence until you were able to alert them to the reason for my visit—"

Realizing she was running on at the mouth, Skye cut off her steady stream of nervous chatter and took a deep breath. "Thank you for consoling me last night, my lord."

His expression remained enigmatic. Shifting slowly onto his back, Hawkhurst propped another pillow behind his head, as if preparing for a conversation he didn't want.

"Do you suffer nightmares regularly?" His raspy voice sounded cautious.

Skye nodded briefly. "Since childhood. They started after losing my parents, when I was sent away to boarding school. But I haven't had them recently. It must be this house, sleeping in a strange place, combined with the storm. . . ."

Her nightmares were her chief weakness, one she couldn't seem to control. It was always the same horrible dream about her parents dying—descending to a watery grave when their ship sank during a storm. The sensation of drowning . . . reaching out to grasp their flailing hands . . . struggling futilely to rescue them.

In any other circumstance, she never needed to be coddled, but she was grateful the earl had provided her solace when the terror struck.

Hawkhurst, however, apparently did not share her view. "I did not mean to take advantage of you last night," he murmured with genuine regret.

"But you didn't," Skye said quickly, wanting to re-assure him.

He cleared his throat in disagreement, but otherwise gave her no reply. After a moment, he threw off the covers, preparing to rise. As he started to swing his legs over the edge of the bed, he happened to glance down at the bed where a faint pink stain marred the white sheets.

Her blood, Skye realized. The same stain had covered the insides of her thighs before she had washed it away.

"Good God. You were a virgin."

His tone was faintly stunned while his entire body had gone rigid. His gaze shot back to her. "I never realized. . . . You seemed more than willing."

Skye felt her flush deepen. Not unreasonably he had taken her wantonness for carnal experience. "I *was* willing."

The grimness of his mouth told her what he thought of her declaration.

"How could you allow me to go so far?" he charged, his tone accusing, and yet she could see his anger was directed as much at himself as her, for he went on without waiting for her reply. "I've compromised you beyond all pardonable limits."

"No one will ever know," Skye protested.

"*I* will know. You are an unattached female guest in my home *and* Isabella's niece." Roughly he ran a hand through his sleep-tousled raven hair and muttered a low oath. "Bella will have my head when she finds out."

"So would my brother. Quinn will likely want to shoot you. But they don't have to find out."

Skye couldn't help a wry wince at the thought of her brother's reaction. Quinn might be something of a rake himself, but he would have an apoplectic fit if he thought his baby sister had given her body to a near stranger, nobleman or not. Quinn's protectiveness was why she hadn't informed him of her plan to come to Hawkhurst Castle in the first place.

"I certainly won't tell either of them," she added for good measure, "and neither should you."

Sinking back against the headboard, Hawkhurst absently drew the covers over his lower body to shield his nudity. "I cannot just ignore what happened." He swore again. "I don't usually go around raping virgins."

Embarrassed laughter escaped her throat. "I would imagine not."

His gaze turned deadly. "You find this amusing?"

"No, not at all. But it was hardly rape. I seem to remember begging you at one point."

"That doesn't justify my actions. I *should* be shot."

She had practically seduced him, and he was taking the blame? Skye couldn't let him feel guilty for what was primarily her fault. "You are not to blame, my lord. You were only comforting me as I asked."

"That is no excuse."

"I tell you, I wanted it to happen."

His gaze pinned her again. "Did you purposely lure me to your bed by feigning your nightmares?"

"No, of course not."

"I didn't think so. Your cries were too real to be pretense."

"They were very real. And I could have stopped you if I'd chosen to."

"Why didn't you?"

"Because I was overcome by passion."

That was undeniably true. She hadn't consciously set out to seduce him. She'd simply been so overwhelmed with desire that she had willingly surrendered her maidenhead.

Skye took a deep breath, deciding to try and reason with him. "Lord Hawkhurst, the damage is done. You needn't flagellate yourself over it."

His silence spoke volumes, since he looked as frustrated as the devil.

"You are making too much of what really is a minor matter," Skye insisted.

"A *minor* matter?" He looked ready to explode at her observation. "Don't pretend you have no comprehension of the position this puts us in," he ground out.

Her brow furrowed. "What position?"

Gazing up at the ceiling, he made a visible effort at control. "We will have to marry. It is the only honorable course."

Skye stared back at him blankly. "Marry?"

"I take responsibility for my mistakes."

"I don't want to be your mistake."

"But you are."

She could scarcely believe her ears. He was actually proposing to marry her, albeit with grave reluctance. "You don't wish to wed me, my lord," she reminded him. "You came all the way to England to claim a certain bride, remember? You are supposed to begin courting Sir Gawain Olwen's niece soon."

"That is beside the point."

She pursed her lips. "Have you married every woman you had affairs with?"

The question seemed to catch him off guard. "Obviously not."

"Why should it be different with me?"

"You know exactly why. Because you are not just any woman."

"We should not be forced to wed simply because we made love. We can pretend it never happened."

"Impossible. You could be pregnant with my child. Have you thought of that?"

Skye's gaze arrested. No, she hadn't thought of that. Aunt Isabella had told her about how to prevent a man's seed from taking root inside her body, but that had been the furthest thing from her mind last night.

"There is no help for it," Hawkhurst stated darkly. "If there's a child, we will have no choice but to wed."

Skye opened her mouth to object, then shut it again. If word got out that she had spent the night in the earl's bed and refused to wed him, she would likely be ruined. Certainly she would be if she bore a child out of wedlock, a transgression that would stain his honor as well. She could weather a scandal, of course; in fact, scandals were practically expected in her family. But she would never sentence a child to a life of illegitimacy. Not when she knew the stigma her cousin Jack had endured, being the bastard son of a European prince.

Yet she didn't want to trap Lord Hawkhurst in marriage because she was with child. If she were to attempt such a calculating scheme, he would always hold it against her. No, she wanted him to love her first.

Perhaps that was a valid argument she could use, Skye realized. Having someone to love, to belong to, was vitally important to her, even more crucial than her desire to find the ideal mate.

There was no question that Hawkhurst was a man she could love. Yet the reverse might not be true. He'd already had the love of his life and buried her. Skye knew instinctively that it would take a great deal to make him fall in love again. And he would never give her that chance if she forced him to wed her.

"I will not marry you under such conditions, my lord," she said firmly. "I want a husband who will love me."

"What you want is also beside the point," he retorted.

His insisting on marriage would upset all her careful evaluations. Skye felt a twinge of panic, but she tamped it down. She had gotten herself in this pickle, and she would have to get herself out.

She managed a calm smile. Sweetness was almost always more effective than stubbornness and belligerence.

"Your sentiment does you honor, my lord, but I cannot accept a proposal from you. I mean to remain in control of my own destiny." Skye made a face and let her tone turn sincerely apologetic. "I confess that being the master of my fate is an irrational obsession of mine. But you see, I cannot marry you to satisfy some moral code of society's."

A muscle hardened in the earl's jaw, but he seemed to realize the futility of further argument. With a grim look, Hawkhurst rose from the bed and snatched up his dressing gown from the floor. Pulling the garment on, he yanked the sash closed, then stood staring at her.

They were at an impasse, however, for she would not back down. Turning, he stalked to the door.

"Do you still mean to make me leave this morning?" Skye called after him in a purposely meek voice.

The look he shot her was withering before he strode out, shutting the door forcefully behind him.

Skye bit her lip hard, uncertain whether her outright refusal to consider marriage had helped her cause or hurt it.

She had meant her declaration about fate. She would never settle for a forced marriage if she could help it. And neither should Hawkhurst.

He shouldn't be compelled to marry her out of obligation. Nor, for that matter, should he have to wed the Olwen girl out of duty, as was his current plan. Everything Skye had learned about young Miss Olwen pointed to her being a milk pudding. Hawkhurst didn't deserve such a cold fate. Being locked in a loveless marriage of convenience with so unequal a mate would only cause him pain. And regardless of whether he was destined to be *her* own mate, Skye wanted desperately to save him from more pain. Which meant somehow preventing his pursuit of the Olwen chit. . . .

Skye went still as a sudden thought struck her. The possibility that she was with child might actually work in her favor. Surely Hawkhurst wouldn't send her away until he knew if she was carrying his child. And until it was confirmed one way or the other, he wouldn't be able to court Miss Olwen, either.

A thoughtful frown turned down the corners of Skye's mouth. Suggesting a waiting period was likely the best way to delay his courtship of his mentor's niece. However, she needed to give the earl a little time for his anger to cool off before making her suggestion.

In the meantime, Skye vowed, she was not leaving Hawkhurst Castle. In the French fairy tale, the beast had imprisoned the beauty. In this case, she would do the imprisoning—holding herself captive until Lord Hawkhurst agreed to let her spend time with him.

And if he never agreed?

Skye let out a shaky breath, knowing everything still depended on her powers of persuasion.

But she was not giving up yet. Not by a long chalk.

Chapter Six

The snorting, prancing stallion was a handful—just the challenge he needed to work off his frustration, Hawk decided grimly. He often rode to conquer his demons, and this morning he was also gentling his newest equine purchase, who was young and fractious and dangerous even to his experienced grooms.

With a touch of his heels, Hawk set the magnificent black Thoroughbred into an easy canter rather than the full gallop needed to expend the horse's excess energy. Normally the quiet meadow was ideal for schooling, but the drenching rain had left the grass slick and treacherous. And, admittedly, Hawk's focus was not solely on his task.

He found it impossible to shake off his anger. Even though Lady Skye had willingly offered her body to him, he was furious at himself for giving in to his sexual need.

He'd been something of a rakehell in his younger days before marrying Elizabeth. And as a widower, he'd occasionally interrupted his solitary life on Cyrene by enjoying the sexual favors and companionship of various Cyprians. But his bed sport had never extended to seducing virgins.

He didn't harm innocents, period. *Bloody hell.* Last night he'd disregarded his deepest principles, seeking oblivion in pure carnal release, losing himself in the hot, sweet comfort of Skye's body.

And now all his long-held plans might be in jeopardy. If he was forced to wed her, he would be unable to fulfill his obligations to the Guardians and their beloved, aging leader.

Some of his anger, Hawk knew, was reserved for Skye herself—for tempting him to want again. She had shocked his numbed carnal hunger violently to life and, far worse, had made him feel long-dead emotions. *Bloody, bloody hell.*

In truth, from their first encounter he'd thought her more sophisticated than she actually was. He should have known better, particularly last night when she'd tried to hide the pain from losing her maidenhead. There had been nothing calculated about their joining, though, he was now certain. She hadn't lured him into her bed with the goal of compromising herself.

If he'd had any doubts, they would have been wiped away by her response to him this morning—the sweet flush of desire on her face, the unguarded openness of her expression, the honesty in her blue eyes. Her shyness was unfeigned, and her nervous chatter was actually endearing to him.

Yet she was perhaps the last woman he wanted to marry, in part because of the dangerous effect she had on him.

Apparently she had no desire to wed him, either. It

frankly astonished Hawk that she'd rejected the idea of marriage so readily. Most ladies her age would have leapt at the chance to snare a wealthy earl, even a reclusive, scarred, ill-tempered one. Initially her refusal had won a measure of admiration from him, until she'd stated her reasons. Her talk of love had roused an instinctive discord in Hawk. She wanted a husband who could love her, and he had absolutely no intention of loving again.

Not that the choice was his to make. He didn't believe he was even capable of loving again. He'd buried his heart with his dead wife.

His discord had stayed with him until this moment—and regrettably translated to his mount. When the stallion shied at a phantom object in the adjacent woods, Hawk brought him up short, then used a firm leg and a soft word to send the horse forward again into a stronger canter. He had no business letting his foul mood affect the nervous animal.

Relying on small circles and more complicated patterns to regain the stallion's attention, Hawk wiped his mind clear of the frustrating beauty inhabiting his castle in order to refocus on his work.

Nearly an hour later, just as he was finishing with the stallion's schooling, Hawk caught a glimpse of a horsewoman riding toward him. Recognizing Lady Skye, Hawk swore another low oath. He should have expected her to do the unexpected and follow him out to the meadow behind the castle.

Just as unexpectedly, she was riding bareback, astride like a man. Her golden hair was down, while the hem of her gown was hiked up a bit to show dark stockings and an expanse of pale thigh.

Remembering those smooth, slender limbs wrapped around him made a rush of heat spike through Hawk.

So did her appearance when she reached the edge of the meadow where he'd come to a halt. She looked as charming and lovely as a summer morning.

Her skin had an enchanting flush that only enhanced her beauty, bringing to mind the potent memory of how she tasted, how she'd responded. He could still feel her beneath him, writhing with the desire he'd awakened in her. . . .

Fiercely disciplining the riot of his senses, Hawk eyed her disapprovingly, making it clear by his stare that he was not happy to see her. "What the devil are you doing here, Lady Skye?"

"I saw you riding off on your stallion from my bedchamber window, so I went to your stables to await your return. When you never appeared, I decided to come to you. I feared you wouldn't give me the chance to speak otherwise." When his frowning gaze narrowed on her mount, she added hastily, "This is one of my own carriage horses. I didn't want to take one of yours without permission."

"You balked at acting without my permission?" he drawled, his gruff reply designed to keep her at a distance. "How astonishing."

His sarcasm won a quick smile from her. "I know you are protective of your horses, and I did not want to get your grooms in trouble."

Lady Skye's consideration impressed him, but Hawk was not about to let her see it. In the face of his dispassion, she went on doggedly.

"I have been watching you from afar these past few minutes, Lord Hawkhurst. I had heard you were an amazing horseman, but you look like a centaur, a seamless part of your horse." She glanced pointedly at the stallion, who was standing quietly and obediently now. "Your grooms told me that splendid creature is said to be rather wild. No one else will dare mount him. How do you manage it?"

"You did not come here to discuss my horsemanship," he returned impatiently.

She offered him another smile, this one conciliatory. "Well, no. I was worried that I had made you angry."

At that vast understatement, a spark of sardonic amusement stirred inside Hawk.

"Actually, I wished to apologize to you," Lady Skye offered.

"Indeed."

"Yes. Not for last night. I am not sorry for . . . mating with you. It was too remarkable to regret. But I am extremely sorry for complicating your life. I truly did not mean to put you in such a quandary."

Hawk didn't know whether to be flattered or exasperated by her efforts to disarm him. He kept his stare level, resisting her charm.

"I hoped we might calmly discuss our dilemma."

"There is nothing to discuss. If you are carrying my child, you will marry me."

Her features remained calm. "You are right. We would have no choice. If it turns out that I am with child, I will marry you. But I hope that isn't likely."

"When were your last courses?"

Her eyes widened, and she looked a trifle embarrassed. Young ladies did not discuss such delicate matters as female bodily functions with gentlemen.

"You are certainly frank, my lord."

"I was married for several years, remember? Carnal relations depended on my wife's courses."

"I finished mine a few days ago."

"So we have several more weeks before the question is settled."

"Yes. We will have to wait and see. Meanwhile, I have a proposal for you."

Hawk cocked his head. "I am listening."

"I want to remain here at the castle until we learn if I have conceived. It will be only a short time, a month at most."

His mouth twisted at her perseverance. "You can wait elsewhere just as well, Lady Skye. You cannot stay here. The risk of scandal is too great."

"My family regularly lives on the edge of scandal. I am not concerned."

"You should be."

She returned his unyielding gaze steadily. "I am not a green girl, Lord Hawkhurst. I make my own decisions, and I am willing to live with the consequences."

"But I am not."

Skye lifted a well-shaped eyebrow. "Do you know your trouble? You are just too honorable."

"I didn't know there was such a thing as being too honorable," he said dryly.

"Oh, there is. A surfeit runs in my family as well. Take my brother, for instance. He might very well call you out to defend *my* honor. Trust me, you don't want Quinn to know what happened between us last night."

It was said lightly but her inference was obvious. At

her audacity, another shaft of unwilling amusement pricked Hawk. Not only had she intruded into his home and upended his hard-won peace, but she was hinting that she had the leverage to blackmail him.

Hawk shook his head. "You can't win with that argument, sweeting. You won't tell your brother for fear he would insist on our marriage."

She sighed and dimpled. "Alas, that's true. You are too astute, my lord. But I still need help finding my uncle's former love, and I cannot do it alone. I *need* you."

Her pretense at helplessness rang false, as Hawk was sure she knew, for she tried a different tack.

"Righting wrongs is your league's primary mission, is it not? Well, what happened to my uncle is a profound wrong. One you could help me set right." Her tone turned earnest. "Just imagine how lonely he is. He has no wife or children of his own. Even if she is no longer alive, it would mean so much to him to know that he had sired a child with his true love."

When he remained silent, Skye offered another argument. "I will make you a simple bargain. If you will help me with my uncle's plight, I will help you with preparing your house for your bride." She quickly raised a hand, preventing Hawk's immediate rejection. "Before you say no, let me explain. I can send for Aunt Bella this morning to act as chaperone. And until she arrives, I'm certain it would be possible to ask your temporary housekeeper or one of the other village matrons to stay a night or two at the castle."

"Searching for your uncle's lover could take weeks or even months. I can't afford that much time away."

"But perhaps you can. You said construction was

set to start at week's end, and you have hired an architect to supervise. By the time you return here, the repairs will be well under way. And I can work on hiring your household staff while you are away. There is so much to be done. . . . Not only clearing out the years of dirt and cobwebs but decorating and refurbishing also. Aunt Isabella has excellent taste, as I'm sure you know. And actually so do I."

Hawk shook his head in disbelief. Lady Skye was trying to commandeer his life and arrange matters to her satisfaction, but ever so sweetly, like a governess making the bitter medicine go down more easily. Only she was like no governess he'd ever seen.

Hawk was struck again by how novel she was. Novel, unique, fresh . . . and strong-willed. She was like a damned burr under his saddle. No doubt she counted on her persistence driving him to distraction until he gave in.

"When we are done with the house," she continued, "I will even help you court Miss Olwen. My family has a great deal of influence in society. With my brother being an earl and my cousin Ash a marquess, we can open doors to her that would otherwise be closed."

He had no doubt that every objection he made, Lady Skye would come up with a solution. Her suggestions were eminently logical but pointless. He had no choice but to refuse her request for help, since he had serious obligations that took precedence.

"Please just say you will think about it," she pleaded. She must have realized he would say no such thing, for she gave an exaggerated sigh. "I suspected you would be this stubborn."

"You are calling *me* stubborn?"

"Yes. But I am not one to admit defeat without a fight. I tend to remain optimistic, even when a cause seems hopeless. And I have faith you will eventually do the right thing," she added serenely.

Hawk gave a grunt of exasperation. "Don't count on it."

"I am very impressed, my lord. You've gone for five entire minutes without making that growling sound." Humor lit her eyes as she surveyed him. "Is that a hint of a smile I see? That is progress indeed. But I would be astonished if you can actually laugh, you are such a grouch."

He had to admit she amused him with her deliberate attempts to provoke him. He was a stranger to laughter and preferred to stay that way. Yet he found himself smiling back at her, damn her.

Skye looked annoyingly satisfied by her achievement. "I will return to the house now and leave you to your work. I was much too nervous to eat breakfast before I spoke to you, but now that I have braved the lion, so to speak, I realize I am famished."

Her blue eyes were perfectly innocent, yet there was a glimmer of laughter there, blast her cheek. She was teasing him in order to coerce him out of his foul humor.

She was succeeding, too. When Hawk met her gaze, something shivered through him, part laughter, part physical desire.

Then her smile faltered and he knew she had felt that same powerful jolt of sexual need. Suddenly she looked shy again, and without another word, she turned her horse away.

Hawk watched her leave with a feeling strongly akin to relief.

Oh, yes, Lady Skye was enormously dangerous to him. In less than a day, she'd incited him to forsake his scruples and possibly ruined his carefully calculated future. And that was nothing compared to the myriad of emotions she roused in him so effortlessly. In the past day he'd been, in turn, suspicious, curious, irritated, protective, passionate, angry, appalled, exasperated, amused, at peace. . . . He couldn't deny that with her he'd enjoyed a deep, dreamless, peaceful sleep for the first time in forever.

What shocked him, though, was how much he still wanted Skye. The desire to make love to her was still stinging his body, when his only burning desire should have been to serve and lead the Guardians.

His predicament would only grow worse with time, Hawk knew, for he couldn't just throw her out, and she wouldn't leave quietly. Her appearance of delicacy hid a spine of steel.

Yet she would have to give up eventually if he remained adamant. Moreover, he could ratchet up his efforts to drive her away, making it as uncomfortable as possible for her to stay.

Wholly aside from the risk of scandal, he didn't want Lady Skye Wilde living in the same house as he. He wanted no warmth and comfort in his life, nothing womanly and soft that would remind him so painfully of what he had lost.

Deliberately Hawk turned the stallion away from the castle. He had meant to return to the stables, but it was wiser to keep away when Lady Skye could be lurking around any corner, ready to ambush him with her vexing, tenacious optimism and her vital, vibrant smile.

Chapter Seven

When the earl remained away the entire day, Skye suspected he was purposely avoiding her, but when dusk fell, she grew worried. He would exhaust himself, riding for so long with no sustenance.

By nightfall, the daily housekeeper and maids had departed, leaving only Thomas Gilpin, the grizzled old man who acted as the castle caretaker. A longtime employee of the estate, Gilpin had been present when the earl's family perished in the fire, but he was not forthcoming in answering Skye's questions about the tragedy, in part, she suspected, because his memory seemed to be failing.

Even so, he was mindful of his master's whereabouts. When Skye made to don her cloak, intending to search for the earl in the stables, Gilpin reported that his lordship was already in his study. Exasperated, Skye realized that Lord Hawkhurst had slipped into the house unobserved, even though she had been watching for him.

She found him there, lounging on a sofa, making steady inroads into his decanter of brandy.

"Good evening, my lord. I came to invite you to partake of supper. I thought you might be hungry."

He barely glanced up at her. "You thought incorrectly."

Skye wasn't inclined to be dismissed so easily. "I met your temporary staff today and introduced myself. For propriety's sake, I told them my aunt should arrive soon." When Hawkhurst eyed her sharply, she hastened to add, "Don't fear. I did not actually invite Aunt Isabella without your permission."

"Thank God for small favors," he murmured.

"I set the maids to cleaning the main rooms today. And I began inventorying the furniture to see what needs repair or replacement. I thought that if I must wait here, I might as well make productive use of my time."

"I trust you don't expect to be accorded laurels for your unwanted efforts."

Skye ignored his sarcasm. "I see what you mean about Gilpin being frail and hard of hearing. He seems a sweet old soul, but he is not capable of heavy work with his rheumatism and aching joints. Nor can he cook well. So I asked the housekeeper to help me prepare your supper. We made a very decent meal, if I do say so myself."

"I said I am not hungry."

"But you need to eat."

"I ate at noonday in the stables with my grooms."

"That was a number of hours ago." When he made no reply, Skye softened her tone. "I laid out the dishes in the small dining room. Please, will you not join me?"

She could tell Hawkhurst was struggling to hold on

to his temper. "Thank you, no. That room holds too many memories for me."

At his admission, Skye instantly felt remorseful for pressing him to relive unpleasant memories. "Then I will bring you a supper tray here."

"You needn't bother."

"It is no bother, truly."

"Lady Skye," Hawkhurst finally said in a gruff tone, "I have no need for a guardian to supervise my eating habits—or my drinking habits, either."

Rather than argue further, Skye temporarily retreated from the field of battle and returned belowstairs, where she prepared a plate of food to take to him. They had roasted a leg of mutton on a spit, and she added helpings of bread pudding, artichokes, and stewed pears, then arranged a tray for him and poured a mug of ale.

Since the elderly Gilpin had retired to bed, the kitchens were deserted and quiet. When a shadow suddenly appeared behind her, Skye let out a soft shriek and whirled to face the threat. Hawkhurst had appeared in the kitchens without warning, his footfall undetectable. Rather than apologize for startling her, he seemed rather satisfied by his accomplishment.

Her hand covering her wildly beating heart, Skye sent him an accusing glance. "You frightened me deliberately, didn't you?"

"It is what a busybody like you deserves."

"Such tactics are beneath you."

"You are welcome to leave if you don't like my tactics."

Skye narrowed her gaze. "That is your aim, isn't it? To be as inhospitable as possible and make me want to leave?"

"Your powers of deduction are admirable, sweetheart."

She smiled. "You should know that I am not easily intimidated. I had to hold my own in a family of overbearing males."

"So you told me."

"What are you doing here in the kitchens? You said you weren't hungry."

"I knew you would not give up pestering me," he commented with a glance at the tray.

"Would you prefer to eat here or in your study?"

"Here will do."

They ate again at the servants' dining table, as they had the previous evening. Hawkhurst seemed preoccupied, though, and barely touched his food, preferring instead to drink his ale.

Disliking the heavy silence between them, Skye searched for something to lighten the mood. She finally settled on ribbing him.

"I confess you are a sore disappointment, my lord. A hero should not frighten innocent women and children."

"You are hardly an innocent—and you continue to overestimate my heroic qualities."

"I don't believe so. You are an extraordinary man."

Hawkhurst grimaced. "If you are trying to butter me up with false flattery, your attempts will fail."

Her admiration was not false flattery. Even though she had built Hawkhurst up in her mind to heroic proportions, he deserved the appellation of hero.

"You are a Guardian. That alone makes you a hero."

His frown deepened. "You know nothing about them."

"True, but I would like to know more."

"Isabella has revealed too much already."

"Only because she wanted me to understand the difficulty I would face in persuading you to put your courtship on hold in order to help my uncle. Your duty to the Guardians comes before all else."

"I don't wish to talk about them."

"If not, then what shall we talk about?"

He downed another large swallow of ale. "Nothing. Some peace and quiet would be very welcome. Have you never heard that silence can be a virtue?"

"Yes, but so can making polite conversation, my lord grouch."

His gaze swung back up to her. "You are set on intentionally provoking me, aren't you?"

"I hoped to prod you out of your stupor, yes."

When he scowled, Skye intuitively knew she had struck the wrong note. He seemed in no mood to be teased just now, so she ceased her efforts.

"I can be silent if I try very hard," she murmured contritely before applying herself to her food.

Occasionally when she cast a surreptitious glance at the earl, she found him staring down into his ale but without seeing much. Sorrow seemed permanently etched into the handsome lines of his face and his thoughts focused deep inside himself.

Skye wished she could do something to break his dark mood, but she bit her tongue. He did eventually begin to eat, more out of habit than hunger, she suspected.

When their meal was finished, he rose without speaking and turned away from the table.

"If you would like some company in your study,"

Skye said hurriedly, "I would be happy to oblige. I swear I won't pester you about helping my uncle. I happen to believe that we could make a good bargain—but I won't mention it again."

She did not get the expected rise out of him. Hawkhurst merely responded with that soft growl she was coming to know too well. "I would prefer you leave me in peace."

Skye watched him walk away. When she was alone once more, a worried frown turned down her mouth. She hated feeling helpless, but even more, she hated that Hawkhurst seemed so burdened by his thoughts. He was only getting more morose by the hour. At this rate, he would resemble a beast in truth. And there appeared to be nothing at all she could do about it.

In actuality, Hawk was contemplating a visit to the damaged wing of his house. He had to credit Lady Skye for inspiring the fortitude he'd been missing since his arrival at the castle. He ought not be intimidated by a mere building.

Even so, he detoured to his study to fetch a fresh bottle of brandy, knowing he might need a dose of liquid courage in order to face the charred remains of his son's nursery. He had to face the past at some point, and this was as good a time as any.

He also took a lamp to light his way and an iron bar to pry open the boards that had blocked the burned corridor for nearly a decade.

The fire had almost destroyed the farthest end of the wing, beginning on the second floor and burning through the servants' quarters and attics above, before collapsing the roof in places. Only a deluge from a massive thunderstorm had kept the flames from incinerating the rest of the mansion and the surrounding outbuildings.

Hawk's gut was tied in knots as he worked the boards loose until he created a wide enough opening for him to squeeze through. The musty, mildewed stench that hit him was mixed with the faint, acrid scent of smoke—although that could have been his imagination playing tricks.

As he slowly negotiated the cluttered floor, shadows played over the walls, sending agonizing memories winging through his mind, making him relive the terror that still haunted his dreams.

Calling on the control he'd so mercilessly taught himself, Hawk banished the images as he carefully picked his way through the ruins. When he reached the end of the corridor, a gaping hole in the floor prevented him from going farther.

This was where the nursery had been.

A great, raw pain surged through Hawk. He'd thought he was mostly over his grief, but he was wrong; it was merely bottled up inside him. Just now it felt as if all his limbs had been severed from his body and his chest had caved in.

Putting his back to the wall, Hawk sank down till he met the charred floor. Memories flooded him with relentless force: The flames, the suffocating smoke. Half-blinded, he'd staggered through the burning rooms like a madman, shouting hoarsely for Elizabeth, for Lucas, smashing windowpanes as he went, letting the drenching rain pour in. Yet he was too late.

He had been crawling on his hands and knees when

he spied their bodies huddled in a far corner of the nurse's bedchamber.

They'd been overcome by smoke, not burned, his sole reason to be thankful. He could imagine their screams, though. How terrified they must have been in their final moments . . .

Hawk raised the brandy bottle to his lips and drank deeply, futilely trying to numb the pain.

Lady Skye found him there some time later—how long he wasn't certain.

"Why're you here?" he demanded, slurring his words. "To shatisfy your morbid curios'ty?"

"I . . . it has nothing to do with curiosity. . . ." She spoke hesitantly, in a low voice, fumbling her words. "I did not want . . . you to be alone at a time like this."

But he wanted to be alone. He *deserved* to be alone. He deserved to have perished with his family.

She sank down beside him, not touching but close enough for him to feel her warmth. He didn't want her warmth, either, damn her.

She was silent long enough that he lost patience with *her* quiet patience.

"Do you wanna know how I losht my wife and child?"

"Only if you wish to tell me."

Hawk dragged a ragged hand over his face. There were streaks of wetness on his cheeks, tears he was hardly aware of crying. " 'Twas my fault."

She turned to gaze solemnly at him. "That is not what I was told. I heard that you tried desperately to save them."

"I should've been here." He drank again, relishing the burn in his aching throat.

"What happened, my lord?" she asked in a soft voice.

He drew an unsteady breath. "The fire shtarted in the nurs'ry. My son's nursh dropped a bloody candle an' the drap'ries caught fire. Sh-she fled, leaving Lucas in his crib. 'Lizabeth went in to rescue him."

"I am so terribly sorry," Skye said after a moment.

"I dragged out their bodies, did ju know?"

"Yes . . . I know."

"They acshually looked peaceful when I found 'em. Carried 'em both out of the flames. Shomeone took 'em from me just before the sheeling fell in. . . ."

"So I heard," she whispered, as if holding back her own tears. "When the ceiling collapsed, you lost consciousness and the servants pulled you from the burning wreckage."

Hawk nodded and brought the bottle to his lips again, annoyed to discover it was almost empty. "When I woke ev'r'thing I cared 'bout was gone." His sharp, humorless laugh was laced with bitterness. "Y' want t' hear the real irony? There was a damned storm that night! It shlowed my carr'age enough so I was delayed reeshing home. Too late for my family. If only I'd been a half hour earl'er . . ."

"Lord Hawkhurst . . . you cannot blame yourself."

"I bloody well *can*! It wash-sh *my* fault. I should've been there. I should've died with 'em."

For years the guilt had swamped him. That and fury that he'd been powerless to prevent the deaths of his beloved Elizabeth and his innocent young son. Hawk let loose a foul oath and threw his bottle against the far wall. The glass shattered, spraying brandy over the floor.

At the sudden crash, Lady Skye jumped, but remained sitting where she was. "I hope," she said softly, "that someday you can forgive yourself."

A savage anger raked him anew at her ridiculous notion. "*Forgive* mysehelf? Go the *hell* away."

She didn't move. "I cannot leave you here like this. As foxed as you are, you might come to harm."

Hawk sent her a fierce glare. If he wanted to drown his sorrows and risk coming to harm, who was she to stop him?

"Go '*way*," he repeated with the same grim conviction.

Skye returned the earl's gaze, feeling the pain that radiated from him. Seeing the bleakness in his haunted gray eyes, she wanted desperately to console him, as he'd done for her last night. His was a living nightmare, and her heart broke for him.

He was more than a little drunk, yet she couldn't condemn his inebriation or begrudge his fit of angry violence. In truth, it might help the tiniest measure if he could let out all that rage and grief.

Still, she couldn't leave him alone and in torment.

"You cannot remain here in the cold ruins all night. If you are staying, then so am I."

He grunted. "Y're a bloody, interferin' busybody, do y' know that?"

"Yes, I know, my lord. Will you come with me anyway?"

He refused to answer and instead sat there in brooding silence.

As time stretched out, Skye began to despair at her own helplessness. There was a stillness about him that spoke of a terrible isolation and loneliness, and she yearned to wrap her arms around him and hold him to her breast.

It took perhaps five more minutes, but he finally uttered a terse oath. "Ver' well, damn you. . . . I'll come."

He rolled onto his knees and struggled to stand. Gratefully, Skye picked up the lamp and rose, then put an arm around his waist, providing a shoulder for him to lean on.

They stumbled forward over blackened wood and damp, rotting carpet. A chill night breeze seeped into the corridor through the gaps in the wooden planks covering the windows. The glass panes were long gone, shattered that fateful evening of the fire by the earl in his futile attempt to let in the rain, Skye had heard.

The going was easier after they negotiated the opening in the boards. Hawkhurst seemed steadier on his feet now, and his words were slightly less slurred when he protested that she had bypassed his study as she guided him toward the stairway. "I need more brandy. . . ."

"I don't think that is wise."

When he started to curse her, she cut him off. "You can growl at me in the morning. For now I am putting you to bed."

They climbed the stairs slowly and trudged along the corridor to his bedchamber. Ushering him inside, Skye supported the earl across the room and left him standing while she set down the lamp and drew down the bedcovers. When she urged him to sit on the edge of the mattress, he remained swaying unsteadily on his feet, ignoring her invitation even as his eyes closed.

"You need to sleep, my lord. You are exhausted."

"Can't . . . won't . . . Don't wan' the nightmares."

She sensed such bleakness in him that the desire to hold him tight intensified. Yet she couldn't show her pity. Her best approach was to treat him like her brother and cousins, Skye decided.

"If you don't lie down and go to sleep, I swear I will comb the house until I find every remaining bottle and cask of brandy and pour every drop out the window."

At her threat, he pried one eye open and tried to focus a glare on her. "You woun't dare."

"You are welcome to test me."

She was only trying to distract him from his grief, but fortunately it succeeded. He sighed wearily and sank down upon the bed, then collapsed onto his side and shut his eyes again.

With effort, Skye pulled off his close-fitting boots, then worked off his coat. When she swung his legs up onto the bed, he rolled onto his side facing her and buried his face in the pillow.

Moving around to the other side of the bed, Skye stretched out beside Hawkhurst and drew the covers up over them both, giving barely a thought to the impropriety. She had already been completely intimate with him. Compared to that, spending the night in his bedchamber was scarcely an infraction. She couldn't let him be alone.

For that matter, she didn't want to be alone, either.

Easing closer, she slid an arm over his waist and pressed her front to his back.

Surprisingly, he was sober and awake enough to notice. "Are y' sleeping with me tonight?"

"Yes."

"You planning t' give me your body again?"

"No."

Regrettably. The taste of desire he had given her was sinfully hot, and she wanted more. But now was not the time. Now she simply wanted to ease his hurt, to warm him, to help him sleep.

When her warmth started to seep into him, he sighed again. It was not long before his body relaxed and his breathing grew more even.

Sleep was significantly more elusive for Skye. She kept seeing Hawkhurst's eyes, so lost and bleak. He didn't deserve such pain, she reflected, not for the first time, and she intended to do everything in her power to diminish it.

Pressing her nose into his hair, Skye breathed in his masculine scent and found her thoughts drifting back to her own dilemma.

Embracing this man felt so natural. She had wondered if he was her life's mate, and she was becoming more convinced by the day that he was.

She could fall in love with Hawkhurst so easily. In merely a day, her girlish infatuation had forged into something far stronger.

Whether she could make him love her was another question entirely. But even if she couldn't, she would do her best to set fate right for him. She would make it her mission to save him from a dark future, wedded to a missish young chit he couldn't possibly love.

And as Skye forced herself to close her own eyes, she made herself another solemn promise: She intended to erase those haunted shadows from his eyes if it was the last thing she ever did.

Chapter Eight

Hawk was awakened early the next morning by a rapping on his bedchamber door. Groggy, his head pounding, he carefully sat up and glanced around the room to find Skye gone. When the rapping sounded again, he bid entrance in a raspy voice.

Thomas Gilpin stepped inside, carrying a large mug. Silver bearded and small of frame, he resembled a gnome. Gilpin had served on the estate for decades, and after the fire, had asked to stay on at Hawkhurst Castle as caretaker rather than seeing the manor shut up completely. He was a man of little conversation, with a surly disposition, which normally suited Hawk.

"Her ladyship bade me bring ye this, m'lord," Gilpin said with remarkable good cheer as he crossed to the bedside.

"What is it?" Hawk asked warily.

"Some concoction that will do yer aching head good, she says. 'Tis a secret recipe, so I canna say the ingredients. I'm to stay until ye drink it down."

Hawk stared at his servant, who unexpectedly grinned, showing several gaping holes where he'd lost teeth.

"When yer feeling more the thing, m'lord, yer to come down to breakfast. M'lady's orders."

"Indeed."

"Aye. She thought to spare me carrying a heavy tray up the stairs with m' weak wrists. She's a kind one, that she is."

It sounded as if Skye had bewitched the old man, but Hawk was determined to resist her enchantment himself.

When he pointed warningly at the door and barked "Out!" in dismissal, Gilpin chuckled and set the mug down on the beside table. "Ver' well, m'lord, I'll leave. But her ladyship will not be pleased."

The servant retreated from the room and shut the door gingerly. Alone once more, Hawk rubbed his whiskered face and took stock of his current state. He felt emotionally drained, yet his outburst last evening had blessedly numbed some of the pain. He had also slept soundly again, in part because Skye had shared his bed. Annoyingly, he missed her warmth this morning.

Regardless of his feelings for his troublesome house-guest, though, it was time he roused himself from his stupor. He'd had enough of self-pity.

Hawk drained the mug, shuddering at the bitter taste, then rose and dressed in riding clothes. He needed a bath and a shave to be presentable, but for now his casual attire would have to do.

He was leaving his bedchamber when he realized the hammering in his head had subsided. More extraordinary, his appetite had returned. Hawk went down to the kitchens, where he found Skye sitting at the servants' dining table, making lists of what appeared to be tasks for cleaning and refurbishing his house.

Her gaze searched his for a moment before she set down her pen and smiled. "It appears you feel a trifle better."

"I must thank you for your potion," Hawk said, tempering his usual grudging tone.

"It is my cousin Jack's recipe—the hard-won result of much experimentation based on Quinn's scientific knowledge. They both swear by its efficacy. Your breakfast is being kept warm for you. Why don't you sit down and I will bring it to you."

Her lighthearted manner suggested that she was prepared to disregard the events of last evening, for which Hawk was grateful. Rising gracefully, Skye disappeared into the kitchen for a moment and returned with his covered plate.

When she was seated again, Hawk made a surprise announcement. "I have decided to take on your uncle's case."

She looked elated. "May I ask why you changed your mind?"

Why? Because he needed to act, as well as to escape the dark ghosts that pulled at him here. Moreover, he wanted to help Isabella. She'd been a good friend to him over the years, particularly during his darkest days when he first arrived on Cyrene, and she was like family to him now. "I owe it to Bella."

"I thought you might feel that way. So where do we start?" Skye asked eagerly.

"I need to determine a plan of attack. First I want to read your uncle Cornelius's letters from his lover—

the lady who reportedly feigned her death and fled to Ireland."

Skye nodded. "Her name was Rachel Pearse before she wed Baron Farnwell, but I expect she changed at least her surname to conceal her identity."

"That would have been the wise course."

Skye went upstairs to her bedchamber to fetch the packet of letters and returned in short order. As he finished eating, Hawk read each letter twice, looking for clues.

Skye remained silent until he folded the last one. "Did you find anything of note?"

"Nothing useful for the moment. And Ireland is a large country. To narrow down the location where Lady Farnwell took refuge, I will need to interview the midwife who acted as go-between for the lovers."

"That should not be difficult. Peggy Nibbs lives in Brackstone in Kent, scarcely two hours from here. We can be there and back in half a day."

He looked up from the last letter. " 'We'?"

"Mrs. Nibbs likely won't talk to you and reveal the secrets she has kept for many years. You are a perfect stranger to her. Besides, I have already quizzed her at length. She doesn't remember much."

"I should be able to get more out of her by asking the right questions."

Skye's blue eyes lit with humor. "Ah, yes, I should have expected you Guardians to employ interrogation techniques we normal civilians know nothing about."

Hawk ignored her provocation. "If you wish to accompany me, you will be ready to leave within the hour."

"As you wish. I won't delay you, I promise."

"And you will do exactly as I say."

She hesitated a moment to consider his demand. "Very well," Skye said genially. "You are the spy so I will defer to your wisdom. You likely know how best to proceed. Should we take your carriage and servants rather than mine? I intend to pay your full expenses, naturally."

"That won't be necessary."

"But it is only fair. You will be going to great expense on my behalf, and I can well afford it. I have my own fortune left to me by my mother. She was a French aristocrat but managed to escape the worst of the Revolution by marrying my father, an English earl."

Hawk raised a quelling eyebrow. "Are you already arguing with me, Lady Skye?"

"No, not at all, Lord Hawkhurst. I would never dare such a thing."

Her false meekness brought the hint of a smile to his mouth.

Skye eyed him in approval. "I am glad you have stopped being such an ogre. You are much more pleasant when you are not snapping and growling."

He chuckled unwillingly. "Don't expect my good mood to last."

"You call *this* a good mood?" she teased.

Curbing his urge to return her banter, Hawk handed her back the packet of letters and gestured toward the door. "You had best leave the kitchens, my lady. I intend to bathe in the storeroom so Gilpin won't have to carry cans of hot water upstairs."

"Yes, of course. I will go change into my traveling gown so I can be ready to leave as soon as you command."

When she dallied, he pulled the tails of his shirt from his breeches in preparation of removing it. To his amusement, Skye quickly gathered her lists and beat a hasty retreat to avoid seeing him undress. But while Hawk thought he might have won this skirmish, he was certain the next ones would not be so easy.

Skye was perfectly willing to let Hawkhurst take the lead in the midwife's inquisition, but she was also glad for the opportunity to drag the beast from his lair. She didn't want him dwelling on his pain, and giving him a purpose was the best way to distract him.

As promised, she was ready to depart within the hour and met him in the stable yard, where his carriage and team awaited. If she'd thought him ruggedly attractive with his jaw stubble and country gentleman's attire, he was breathtakingly handsome with his face clean shaven, his ebony hair washed and shining, and his tanned, chiseled features set off by a sparkling white cravat. His clothes fit his noble station also, his superbly tailored coat molding his broad shoulders to perfection and a caped greatcoat flung over his arm. Skye felt the familiar riotous fluttering in her stomach as he handed her inside and settled next to her.

The journey to Kent went by rather quickly. Hawkhurst spoke little, but Skye found herself telling him all about her family and their history with Isabella. It was only when they reached the small village of Brackstone that she realized how skillfully he had drawn her out with his subtle probing, while she had learned practically nothing more about him.

He was the most enigmatic man she had ever met, she decided, marveling at how his gray eyes cloaked with heavy black lashes hid his every emotion. She suspected the previous evening's heartrending revelations were the last she would get for quite some time.

The ivy-covered stone cottage where midwife Peggy Nibbs lived was pretty and well kept but common enough that the earl looked out of place with his aura of elegance and power. When Skye made the introductions, the elderly dame seemed intimidated at first, but over cups of steaming tea, which Mrs. Nibbs shyly offered, Lord Hawkhurst successfully put her at ease with gentle questions designed to enhance her memories and unearth clues about Lady Farnwell's trail more than two decades ago. Skye listened to their conversation with growing fascination.

Mrs. Nibbs knew the general area of Ireland where the fugitive had intended to seek refuge but not the specific county, although she thought the name began with "Kil."

She did recall that it was not a large town like Dublin, but a small village. When asked about weather and key geographical markings such as lakes or seaside or mountains, the only detail that came to mind was a castle.

As for pseudonyms Lady Farnwell might be using, she had hoped to find shelter with a distant female relative whose surname sounded a bit Spanish . . . something that brought to mind the celebrated lover Don Juan. When Hawkhurst suggested "Donovan," "Donoghue," or "O'Donnell" as possibilities, Mrs. Nibbs nodded slowly at the last. "Perhaps Donnelly. Yes, that might be it. I know her ladyship mentioned liking the name 'Meg' because it rhymed with mine—Peg."

When he concluded his questioning, Mrs. Nibbs expressed her relief. "I am sorely glad the secret is finally out. I did not want to carry that to my grave." A tear rolled down her wizened cheek. "Now I pray you can find her ladyship and lay my worst fears to rest. It has been a terrible burden, not knowing what became of her."

"If she is still alive, she will be found," Hawkhurst assured her.

Mrs. Nibbs appeared to believe him, for she sniffed in gratitude and pressed more tea upon him. "If by some miracle you do locate her, my lord, you must not let the new Lord Farnwell know her whereabouts." Her gaze darkened. "Edgar is not a very good man. Sadly, he is miserly and mean, much like his late father, although perhaps not outright vicious and cruel. He has not been kind to his half sister, Miss Daphne."

The Honorable Miss Daphne Farnwell was the daughter that Rachel Farnwell had abandoned as a baby, Skye remembered, while Edgar Farnwell was the present baron and two years younger than Daphne. Edgar's father—and Rachel's abusive husband—William, had remarried barely a year after her supposed death by drowning.

When it was time to leave, Skye embraced the elderly midwife and thanked her for her help, promising she would be among the first to know if Lady Farnwell was found.

On the return drive to Hawkhurst Castle, Skye expressed her genuine admiration to the earl. "You learned a good deal more helpful information than I thought possible."

"You should have had more faith in me," Hawkhurst responded.

"True. What comes next?"

"I'll start by studying maps of Ireland. Fortunately it should be easier to find her in a village than a metropolis. But I think I will summon a colleague of mine from London to aid me."

Skye frowned slightly. "Must you involve someone else? I hoped the search could be done discreetly. We ought not expose Lady Farnwell's secrets to the world, especially since it could result in serious repercussions for her daughter, Daphne."

"Macky happens to be Irish and may have some insight on where best to begin the search."

"Is he a spy like you?"

Hawkhurst didn't deign to answer her provoking question. "I would have traveled directly to London to meet with him this afternoon, but I must see you home instead."

She couldn't dispute his decision. It would not be prudent for her to travel to London with him where she might be seen by her many acquaintances. The ton thought she had retired to Tallis Court, the Traherne family seat in Kent, and she would just as soon maintain that fiction.

"How may I help?" Skye asked the earl.

"You needn't worry. I will proceed from here."

"Do you intend to look for Lady Farnwell yourself?"

"Perhaps. I want to discuss the plan with Macky."

"If you go to Ireland, I ought to accompany you. Uncle Cornelius is my family. I should be part of finding his true love. If we do, I hope to persuade her to return to England to be reunited with him and her daughter."

"You can write her a letter."

"Lady Farnwell might not heed a letter. I would stand a better chance if I make my request in person."

"You are jumping the gun," Hawkhurst replied patiently. "We must find her before moving on to the next step. You may trust me to act appropriately."

She did trust him, Skye acknowledged. He was intriguing to watch in action—dynamic, decisive, sharp-witted, but with a kindly touch that had put an old woman at ease. This was the real Lord Hawkhurst, she decided . . . a far different man than the dour recluse or the grieving widower she had known over the past two days.

When they reached his home, however, the familiar grimness seemed to descend over Hawkhurst once more. His tone was curt when he escorted her inside the front hall. "I have asked the housekeeper to stay the next few nights at the castle to act as your chaperone."

"Do you fear being alone with me?" Skye asked lightly, but apparently he was done bantering. He gave her a dismissive look before turning to stride off toward his study.

"May we at least dine together this evening?" Skye called after him.

"Yes," he answered gruffly. "For now I have your uncle's business to attend to. I will see you at seven."

At the arranged hour, Hawkhurst appeared in the kitchens, dressed once more in his casual attire. Her body was instantly aware of him, but Skye tried to suppress her desire when he joined her at the servants' dining table.

The dinner this time was more in keeping with the usual fare suitable for an earl. They enjoyed less privacy also. Mrs. Hannah Yeats, the housekeeper, along with two of the maids, Maria and Betty, bustled to and fro, serving a variety of dishes.

Over the meal, Hawkhurst reported that he had sent a messenger to London to summon Macky. Beau Macklin was his real name, Skye learned, and he had formerly been an actor, but she gleaned nothing more except that he would likely arrive on the morrow.

When they were finished eating, Hawkhurst made to excuse himself.

"Would you care for a game of chess?" she asked. "Aunt Isabella says you play, and I brought my own set."

"Indeed?" His gaze fixed on her. "You were awfully certain of gaining admittance, weren't you?"

She sent him a bright-eyed look. "Not certain, merely hopeful. I must warn you, I am rather good at chess since my brother taught me. Quinn is actually quite brilliant when it comes to strategy."

"Perhaps some other time."

"Are you afraid you will be beaten by a woman?"

A knowing glimmer lit his eyes and turned the hue to silver. "This is your latest attempt to distract me, isn't it, Lady Skye?"

She dimpled. "Well, yes—but I think a little distraction would stand you in good stead at the moment. Otherwise you will just hide away in your study and drink brandy all evening."

His mouth twisted. "After last night, I have temporarily lost any taste for brandy."

Skye felt it was progress if he could refer jokingly to his overindulgence.

He was a superb chess player, she soon discovered

when they repaired to his study. He beat her soundly twice, although the third game was closer. When she stifled a yawn, he proposed they retire for the evening.

"Separately?" she asked although she knew the answer. "I suppose with Mrs. Yeats here, we ought not sleep together in the same room."

His response was very dry. "You suppose correctly. In fact, we will never sleep in the same room again."

Skye refrained from arguing that point, even though she had every hope of changing his mind. "What if I have another nightmare? Or what if you do?"

"We will just have to suffer through."

Hawkhurst escorted her upstairs to her bedchamber door and parted ways.

It was with great regret that Skye watched him walk away, yet more than any time since her arrival, she felt hopeful that she was at last slipping under his guard a small measure.

Hawk dreamed about her that night—one of the most erotic dreams he'd ever experienced. He woke the next morning with his cock stiff and aching, his mind filled with lingering sensations: his fingers tangled in her golden hair, her breast in his mouth, her bare legs wrapped around his hips as he took his pleasure of her and gave her pleasure in return.

When they met in the kitchens for breakfast, the lucent memory of making love to her hit him like a fresh blow. Unwanted images flooded him . . . Skye beneath him, sobbing with ecstasy as he sheathed himself deeper within the haven of her body.

The thought of bringing her to passion again made his loins grow heavy, and he had difficulty hiding the result. Thankfully Macky arrived by midmorning and served as a distraction from his erotic fantasies.

Macky was indeed a member of the Guardians. The chestnut-haired Irishman was also a charming ladies' man who had recently—and surprisingly—met his match with a quiet young beauty, Lady Claire Montlow. Claire's elder sister Eve, Countess of Hayden, had less-surprisingly married Hawk's fellow Guardian, Sir Alex Ryder. Macky and his new bride continued to reside in England, while the Ryders made their home on the Isle of Cyrene.

Lady Skye, who had a natural charm even more potent than Macky's, worked her wiles on the Irishman, enough to coax him to admit that he was occasionally employed by the Foreign Office. It didn't satisfy her rabid curiosity about the Guardians, Hawk could tell, but she didn't press further.

Hawk had her repeat the story about her uncle's suspected love affair, then related the details he'd uncovered during his interview of the midwife, Peggy Nibbs. Afterward he allowed Skye to sit in on their deliberations as he and Macky pored over maps of Ireland.

Eventually they decided to concentrate the search in the area closest to England that matched Mrs. Nibbs's recollections. The southeastern county of Kilkenny boasted a town of the same name built around a medieval castle, as well as a smaller town, Castlecomer, a short distance to the north.

The region even farther to the north had the additional advantage of being a horse-racing center with a National Stud and a celebrated racecourse. The broad plain of the Curragh in County Kildare was home to a number of studs with top breeding stallions.

Acting as an advance scout, Macky would travel in the guise of purchasing agent for Lord Hawkhurst, who, he would say, wished to add some champion bloodstock to his stables. Hawk had various contacts in Ireland from his former visits there, but Macky could blend in with the local citizenry with remarkable ease and so could ask questions more easily, he explained to Lady Skye.

"Then you have played these roles before?" she observed.

"Aye, that we have, my lady," Macky answered, his eyes twinkling.

Hawk explained his rationale. "It will raise less suspicions if Macky goes first, besides making the search progress more quickly. I will follow him a few days later, after I put my affairs in order here at home."

Before Macky took his leave, Hawk gave him some additional instructions. "When you return from Ireland, I will want you to find out everything you can about the late baron William Farnwell, and his son, Edgar, as well as Lady Farnwell's daughter, Daphne. In fact, you should hire Linch to begin inquiries while you are gone."

"Who is Linch?" Skye asked.

"A London Bow Street Runner who has a keen eye for details."

The Runners were private thief takers, but Horace Linch possessed a number of skills the Guardians had relied upon in the past.

When Skye looked concerned at yet another stranger becoming involved in her uncle's tragic love story, Hawk reassured her. "You may trust Linch to be discreet."

Macky made her a similar promise before collecting the miniature portrait of Rachel, Lady Farnwell, to use in his inquiries, then bowed himself out.

When Hawk was alone with Skye once more, she thanked him for personally conducting the search for the missing Lady Farnwell. "So you mean to leave for Ireland in a few days?"

"Yes. The sooner the better. I have a great deal of work to do here first, but a delay will allow Macky time to narrow the search area."

She nodded sagely. "This is a good time for you to be away. Even if you weren't inclined to traipse all over Ireland on my uncle's behalf, you ought not stay here while the damaged rooms are being torn down."

Hawk gave her a sharp look. "I don't need you to coddle me, sweeting."

"Certainly you do. Everyone needs a little coddling now and then, and you have no one else to do it for you. I am well practiced at coddling, since I have a large family and any number of good friends."

Hawk managed to hide a smile. In some respects, he appreciated her concern for him. Her heart was soft enough that she wouldn't let him wallow in his pain. But it went against the grain to accept her succor.

For the next two days, he made it a point to keep away from Skye as much as possible. He did have major preparations to make before he could leave. The first was to send for the architect in order to finalize arrangements for rebuilding the house. The workmen would start sooner than planned, so that the razing of the damaged wing would be well under way by the time he returned to England.

Another critical step was to summon Isabella here

to stay with her niece. It would never do to leave Lady Skye alone in his home for such a length of time without a respectable relative to quell the inevitable gossip.

Hawk was actually glad to have a mission to occupy him, though. Skye was right. Leaving would allow him to escape the inevitable din of reconstruction as well as the ghosts.

He was even gladder to delay beginning his courtship of Sir Gawain's niece. The onerous chore of wooing a shy young miss held no appeal whatsoever.

Surprisingly Lady Skye made no requests to accompany him on his journey to Ireland. Instead, she claimed to have plenty to occupy her while he was away. She was already supervising his temporary servants and had enlisted the stable hands, including her own grooms, in cleaning and refurbishing the house. And she wrote her cousin Lady Katharine Wilde to ask for help hiring staff from a London employment agency, starting with a permanent housekeeper and butler, although she vowed to leave the final decisions to Hawk.

His plans progressed much as he wished. Even his relationship with his meddlesome houseguest settled into an amiable truce where she no longer pressed him about his past. Skye didn't seem particularly sorry that he would be leaving, either.

The night before his scheduled departure, he was awakened in the wee hours by a creaking sound outside his bedchamber door. Wondering if perhaps Skye had suffered a recurring nightmare, Hawk went to his door and opened it wide enough to see her tiptoeing down the hall, carrying a partially covered lamp.

"I am returning to my rooms," she murmured in

explanation when she spied him. "I couldn't sleep so I went downstairs for a glass of warm milk."

In the dim light, he could just make out her attire. "Then why are you wearing your traveling cloak?"

His suspicious tone didn't seem to faze her. "I have no proper dressing gown with me."

Hawk remembered deciding not to loan her any of his late wife's garments. He could have offered her one of his own dressing gowns, but picturing Skye in his clothing would only have led to unwanted fantasies about removing it.

When she said a pleasant good night, he made no response. With a frown on his face, Hawk watched her slip inside her room, then returned to his own bed. He rose early, but she must have slept in. He was conscious of a faint, nagging disappointment that Skye was not at breakfast in order to wish him farewell.

When he arrived in the stable yard where his coach and team awaited him, his footman opened the carriage door and stood back. Hawk was halfway inside when he realized the vehicle was already occupied. Lady Skye sat in the far corner, dressed in her traveling gown and cloak. Evidently she had snuck into his coach while he was breakfasting, or perhaps even earlier.

He settled slowly on the seat and shook his head in admiring disbelief. "This was the reason for your midnight endeavor, wasn't it? You weren't after warm milk to help you sleep."

"Oh, but I was," Skye avowed. "I needed a good excuse in case you caught me roaming the corridors. I put my valise in the boot last night and hid myself here this morning, since I didn't want you to see me and provoke an argument in front of the servants."

"Why ever would we argue?" he drawled sardonically.

"Because you will no doubt object to my intentions. I am coming with you to Ireland," she announced serenely.

"No, you are not."

"If you wish to stop me, you will have to throw me bodily out of your carriage."

"Don't think I won't."

"If you do, I will only follow you in my own carriage. And I see no point in doubling the expense of searching for my uncle's true love."

"You cannot travel all that distance with me. My inquiries could take a fortnight or more."

Lady Skye had an answer for that also. "I am not concerned about scandal, remember? To conceal my identity, I will wear a veil in public and pose as your widowed cousin, at least while we are in England. See"—she held up a black bonnet with a swath of black netting—"Mrs. Yeats loaned this to me. It should be adequate to prevent me from being recognized by anyone who happens to know me."

Hawk felt an urge to grind his teeth. "Your brother will be angry."

"My brother has no say in this matter," Skye assured him. "I can manage my own life. Moreover, Quinn will be mollified if we succeed. He loves our uncle and wants his happiness almost as much as I do."

Her expression grew earnest as she leaned closer to Hawk. "Please, my lord. . . . Fate played a horrible trick on my uncle, but now I have a chance to set it right. I would never forgive myself if I let it pass by without trying to help."

"You have already done more than enough."

"No, I have barely begun."

Hawk eyed her with a baleful look, half-exasperated and wholly vexed. He believed Lady Skye when she threatened to follow him. He couldn't let her go haring off to Ireland alone. If nothing else, he would have to protect her from herself.

With a disgruntled sigh, he rapped on the coach roof, giving his coachman the order to start his team. This was not surrender, Hawk told himself. He merely wanted to accomplish his task quickly so he could be rid of Skye and temptation.

"Do you always get your way?" he grumbled when the carriage was moving.

She flashed him a brilliant smile and laughed softly. "Almost always," she replied without even a pretense of humility.

His lips twitched. "You are an aggravating, conniving little wretch, do you know?"

"Yes, I know, but I will grow on you over time."

Hawk gave a snort. "I doubt that."

He wouldn't give her the opportunity to grow on him, he promised himself, but for now it appeared he was stuck with her.

Determined to ignore her as much as possible, Hawk stretched his long legs out on the opposite seat and leaned back against the leather squabs. Then he crossed his arms and shut his eyes, prepared to get some of the sleep that had eluded him the previous night because of his erotic dreams and pretend he wasn't acutely aware of the charming beauty who sat there on the seat beside him, smiling so sweetly and smugly.

Chapter Nine

Skye was vastly relieved that Hawkhurst had agreed to let her accompany him, albeit under duress. Yet he was distancing himself from her, she could tell. When he woke from his slumber, he unbent only enough to tell her the route they would take.

They were now heading for the seaport of Bristol, where they would likely have to wait for a passenger ship to ferry them to Wexford Harbor in Ireland. From there they would travel northwest to Kilkenny, the closest county to England that matched the details Mrs. Nibbs remembered. Hawkhurst had made this exact journey several times in the past, in search of champion bloodstock for his racing stables.

Otherwise, he withdrew from conversation the first day, hiding any emotion in his eyes behind that dark fringe of lashes. Skye resolved to bide her time, but it was difficult in the close confines of his coach. Her physical awareness of him grew with each mile they traveled. Sitting so near to him, she could feel the warmth of his splendid body and smell the now-familiar scent of his skin mixed with the freshness of soap.

When they reached Bristol late that evening, they took separate rooms at an inn but ate supper together in a private parlor. Over the meal, he made one more effort to dissuade her. "I will happily hire a carriage to convey you home in the morning."

Skye shook her head. "You will not change my mind, my lord."

The stakes were too high, she added silently, both for her uncle and for herself. This was her best and perhaps sole chance to win Hawkhurst as her heart-mate, and she wasn't giving up.

He continued pressing her, however. "Bella is scheduled to arrive at my estate tomorrow. She will worry when you are not there to receive her."

"I left her a note of explanation. She will not only understand, she would encourage me to accompany you. Besides, I might actually be able to help you find Lady Farnwell. Two heads are often better than one."

"I already have two heads with Macky. Three, counting Linch."

"It is not the same thing. You obviously haven't considered Lady Farnwell's perspective. If a number of strange men come hunting for her after all these years, she may take fright. As a woman, I will stand a better chance of soothing her fears. Especially since I am related to her former lover."

Hawkhurst gave her credit for the point but said he would be able to manage Lady Farnwell on his own. "Furthermore, I have no desire to be burdened with a meddlesome pest the entire journey."

Skye smiled up at him. "Instead of chiding me for

meddling, you should be thanking me for providing you a reason to leave home."

His mouth curled. "You are all consideration."

"Indeed, I am. It is not healthy to dwell on your sorrows. I can provide you a distraction and keep you company."

"I have no desire for either."

When she offered to play chess—or cards, if he preferred—to break up the monotony of their travels, he agreed to chess but didn't seem to appreciate the teasing note in her voice when she added, "If I win, you must tell me more about the Guardians."

Hawkhurst responded with more than a hint of exasperation. "You will learn nothing more about them from me."

"Why is it so imperative that your league remains a secret?"

"If I tell you why, it won't be a secret anymore, will it?"

Other than their chess matches and meals, however, Hawkhurst spent as little time as possible with her. Two mornings later, they boarded a ferry, along with the earl's carriage and servants. As they sailed out of the mouth of the Severn, heading for the Irish Sea, Skye stood at the prow of the ship beside Hawkhurst, unable to contain her excitement, despite a chill wind and rough seas.

"I have never been to Ireland before. In fact, I have seldom left England, although I accompanied my family across France this past summer to support Jack when he visited his father's principality of Navartania, so this will be an exciting adventure for me. The Wildes are known for their audacious exploits, but I never am allowed to enjoy any."

Judging from Hawkhurst's skeptical glance, he didn't appear to believe her. "What do you call camping on my doorstep in a thunderstorm?"

"That was unnerving, not exciting. And I am speaking in generalities. My brother is overly protective of me and firmly resolved to keep me out of danger."

"Can you fault him for that?"

"I suppose not. But it is hardly fair. Quinn is the daredevil in our family and is even an intimate of Lord Byron. He risks his own skin far too frequently to my mind, and his cavalier attitude toward his own safety is our greatest source of disagreement. After losing our parents, I couldn't bear to lose Quinn also. And he feels similarly about me. But my gender is a significant additional disadvantage."

She glanced up at Hawkhurst. "You have traveled the world, so you wouldn't understand how liberating this journey to Ireland is for me. You have never had to bow to the dictates of society, either. It is enormously frustrating, being hemmed in by the strictures governing women—especially unmarried young women."

To underscore her complaint, Skye raised the face veil she had worn in public since leaving his estate in East Sussex. She had always wanted to do more, to *be* more than genteel young ladies were permitted to be. But this was actually the first time she had ever struck out on her own in a major way, without her family close by. Even when she'd gone away to boarding school as a girl, her cousin Katharine had been with her. Kate was privy to her current plan to romance Lord Hawkhurst, but wouldn't interfere unless Skye specifically asked for help. She didn't intend to tell Quinn at all, for he would likely drag her home.

"Please, allow me to enjoy this moment, Lord Hawkhurst," she entreated in a low voice.

He held her gaze for a long moment, studying her as if judging her sincerity. Then surprisingly, he relented. Rather than retire belowdecks, he summoned one of the crew to fetch her a blanket, then wrapped her in it to keep her warm and stood beside her, answering her questions about Ireland and relating interesting facts about his travels there.

As the ship crossed St. George's Channel, the vivid green land mass grew till it resembled a jewel rising from the water.

"How striking," Skye murmured. "I can see why Ireland is called the Emerald Isle."

Later, as they grew closer, Hawkhurst pointed out various features along the coast, which led to a discussion about horses.

"You seem to know Ireland well," Skye observed. "You said you come here often to purchase bloodstock?"

"Every few years. Some of the best stock comes from Ireland."

"Have you always bred horses?"

A dark cloud momentarily claimed his features. "Not until I moved to Cyrene. I began breeding as a diversion but continued in earnest when I had success crossing Berbers and Arabians with Irish and English Thoroughbreds."

"Why would you want to mix breeds?"

"To leaven stamina and endurance with speed and grace."

"And you sell the horses you raise?"

"Most of them. Not for the income as much as the satisfaction of creating spectacular results."

"But you train them as well, do you not?"

"Sometimes. That *is* purely for the satisfaction." His warm tone seemed to verify his statement.

"I think I can understand why," Skye observed. "Horses are magnificent creatures, and you clearly have a magical touch with them, judging by the stallion you rode the other day. How do you ever manage to gentle a horse like that so easily?"

"I start by letting him know my voice and scent and touch to persuade him to trust me."

That was precisely what she was trying to do with Hawkhurst, Skye thought. Not that she could allow him to know her strategy. She would drive him away if she let on how badly she wanted him. That was one of her Aunt Isabella's prime rules in the game of love: *A lady should never appear to chase a gentleman. She must contrive to let him pursue her instead.*

Skye had quizzed her aunt in great detail about how to approach Hawkhurst. *You must be his friend and confidant, simply be there for him when he needs comforting,* Isabella had warned her.

Easier said than done, Skye had quickly discovered, given the way he closed himself off from the world. Except for that one night of drunken revelations, he was clearly an intensely private man who'd finely honed the art of protecting his secrets. He was maddeningly remote and elusive. Undoubtedly numerous other women had attempted futilely to overcome that elusiveness.

Skye had every intention of succeeding, however. She

had made her choice. Hawkhurst was her future mate, she was sure of it. She had only to make him see it.

That, and win his heart.

Glancing at him now, she swallowed her misgivings. Despite the earl's rakish behavior in his salad days, he had fallen in love and become a devoted husband and father. Skye devoutly hoped that if he had loved once, he could do so again.

But first she needed to help him put to rest his tragic past. From practically the first moment of meeting him, she had felt his overwhelming sadness, his loneliness, and she meant to put a stop to both. She was most haunted, however, by Hawkhurst's guilt that he hadn't perished with his family.

Skye pressed her lips together in determination. She would give him a new reason for living by making him fall in love with her.

A difficult task, yes, but not impossible.

She was a Wilde, after all.

They spent the night at the small seaport of Wexford, and then set out for the town of Kilkenny early the next morning, where Hawkhurst had arranged to rendezvous with Macky. When they arrived at the designated inn, a message awaited them from Macky about his lack of progress, saying that he had ridden to the smaller town of Castlecomer and should return by the next afternoon.

They were met with additional news that did not sit well with Hawkhurst. Due to the traveling fair in town, the inn was nearly full, so they were able to book only a single bedchamber and no private parlors.

To Skye's disappointment, Hawkhurst said he would

spend the night with his male servants. Perhaps to avoid being cooped up with her for the remainder of the day, however, he offered to show her the sights while they waited for his colleague, much to her surprise and delight.

In medieval times, he told her, Kilkenny had once rivaled Dublin in historical importance but had not grown apace. Even so, it boasted both a cathedral and a castle of gray stone overlooking the River Nore, as well as shops and a market. Upon attending the fair, Hawkhurst bought her an ice and took her to watch the jugglers and acrobats and a troupe of actors performing parts of the Shakespearean comedy *A Midsummer Night's Dream*.

The engaging entertainments made Skye feel as if she were celebrating a holiday rather than pursuing a somber investigation. Hawkhurst himself seemed to relax a small measure and even cracked a smile once or twice when she teased him about his solemnity.

At the conclusion of the long day, she was pleasantly weary but returned to the inn with reluctance. She hadn't wanted the enchantment to end.

"Thank you for a lovely day, my lord," she told him earnestly as they entered the Green Goose. "I can't remember when I have enjoyed myself more."

Perhaps Hawkhurst might have answered had the innkeeper not greeted him just then. "My lord, a message arrived for you barely moments ago."

Hawkhurst took the proffered letter but waited until they had climbed the stairs to her room before breaking the seal and scanning the contents.

"Is it from Macky?" Skye asked.

"Yes. He discovered a possible lead to Rachel Farnwell's whereabouts."

Excitement filled Skye. "What does he say?"

"A shopkeeper in Castlecomer recognized the subject in the miniature portrait. It resembles a woman by the name of Meg Donnelly, who lives in a small village close to Castlecomer."

"That is famous!"

"Don't raise your hopes too high," Hawkhurst warned. "It might not be Lady Farnwell."

"But it might be. So what is our next step? Should we travel there tonight?"

"Such haste isn't necessary. Macky wishes to investigate further and try to confirm her identity. If so, he won't approach her alone. You and I will leave in the morning in time to meet with him at noon. It is less than two hours' drive."

Skye found it difficult to contain her anticipation, but she realized that no purpose would be served by racing to reach Castlecomer that evening.

They could have dined in the public room of the inn, but Hawkhurst ordered supper to be brought upstairs to her room. Even though she'd given up her face veil once they'd disembarked in Ireland, they wanted to avoid her needless exposure.

Over their meal, Skye became conscious that this might be her last opportunity to be alone with him for a while, since they would be joining his colleague the next morning. She dallied as long as possible over the game of piquet that followed, knowing that Hawkhurst intended to spend the night elsewhere.

When it was time to retire, she stopped him before he rose from the table. "You needn't leave, my lord.

There is no reason to inconvenience yourself by sleeping with your servants when a perfectly good bed is right here."

He glanced dismissively at her. "There is only one bed."

"We have spent two nights together already. What harm will there be in doing so once more? Please, won't you consider staying here with me tonight? I have not slept well on this entire journey, being alone in strange inns."

That was completely true. She'd had another nightmare last night, although not a severe one. But she also wanted him to sleep with her so she could comfort him. There were still shadows lingering in his eyes—shadows she longed to banish.

"It would be the gentlemanly thing to do," Skye added lightly. "You are supposed to be a hero. You should act like one and console me."

Faint amusement curved his lips, even as he studied her skeptically. "This is another of your connivances, isn't it?"

There was no avoiding the perceptive depths of his eyes, so she didn't even try. "I may be conniving," she readily admitted, "but I usually have good reason. In this case, I can sleep much more peacefully with you. Nothing needs happen between us. We can remain perfectly chaste."

Hawkhurst hesitated a long moment. When she was about to give up hope, he shook his head in self-deprecation, as if hardly believing he would agree to her proposition. "Very well. I'll stay."

Feeling a great surge of relief, Skye smiled. Rising,

she moved around the table. "Here, let me help you off with your coat."

"I can undress myself," he said dryly.

"But you have no valet present, and I don't mind. Besides, I would like you to reciprocate. It is not easy untying a corset by myself."

He allowed her to take his coat and waistcoat. While she hung the garments on a wall peg, he removed his boots and cravat.

Drawn by his irresistible allure, Skye couldn't help watching him. His well-tailored shirt and breeches clung to his body, accenting his lean, muscular grace. His shirt followed, revealing the powerful play of the sleek muscles of his chest and shoulders and arms. Her pulse quickened as he stripped down to his drawers. He was so beautiful he took her breath away.

Then he crossed to the bed to turn down the covers, giving her his ravaged back, reminding her once again of his tragic past.

Feeling less steady at the sight of his burn scars, Skye started to undress herself. She managed her gown and half boots and stockings easily, but when it came time to untie her corset, she presented her own back to him.

"Why do I get the feeling you are working your female wiles on me?" Hawkhurst asked as he loosened the strings.

"Perhaps because I am. How else am I to deal with so irritable a grouch as you?"

"I am not such a grouch. I displayed admirable forbearance for not tossing you out on your ear when you snuck into my carriage."

"So you did. You have been much more pleasant

these past few days. My influence must be wearing off on you."

The slight huff he gave was part scoff, part chuckle. Skye glanced back over her shoulder at him. "Can you blame me for making use of my feminine wiles? I am not ashamed that I have a knack for dealing with men. As Aunt Isabella says, we women don't have the advantages you men have, so we must rely on whatever talents we possess."

Hawkhurst's eyes flickered with amusement again. "I won't let you run roughshod over me, sweet wretch."

"Of course you won't," she agreed congenially, but inside she was debating with herself. She well knew she couldn't have her way as easily with Hawkhurst as with other men. But she intended to try.

When he had loosened her corset, Skye removed it, leaving her wearing only her shift. She meant to sleep that way rather than change into her nightgown. Disappointingly, he seemed impartial to her scant attire, for his gaze barely skimmed over her. Instead, he went around the room, putting out the lamps while she climbed into bed and pulled the covers up to her arms.

Hawkhurst paused another moment before joining her. Rather than move closer, however, he lay on his back, not touching her.

His honor was taking control again, Skye decided. To her, however, it did not seem at all dishonorable for them to share a bed. Not now that she was beginning to think of him as her future husband. Nor would it be shameful if they were to go even further. Yet convincing him of that would be difficult.

But what if she were to resort to more direct measures? Seduction might be her only hope in getting

Hawkhurst to consider her as his potential bride, and more crucially, to fall in love with her.

Her aunt strongly believed that physical passion could lead to love. It was one of many kernels of wisdom Isabella had imparted to her. Skye very much wanted to make love to Hawkhurst, not only for the pleasure, but to force him to recognize the bond that already existed between them: a powerful, potent bond that made her body yearn at the same time it soothed her soul. She had never felt this sweet mixture of desire and comfort before—this delicious arousal warring with tender contentment.

Letting her eyes fall shut, Skye willed herself to relax. This was not the right moment, but when morning came, she would be prepared to take the next step.

Hawk remained awake for much longer. He should have known better than to stay the night with Skye, but the truth was, he could sleep peacefully with her beside him.

Or, he *should* have been more peaceful. At the moment it was pure torment, with his cock throbbing and ready to burst, his body aching to ease over hers and fill her with his flesh.

The bald reality was, Lady Skye Wilde fired his blood whether she was awake or sleeping. And having made love to her once made resisting her much, much harder. He wanted her more than any woman he could remember, including his late wife.

A disloyal thought, Hawk acknowledged. Yet he couldn't bring himself to feel guilt, not when it had been so long since Elizabeth's passing.

Moreover, his desire for Skye stemmed from more

than mere physical lust. He was actually startled by his enjoyment of their journey thus far.

Of course, it wasn't surprising that this was the first time in months that he'd felt mentally challenged. Her quest to find her uncle's lover had given him an intriguing problem to focus on. Worthy challenges were much less frequent now that the decades-long war with Napoléon was over; the Guardians were not needed nearly as much as in past years.

And Skye herself kept his wits sharp. He liked that about her, but her ability to always put him at ease unsettled him. Her tone was often warm and teasing, as if she'd known him intimately for years. Every time she used that provocative, affectionate tone, Hawk instinctively stiffened. Bantering—even flirting—was not his style.

The trouble was, he found her impossible to shut out. Since she'd appeared on his doorstep a mere nine days ago, she'd caused long-dormant emotions and desires to surge to life within him—almost as if he were actually living a normal existence again.

Her liveliness was a vivid contrast to his own bleakness, Hawk knew. That mischievous light dancing in her blue eyes was utterly delightful. And her smile . . . Each time she flashed that enchanting smile, something inside of him stirred, responding as naturally, as inevitably, as breathing.

She invited too much vulnerability, though. He needed to set strict limits on how close he would let her come. With her enticing power over him, she would constantly test his strength of will.

Intellectually, he understood her success: Lady Skye Wilde might be calculating and manipulative, but her manner was so charming, she made a man *want* to succumb. She used flattery and praise and reason to bend males to her will effortlessly.

No doubt her many beaus were at a severe disadvantage. Most normal men wouldn't stand a chance against her. Hawk, however, was not normal. In his decade as a Guardian, he'd faced down numerous murderers, traitors, and other villains. Surely he could avoid being conquered by a delicate-looking enchantress who was doing her best to get under his skin.

Hawk rolled over on his side, facing away from her, and shut his eyes, knowing it would be a long night. He would likely dream of Skye, although his erotic fantasies were better by far than the haunted, twisted dreams he'd had since returning to England.

For that reason alone, he was glad for his decision to share a bed with her again. The physical pain of unremitting arousal was a small price to pay for such welcome release from his memories.

Chapter Ten

Sometime during the night, they moved closer to each other. As dawn broke, Skye came slowly awake to feel Hawkhurst's arm encircling her waist, his face very near to hers. For a long moment she lay there luxuriating in his warmth. When she opened her eyes, she found him watching her.

In turn, her gaze lingered on his beautifully chiseled features. The proud bones and angles were softer now; the contentment in his eyes unmistakable.

She relished that peaceful look. He was a man who had been in pain far too long. Alone, isolated, severed from any sort of pleasure in life. He wasn't alone any longer, though, and it was time she made him realize it. They had comforted each other through the night, but she yearned for so much more.

The nearness of his mouth made her long to thread her fingers in his hair and pull him close enough to kiss her, but she settled for reaching out silently to brush his bare chest with her fingertips, feeling sleek skin over hard muscle.

His body tightened at that simple contact.

Not letting his instinctive resistance deter her, Skye eased closer and lowered her lips to press a tender kiss on his breastbone, near his heart. His hand rose to cup her shoulder, keeping her at a distance.

Her gaze dropped down his body to his flat, hard abdomen. Below the waistband of his drawers was an enormous bulge. She knew what that swelling meant.

"You are in pain."

Her voice was raspy with sleep, and his was just as low and husky when he replied: "A natural response to sleeping with a beautiful woman."

He wanted her, Skye thought with satisfaction. Although she doubted his desire was any greater than hers. "I am in pain as well. I am aching for you."

Taking a shallow breath, she grasped the arm that was curved around her waist and drew his palm to her breast. "I know a remedy for our pain."

Heat flared in his eyes, but he tamped it down. "It is not a remedy I can permit."

"Would it really be so wicked if we were to make love again?" Skye asked softly. "We have already been intimate, so there should be no moral dilemma."

His reply was droll. "You are overlooking the practical dilemma. At present we are waiting to learn if you conceived the first time. If not, I am not about to risk getting you with child."

"But I know how to prevent conception."

His eyebrow rose a fraction. "How would you?"

"My Aunt Isabella told me of an old courtesan's trick. A woman can use sponges inside her passage to prevent a man's seed from taking root inside her. Have you never heard of it?"

His mouth curved subtly. "Yes, I have heard of it. I just can't believe Bella corrupted you so thoroughly."

"She did not corrupt me. She wanted to educate me. Isabella believes women should have a modicum of power over men. Knowledge is power, in her opinion."

Her aunt had outlasted three husbands and knew a thing or two about passion. After much begging, she'd shared her secrets of seduction so Skye could arm herself for the battle ahead. She'd wanted to learn how to make Hawkhurst love her.

"We needn't have a full consummation, do we?"

Hawkhurst momentarily shut his eyes, as if striving for control. "We needn't have any consummation at all."

"I would never have expected you to be so craven," Skye complained lightly. "You are afraid even to kiss me."

At the charge of cowardice, irritation crossed his features—until he caught on that she was deliberately provoking him again. Then he laughed softly. Something he didn't do often, she knew.

"Take care, sweetheart. You are playing with fire."

"What if I am?"

"At some point, you will push me too far."

"The prospect does not frighten me."

Deliberately she reached down to fondle the swollen bulge at his groin. His jaw clenched as he held her hand away.

"*You* don't frighten me, Lord Hawkhurst," she vowed in an even softer voice.

Pushing himself up on one elbow, he stared down at her for an endless moment, searching her face. Then muttering a low oath, he lowered his head to capture her mouth possessively.

A feeling of triumph filled Skye. She had *finally* broken through his resistance. His kiss was hard and compelling, his mouth hot and tasting of need. For all that he strove to bury his emotions, he was the most passionate man she knew. His raw intensity set her senses whirling. She strained toward him, her breasts seeking closer contact with his naked chest.

In response, he cradled her face with his hands to give his tongue better access and kissed her deeply, ravenously, as if he couldn't get enough of her taste. At his savage-tender assault, desire flooded Skye in a mad rush . . . but then suddenly Hawkhurst drew back and dragged in a shuddering breath.

Disappointment surged through her, but only fleetingly. Grasping the hem of her shift, he pulled the garment over her head, practically ripping it in his urgency.

She had riled the beast enough, apparently. Perhaps he was merely re-exerting control, Skye conceded. Perhaps he was tired of letting her hold the upper hand and this was his means of reprisal for prodding and teasing him.

If so, it was extremely effective. At his dangerous look, the pulsing quickened between her legs.

"You are wrong, darling," he said silkily. "You haven't begun to ache yet."

Heat seared her as his fingertips skimmed the underside of her breasts. "What . . . do you mean to do?"

"To see how much more pain I can give you."

His deep voice hinted at a smile, though, belying his threat of painful punishment. Suiting action to words, he cupped her breasts, his fingers spreading and fanning over the swells, his thumbs passing in scorching circles over her nipples. Pleasure shivered through Skye at the sensation of his hands on her soft flesh.

He plucked at the tight buds, pinching lightly and soothing in turn. Then his mouth dipped to her bosom. He kissed both nipples, laving the swollen tips with his silk-rough tongue. When his hot mouth closed over one peak, sucking it strongly, she gave a breathless whimper. The throbbing heat between her thighs was an insistent drumbeat in her blood now.

He wasn't content with fondling and caressing her aching breasts, though. Slowly he swept a hand down her body, his reach stretching to graze her legs, stroking her thighs, seeking her feminine center. The trail of his fingers burned, while his tantalizing, arousing caresses sent a sweet arrow of lust streaking down below her belly.

He paused at the vee of her thighs before drawing his fingers between her feminine folds. Skye let out a soft moan as he spread a hot ache through her.

"Your first time I was too harsh," he murmured. "This time I intend to make it pleasurable for you. I mean to make you scream with pleasure, love. . . ."

The soft words were tauntingly seductive, threatening and promising at the same time. They made her entire body clench in anticipation.

His lips abandoned her breasts then and left a trail of fever over her skin as he moved lower. Skye felt his warm breath dampen the golden curls of her mound, then the tender flick of his tongue over the bud of her sex, and she quivered at the shock of it.

For long moments, his tongue played in a leisurely

dance, tasting her, tormenting her. Her skin seemed to melt under his erotic attentions. Under the intoxicating influence of his mouth, she felt weak and helpless. She had thought to seduce Hawkhurst, but *he* was the one entrancing *her*. His mouth enthralled her—

When he pressed his face harder between her parted legs, she whimpered and arched her back.

"Steady," he murmured.

How could she be steady when he was touching her with fire?

His hands moved beneath her buttocks, holding her hips still, keeping her thighs spread wide as he went on nuzzling, nipping, suckling. Skye closed her eyes against the rush of ecstasy building inside of her. His mouth dazzled, his tongue stroking in relentless rhythmic stimulation that sent shuddering thrills through her pleasure-flushed veins.

He paused only long enough to ask a rasping question, his tone low and provocative. "Do you remember the feel of me inside you, angel? Pretend this is my cock taking you."

His voice was maddeningly sensuous now, and so was the hot invasion of his tongue. Skye gasped for breath at the incredible feel of it.

Her breath coming in hoarse whimpers, she shut her eyes more tightly. She was unbearably hot, unbearably aroused. She heard her own moans as she writhed blindly beneath him. All she knew was the devastating heat of his mouth, the hot pounding of her blood, the fierce delight of what he was doing to her.

Suddenly, the pleasure was too keen to be borne. Frantic, she grasped at his shoulders. A primal sound that was half sob, half scream escaped her as wave after wave of shuddering pleasure ripped through her. Her body shook before falling limply back against the pillows, boneless with sensation.

Skye was only vaguely aware when Hawkhurst stretched out beside her. She knew he could feel the fine tremors still running through her though, for he was stroking her hair soothingly, caressing the curve of her hot cheek with a gentle finger.

Finally, Skye opened her eyes to find him watching her again. The perception and tenderness she saw in his eyes made her throat ache. She tried to speak, to say something that would praise his marvelous lovemaking, but her voice was too hoarse, so she contented herself with burying her face in his warm chest.

His arms came around her and drew her close. It was a long while before her ragged breathing slowed and her racing heartbeat returned to anything resembling normal. Only then did she become conscious that although he had given her astonishing pleasure, he was still in dire pain.

"I want to pleasure you now," she murmured.

His hand, which had been drifting through her hair, went still. When she reached down to open the front placket of his drawers, he didn't stop her.

Encouraged, Skye pushed herself up on her elbow. She badly wanted to reciprocate. Hawkhurst had set her afire, and she wanted to kindle an answering fire in his body.

When she parted the fabric, his shaft sprang out, heavy and aroused. In the growing daylight, she fixed her fascinated gaze on his naked loins, unable to look away. The huge, thick length was standing nearly erect between his powerful thighs.

Skye bit her lower lip. Her aunt had told her something about the male body, how to arouse a man, but putting theory into practice was another matter altogether.

"What should I do?" she asked.

"Whatever you like."

"I want to see your body," she said honestly, knowing she was blushing.

"As you wish."

Raising his hips, he stripped off his drawers in one smooth motion, then lay back, allowing her to look her fill. She was captivated by the sight of his magnificent body . . . his nakedness, his intense beauty . . . virile, masculine, hard, corded with lean muscle.

He had invited her to do as she wished, and she was hungry to touch him, but still she hesitated.

"Run your fingers over my skin," he suggested.

Obligingly, she let her fingers drift over his torso. She stroked his chest for a time before moving down to his sinewy thighs, savoring the exquisite textures of him, the heat and strength that was so profoundly male.

Feeling shy and daring at the same time, Skye trailed her hand upward again to brush her fingertips over his hard, silky flesh. When she let her fingers close around his hard member, his breath quickened.

"Stroke me with your hand," he urged.

Skye looked up to find the eyes that were fixed on her face had grown darker.

"Like this?" she asked, lightly fondling his rigid, straining arousal.

His body tightened as hers had done moments before. "Yes," he replied, his voice suddenly hoarse.

She watched his storm-silver eyes as she explored,

cherishing the pleasure she saw reflected there, the tenderness. She learned him with her hands, cupping the heavy sacs beneath his manhood, running her thumb over the blunt, velvety head.

When her fingers curled again around his shaft and squeezed, the whole length surged and quivered at the pressure. Yet Skye was not satisfied.

"I intend to touch you as you touched me . . ." she murmured. She was not nearly so confident as she let on, but she bent down to kiss his swollen flesh.

His body tensed at the first warm touch of her mouth. And when she tasted him with her tongue, his breath drew harshly between his teeth.

"This is what you did to me, is it not?"

"It is similar, yes."

At the delicate searching of her tongue, his hips stirred restlessly. And when she suckled him harder, he gave a soft groan.

"Am I doing this correctly?"

"Yes . . . quite correctly."

A shudder ran through him. In response, her own body shivered in purely sensual reaction. She had resumed control, Skye realized. Hawkhurst's weakness was both intoxicating and arousing. His need called to something womanly and powerful inside her.

Her lips played on his arousal while her fingers continued caressing the velvety, swollen sacs beneath. She glanced up to see that he had shut his eyes, looking as if he might burst. Then, as if he could bear no more, he took her hand and placed it on the crest of his pulsing erection.

Heat emanated from him in waves as he thrust against her palm. Her gaze was drawn irresistibly back to his loins. He kept his fingers around hers, stroking his sex within their joined grasp.

His jaw locked as his fingers kneaded harder, sweeping up and down his tumescence in swift jerky motions. His breath was harsh and uneven, the pleasure on his face almost pain . . . until his climax came abruptly and he exploded into his cupped hands.

Several heartbeats later, Hawkhurst sank back against the pillows, much as she had done earlier. The taut lines straining his features relaxed, even though his breathing was still very ragged.

Eventually, he pulled her down to join him and gathered her close, so that her head rested on his shoulder, his chin on her hair. He seemed weary but totally sated.

Skye exhaled a soft sigh of contentment. To lie in his arms like this, to breathe in his scent, to absorb his warmth, was indescribable bliss.

"You are a most marvelous lover, Lord Hawkhurst," she murmured.

"Lord Hawkhurst?" he repeated in a hoarse, wry voice at her formal address. "I think by now we are familiar enough that you can call me Hawk."

"Very well . . . Hawk. Thank you for relieving my ache."

"It was my pleasure—but you gave me little choice."

"That was my intention . . . although it is actually very unlike me. I have never been this wanton. I am known as the *good* Wilde cousin."

"I would never have guessed," he said, sounding amused.

"It is true. But I am rather tired of being angelic."

"*You*, angelic?" His tone was roughly edged with humor.

"Comparatively, yes." She'd committed her own share of troublemaking, but nothing truly scandalous. And being good had gotten her nowhere in finding true love as her Wilde ancestors—and more recently, her cousins Ash and Jack—had done.

"It is time for me to live up to the Wilde name and reputation. I want to have a grand passion like the rest of my family."

She hesitated, waiting for a response from Hawkhurst—Hawk, she amended. When none came, she added wistfully, "You could show me what real passion is like."

"No, I could not."

"Why not?"

"You know very well why not. A small thing called honor—not to mention the risk of scandal."

"It isn't fair that ladies cannot enjoy lovemaking the way men can."

"Perhaps." He sounded sympathetic but not enough to accede to her request.

"The damage is already done," she contended. "We might as well continue what we began. Who better than you to educate me in the arts of lovemaking?"

When Hawk didn't reply, she shifted her head to glance up at him. His eyes were still shut, and it didn't appear as if that would change anytime soon.

"I want to know about lovemaking so I can have a fulfilling marriage with my future husband."

Hawk pried one eye open. "You can ask your aunt for advice."

"I already have. But at some point I need actual experience, not just theoretical guidance. Please, will you show me?"

"No."
"Please?"

At her pleading tone, Hawk stifled an exasperated laugh. She was drawing a sensual pattern on his chest with a forefinger, gazing up at him with her wide, imploring blue eyes. Her persistence was unbelievable. And once again she had surprised him with her boldness, practically ravishing him and then asking him to teach her about lovemaking.

He shook his head mentally. No one had ever given him so much aggravation or put him on the defensive so easily as Skye Wilde. No one had ever tempted him as fiercely, either. It was all he could do to hold his own with her.

In fact, he had to admit his miscalculation just now. He'd had some thought of scaring her off with his aggressive embrace, but he should have known she wouldn't scare easily. Nor would she back down once she'd set her sights on something.

At the moment she had her sights on overwhelming his good sense, not only with rational arguments but with the lure of her delectable body. And as usual with Skye, his feelings were a complex mix of amusement, exasperation, vexation, and desire.

Desire was strongest just now. She'd set him alight with her innocent eroticism—and that was *after* giving him the most peaceful night he could remember in years. And then the pleasure of waking up beside her this morning . . .

He'd awakened to find her close enough to kiss. He'd spent several quiet moments watching her, taking in her bright, sleep-tumbled hair, her lush lips that were slightly parted as she breathed in slumber. She'd looked tousled and drowsy, and soft—and beautiful enough to make him ache.

He was still aching now, even after she'd temporarily relieved his painful, carnal hunger. He wanted to be inside her again in the most desperate way.

A bloody dangerous sentiment.

Yet another part of him was urging him to ignore the danger. Skye was offering herself to him fully. What red-blooded male could refuse?

Hawk shut his eyes, trying to bolster his fading willpower. He couldn't give in, of course. Complying with her request to tutor her would only compound his problem—what to do with an enchanting siren who didn't understand the word "no."

He had to exert better control over his lust, Hawk reminded himself. He was determined to focus solely on finding her uncle's lover and nothing more.

Repeating that silent declaration, Hawk eased away from her embrace, then rose and went to the washbasin to clean his seed off his hand.

He could feel her gaze on his body, studying his backside, though. For all her curiosity, Skye was inexperienced with nudity, and her examination made his loins hard all over again.

"Do you mean to dally in bed the rest of the morning?" he asked curtly over his shoulder. "I thought you didn't wish to be late in meeting Macky."

When Skye made a soft exclamation of agreement and climbed out of bed with alacrity, Hawk hid a smile.

His only chance in dealing with her was keeping

their relationship all business, but it would be damned hard.

Maybe impossible.

Particularly when she had the tactical skills of a Napoléon Bonaparte and the allure of a ravishing seductress all rolled into one.

Chapter Eleven

Hawkhurst's carriage made good time driving to Castlecomer and by late morning reached the town square, which was surrounded by lime trees and elegant Georgian houses.

The Fox and Hound, where they were scheduled to meet with Macky at noon, was a quaint inn with mullioned windows. Hawk hired a private parlor, where they dined on a tasty shepherd's pie for lunch. As Skye kept one eager eye out the window, their loquacious host treated them to a display of charming Irish wit as he related that the town had been partially burned some two decades ago but rebuilt by a wealthy, noble benefactress.

Hawk dismissed the innkeeper when Macky arrived a half hour later. After quaffing half a tankard of ale to quench his thirst, Macky reported on what he had learned to date.

"Your hunch about quizzing local proprietors paid off, m'lord. As you instructed, I fabricated a claim that my wife's friend was coming to Ireland soon and was eager for news of her long-lost relative, a genteel Englishwoman who settled somewhere in County Kilkenny some twenty-five years ago. I first made the rounds in Kilkenny and showed the miniature to every dressmaker and milliner I could find, with no results. But in Castlecomer, three different shop owners recognized the Widow Donnelly, who goes by the given name of Meg. I have little doubt it is the fugitive Lady Farnwell."

"She is posing as a widow?"

"Yes. She has been living these many years past with a cousin, Bridget O'Brien, and her husband Shamus on a farm near the village of Clogh."

"How far is Clogh from here?" Hawk asked.

"Not more than five miles. I scouted the O'Brien farm a short while ago but never approached, since I gathered you wished to make the first contact."

"You did well, Macky."

Skye felt her spirits soar at the welcome news. "Yes, *thank* you, Mr. Macky."

According to Macky, Clogh was a thriving coal-mining village but too small to boast an inn of its own, so Hawkhurst bespoke separate rooms at the Fox and Hound in Castlecomer before he and Skye set out north in his carriage once again, following Macky's detailed directions.

Shortly after their departure, a drizzling rain began and slowed their progress over roads that were little more than rutted lanes. Although it was autumn, however, the countryside glowed a verdant green, and the farms they passed looked prosperous and well kept.

The O'Brien farm appeared larger than most, yet the main house was no manor but a pretty whitewashed stone cottage with a thatched roof—a far cry from the wealthy estate where Rachel Farnwell had once reigned as baroness. Skye found herself wondering if Lady Farnwell—presumably now Mrs. Meg Donnelly—ever regretted exchanging her wealthy, aristocratic lifestyle for the quiet, remote existence of an English widow in hiding.

As Hawk's crested carriage drew to a halt before the cottage, Skye felt a surge of nervous anticipation, knowing how crucial this initial meeting with the fugitive could be for her uncle Cornelius.

Hawkhurst seemed to understand her apprehension. "Would you like me to speak to the Widow Donnelly first?"

"No, I think it best if I explain who I am and then see how she responds."

Skye took a deep breath, then allowed Hawk to help her down, into the rain, and escort her up the flagstone path to the front door.

Before they could knock, however, the door swung open abruptly. A gray-haired woman stood there, blocking their way, brandishing a pitchfork.

At the threat, Skye's eyes widened, but Hawkhurst stepped forward, his body shielding her in an instinctive, protective gesture. "Mrs. O'Brien, I presume?" he said calmly.

"Who is it asking?" the woman demanded.

"I am the Earl of Hawkhurst, and this is Lady Skye Wilde, here to see Mrs. Donnelly. We mean her no harm. Pray, would you ask her if she will receive us?"

His polite manner soothed Bridget O'Brien's defensiveness a small measure. Although still wary and suspicious, she gave a curt nod. "Wait here, the both of you." Stepping back, she slammed the door in their faces.

Hearing the latch being set to lock them out, Skye bit her lower lip.

"Don't fret yet," Hawk reassured her. "It is only to be expected that she would be cautious and defensive."

His serenity calmed Skye somewhat as she peered up at him from beneath the brim of her dripping black bonnet. "You have conducted this sort of investigation many times before, haven't you?"

"Yes, many times. And if you won't pester me to reveal the particular circumstances, I might even tell you about one or two of my more interesting cases."

His easy smile won a faint one from Skye. "I suppose we should be glad Mrs. O'Brien was waving a pitchfork and not a more lethal weapon."

"Indeed," Hawk agreed.

Skye was certain he could have handled any weapon with aplomb, though. She felt her tense muscles relax. It was curious how implicitly she trusted Hawk, how safe and protected he made her feel. The Guardians were aptly named, she decided.

Perhaps two more minutes passed before they heard the scrape of the latch again.

When the door slowly swung open, a slender, elegant, middle-aged lady stood in the entryway. Ample gray streaked her dark hair, and sadness lined her pale features, but her beauty was similar to her miniature portrait, leaving no doubt in Skye's mind that this was Rachel Farnwell.

Lady Farnwell stared at them, drinking them in, her expression fearful yet hopeful all at once.

Taking a cue from Hawk, Skye flashed one of her gentlest smiles. "Mrs. Donnelly? I have so longed to meet you. My uncle is Lord Cornelius Wilde."

The lady clearly recognized the name. Her gaze shifted furtively to search the carriage behind Skye. "Is Cornelius . . . here with you?"

"No, he has no notion you still exist. I did not want to raise his hopes until I was certain you were the woman he once loved."

Her trembling hand rose to her throat. "Then you know what happened," she breathed.

"We know some of it. Recently I found your letters to my uncle and couldn't rest until Mrs. Nibbs shared what she could remember. Her memory is failing significantly, poor woman, but thanks to this gentleman, Lord Hawkhurst"—Skye glanced up at Hawk—"we were able to guess in general where you might have gone all those years ago. So we acted on our theory and traveled here to Ireland in hopes of finding you."

Lady Farnwell's gaze lingered on Hawk a moment, then returned to Skye. "Why . . . would you wish to find me?"

"Because I believe my uncle would want to know that you are safe and well."

Her face crumpling, the baroness turned away and covered her eyes with her hands. Her body shuddered as she struggled to breathe. When long moments later, she turned back again to her unexpected guests, her eyes were wet with tears.

"Please . . . come in, Lady Skye, Lord Hawkhurst," she bid in a shaken voice.

When they stepped into the cottage, Bridget O'Brien came forward, much less aggressively this time, and took Skye's wet cloak and bonnet and Hawk's great-coat and tall beaver hat.

"Where are my manners?" Lady Farnwell murmured weakly. She introduced her distant cousin, who was a Donnelly before marrying Shamus O'Brien, then added, "You must be chilled. May we make you some hot tea?"

"That would be very welcome," Skye replied, not so much needing the warmth as wanting to allow the baroness time to compose herself.

While Mrs. O'Brien went to the kitchen to fetch tea, they were shown into a small parlor where a cheery fire burned, and took the seats offered. The baroness sank down upon a sofa beside Skye, looking slightly dazed. "What did Peggy Nibbs tell you?"

"That you were forced by circumstances to stage your own death and sought protection with relatives here in Ireland. It was because your husband was unimaginably cruel, was it not?"

"Yes," Rachel whispered. For the next few minutes, she haltingly confirmed her dire story . . . that she'd had a secret love affair before her engagement and that her husband, William, had become so abusive, she feared for her life.

"I promise you, I was never unfaithful to my marriage vows," she said earnestly. "But William did not believe me, and for that I am to blame. Even though I ended my . . . romance . . . with Cornelius when I married, I foolishly continued to write him letters that I never sent, and William found them shortly after I gave birth to my daughter. He never learned the identity of the man I loved because I never addressed Cornelius by name. But William couldn't bear the thought that he had been cuckolded. He was much too prideful."

Skye hesitated, wondering how to tactfully ask the most important question. "There is one thing I would dearly like to know," she said gently. "Is your daughter my uncle's child?"

Rachel swallowed. "Yes . . . but I never told Cornelius. He could never claim Daphne as his own, and I couldn't bear to cause him the pain of knowing another man was raising his daughter."

"Did your husband realize her lineage?"

"I don't believe so. Or perhaps he didn't wish to contemplate the possibility. You see . . ." An embarrassed flush rose to her face. "Peg helped me to hide the evidence that I was not . . . chaste when I came to the marriage bed."

Skye supposed that the midwife would have known how to smear bloodstains on the nuptial sheets to fool a bridegroom. "I don't believe my uncle ever suspected that Lady Daphne was his daughter."

Looking remorseful and sad, Rachel glanced down at her clasped fingers. "My silence was for his own protection. Farnwell would have killed him had the truth become known. As it was . . . he nearly killed *me*."

Rachel's gaze grew distant in remembrance, and tears filled her eyes again. "Farnwell became so cruel. . . . He enjoyed seeing me suffer. I couldn't bear it any longer. But leaving my baby daughter was the hardest thing I have ever d-done—"

Her voice broke, and Skye felt her heart go out to the woman who'd been forced to abandon her child in order to save her own life.

When she began weeping in earnest, Skye moved nearer in sympathy and slipped an arm around Rachel's slender shoulders. "I am certain you did what you knew to be right. You had no other choice."

She drew a gulp of air as she labored for control. "You are r-right. . . . I had no choice. While I still remained alive, I f-feared he would punish Daphne for my s-sins."

After a time her sobs quieted, and she took Hawk's proffered handkerchief to dry her eyes. "Please forgive my hysterics," she begged in a rasping voice.

Skye felt a spurt of anger on her behalf. "It is not hysterical in the least to mourn the loss of your only child."

Rachel nodded silently. Eventually she sniffed once or twice, then took a deep breath. "Daphne . . . tell me, how . . . how is she? I only remember her as a tiny babe."

From her expression, she seemed pitifully eager to learn about her daughter, and Skye was happy to oblige. "Lady Daphne is a lovely, intelligent young woman now. She is something of a scholar—a talented artist and an expert on roses. Quite an achievement for one so young. She is barely my age."

Rachel's response was a watery smile. "I always loved roses . . . my garden was my one solace during those terrible times. But tell me . . . she never married? She is a spinster?"

Skye hesitated to brand Lady Daphne with the spinster label. "She is still unattached, I believe, but I don't know her reasons."

"I imagine she would not wish to follow my example

and marry without love," Rachel muttered in a stronger tone.

Then she abruptly changed the subject, seeming eager to learn about her former lover also. "Tell me . . . How fares Lord Cornelius?"

"He is well enough, I suppose," Skye answered. "Or to be more specific, his health is good. But his spirits . . . not so much. After your tragic death, he turned to his books for comfort and became quite the literary scholar. He never married, but it was only when I found your letters hidden away in his library that I understood why."

"I never thought he wouldn't marry and have a family."

"You were the love of his life," Skye said simply. "When you harbor a love that deep, it is difficult to move on. Uncle Cornelius kept all your letters. He even kept a dead rose pressed among them, in remembrance of you, I imagine." From her reticule, Skye pulled out the box of letters.

Rachel's mouth trembled as she opened it and unwrapped the scrap of muslin on top. The red rose, now brittle and faded with age, had a delicate blue ribbon tied around the stem.

"This was from the last time we met . . . a pledge of my love."

She put her hand to her mouth to stifle another sob. "I could never have married him, though. My parents insisted that I accept the wealthy baron instead."

Hawk spoke for the first time in several minutes. "Did you know that Farnwell died eight years ago?"

"Yes. . . . Bridget has corresponded with some of her family in England over the years. We heard about my husband from time to time. His son from his second marriage inherited the title."

"But you have never thought about returning to England?"

"Oh, I have thought about it . . . every day of my life. But I have never dared. The temptation to see my daughter would have been too great. It would have been unforgivably selfish of me even to try to contact Daphne. No good could come of it. She has her own life to live."

Skye was not thinking only of Daphne, however. "Do you still have feelings for my uncle?"

"Yes," Rachel admitted hoarsely. "I love him dearly still. As you said, love like that does not die easily, not with time or distance or even death."

"Then would you consider returning with us to England? I know Uncle Cornelius would be overjoyed to see you."

Rachel shook her head slowly, despairingly. "I . . . am sorry but I cannot. I fear for Daphne if my secret ever came out."

"There is no reason for your secret to come out unless you wish it to," Hawk told her. "I believe we can conceal your past identity from society, particularly if you continue to use your assumed name."

"Yes," Skye pressed. "I think it is time for you to come home. You have suffered more than enough." When Rachel hesitated, Skye added, "This is your chance to see your daughter again."

The pain on her face was evidence enough. "It is, and I would like nothing more than to gaze upon her face and hold her in my embrace. But the ramifications . . . Just think of the harm the truth could cause her. The man she always thought was her father was not really her flesh and blood after all."

"I agree that any revelations will have to be handled delicately and that we should not rush to tell Daphne of her parentage. Perhaps you might never choose to divulge the truth about her birth. But we will help you negotiate the dangers every way we can."

Apparently Rachel was not convinced. "But William's son—the present Baron Farnwell. He is said to be much like his father." Her voice dropped to a whisper. "I have lived in fear for so long. William was in London at the time of my supposed drowning, and I know he was relieved to be rid of me, but I always feared he would find me."

"You needn't be afraid any longer," Skye declared softly. "I have every faith that Lord Hawkhurst will ensure your safety, and your daughter's as well."

"I cannot risk it."

"I believe Daphne would want to know her mother, don't you?"

When Rachel looked anguished, Skye softened her offensive even more. "Will you at least consider our proposal, Mrs. Donnelly?"

Bridget O'Brien brought in the tea tray just then, so Rachel never replied.

Accepting that Rachel needed time to digest all their revelations, Skye purposely changed the conversation to lighter matters, telling the baroness about the Wilde family—how Lord Cornelius had taken over the raising of five orphaned cousins when their parents had perished at sea, with often humorous results, since he had little experience with children.

A short while later, Skye met Hawk's eye, silently

asking if they should end their call. When he gave a brief nod, she rose to her feet and purposely called Rachel by her assumed name. "We will leave you now, Mrs. Donnelly, but may we return tomorrow?"

"I . . . would rather you did not. I need time to think."

"Yes, of course."

"I will let you know my decision soon, Lady Skye. I hope you can understand. I believed that part of my life was over. After all these years, I . . . I don't know that I want to resurrect it again, even if I could."

Disappointment filled Skye, but she strove hard not to show it. "Of course we will respect your privacy. We are staying at the Fox and Hound in Castlecomer, should you wish to contact us. I will leave these letters for you to read. . . ." Skye indicated the box. She did not want to give up her uncle's treasured correspondence, but perhaps they would help Rachel remember the tender feelings she'd once borne for him.

They left her sitting in the parlor while Bridget showed them out. On the return drive to Castlecomer, Skye was unusually quiet—a state that Hawkhurst apparently noticed.

"I thought you would be more pleased at finding Lady Farnwell."

Skye hastened to reassure him. "I am pleased. Truly, I am ecstatic. But I worry that she will never return home where she belongs. Her fortitude is remarkable, but she will always put her daughter's welfare above her own, which means Uncle Cornelius may never have a chance to rekindle the love they once shared."

She shook off her solemnity. "Thank you for finding her, Hawk. Your talents are remarkable."

"I was not fishing for compliments," he responded, evidently suspecting her of trying to butter him up again.

"I am only giving praise where it is due. I could never have done this on my own."

"Macky deserves the credit."

"But it was your keen questioning that led us here."

But locating Lady Farnwell was only the first step. Realizing how far they had yet to go, Skye exhaled a sigh. "I did not expect her to be so adamantly set against returning with us."

"I have every faith that you will succeed in convincing her. Your powers of persuasion are first-rate."

Now he was trying to bolster *her* spirits. "But it may take quite some time. You cannot remain here in Ireland for very long."

"I can spare another week or so."

Skye searched his face in surprise. "You would do that for her?"

Hawk gave her a wry look. "I would do it for you, sweet wretch. We came here for a purpose, and I dislike leaving a mission unfinished. While we wait, I can resort to my original excuse for coming to Ireland— searching for brood stock."

"I thought that was a ruse."

"It was, but I am not letting you give up so soon."

Skye pressed her lips together in new resolve. "Oh, I am not giving up. As soon as we reach the inn, I will send Lady Farnwell a note. There are many more arguments I can make for our case. And I will keep sending her messages each day until she sees the merits of our plan. I agreed I would not visit her, but I never said I would not write."

Her vow brought a glimmer of amusement to Hawk's eyes, but Skye would not apologize for her zeal in saving her uncle from a continued loveless, lonely existence. "Even if it takes an entire year, I am not leaving here empty-handed. Still . . . the decision must be hers. Happiness can yet come out of her tragic past, but she will have to reach out and seize it."

Hearing the fervor in her declaration, Skye realized she ought to heed her own advice. If she was ever to realize her dream of finding true love with Hawk, she had to take advantage of their journey together and not let her chance slip through her fingers.

When they returned to the inn, she immediately began composing her first missive to Lady Farnwell. Hawk spent the afternoon reviewing his list of stud farms in Kilkenny and the neighboring counties, then wrote to two of them, stating his intentions to call the next day, and sent a messenger off.

"May I come with you tomorrow?" Skye requested as a way to keep up her own spirits and not dwell on what she hoped was only a temporary setback with Lady Farnwell. Hawk agreed without apparent reluctance.

However, when it came time to retire and Skye asked if she could spend the night with him, he refused in no uncertain terms, even when she reminded him that they could relieve each other's carnal pain.

Her tone was lighthearted, but for an instant as she met his suddenly smoke-dark eyes, she glimpsed the smoldering passion he was striving to repress.

His sense of honor won out, though, and he resisted her entreaties when he escorted her to her room, even when she turned to gaze up at him with her most imploring expression.

In fact, judging from his ironic smile, Hawk enjoyed thwarting her designs as he gently pushed her inside and shut the door in her face.

As Skye stared at the wood panel, she bit back a mild oath, then sighed heavily. She supposed it was admirable that Hawk was putting her reputation and welfare first, but it frustrated her keenly that he refused to cooperate in his seduction.

The man had the self-control of a monk, and she had no idea how to break it.

Hawk was not nearly as sanguine as he appeared, yet he repaired to his own bedchamber quite alone, resolved to be ruthless with himself in fighting his powerful attraction for Skye.

She was temptation incarnate. His hands hungered for her—bloody hell, his entire body hungered for her. Her alluring invitation was nearly impossible to withstand, especially when she was promising him another blazing night of passion.

It was only in the darkest hours of the night—when sleep completely eluded him—that Hawk let himself give in to temptation, remembering the memory of her flesh pliant against his fingers and mouth, and the reverse: Skye kissing his hard male flesh with her soft lips, teasing him to painful arousal, the silk-bright curtain of her hair draped over his loins. . . .

Then she moved upward to take his mouth with hers. Feeling a warmth so rich he could taste it, he eased her onto her back and settled between her thighs, wanting to impale her till he drowned in her. Curbing his urgency with effort, he slowly thrust inside her, feeling her moist flesh close around him tightly, feeling her surround him. The pleasure began, her perfect breasts rising to mold against his chest, her hips arching to meet his. . . .

The tantalizing fantasy was the only thing that finally allowed him to sleep.

Chapter Twelve

For the next two days, Skye persisted in her efforts to persuade both Lady Farnwell and Lord Hawkhurst to embrace her goals, with precious little success.

She spent that time viewing Hawk in his element as they toured the countryside, inspecting broodmares and blooded stallions. He rode several prospects; thus she had another firsthand demonstration of his magical touch with horses. Skye's frustration grew, however, at the failure of her romantic schemes. Not only did Hawk markedly ignore her attempts to deepen their intimacy, he seemed to relish acting contrarily just to see her reaction. Either that, or he was deliberately provoking her in order to take her mind off her worries.

To her dismay, Lady Farnwell had responded to none of her messages, even though the courier was instructed each time to await a reply. Yet whenever Skye grew overly earnest, Hawk found some way to lighten her mood, usually by teasing her much as she'd done to him, or ribbing her about acting cowardly and giving up. His riling was reminiscent of her own family, where she had to hold her own with her provocative brother and cousins.

Their sparring generated some lively conversations, and Skye looked forward even more to their solitary evenings together playing chess or cards, where there were no grooms or stable masters or inn servants to interfere with her pursuit of Hawk. Otherwise, he was the same enigmatic, elusive "beast" she had known from the beginning of their relationship. He refused to answer a single question about his work with the Guardians and wouldn't reveal an inkling about his life on the Isle of Cyrene, about which she was highly curious.

Once, Skye was exasperated enough to issue a warning: "You had best take care, my lord. I will ply you with brandy, then tie you up and force you to reveal your secrets."

He laughed outright at her threat. "I should like to see you try."

She liked his laughter, but there were still too few incidences of his lightheartedness to her mind.

The second afternoon, she was preparing to visit yet another stud farm with Hawk when "Mrs. Donnelly" was announced. Hope mingling with apprehension, Skye invited Lady Farnwell to join them in their private parlor. After ordering tea from the inn footman, she held her breath while awaiting the baroness's decision.

Yet Rachel did not immediately state her intentions. "I have carefully considered your rationale in favor of my returning to England."

"And?" Skye prompted.

"I don't believe it would be wise."

Skye wanted to retort that sometimes love was *not* wise but worth the risk. Although Rachel had escaped her abusive husband, she still badly needed healing; love—from both Daphne and Cornelius—could help her to heal.

Another argument Skye had championed in her missives was that life was too short to let the rare chance for happiness pass by. But rather than repeat her logic, she schooled herself to patience, hoping that in this case, heart would win out over mind. Rachel had not refused outright, which meant she was still debating.

She seemed most interested in how Lord Hawkhurst's plan might work. "You said my past could be kept secret, my lord. Is that even possible?"

"It's quite possible," Hawk answered easily. "As I said, you can maintain your current identity as Mrs. Meg Donnelly. If you refrain from public appearances—specifically if you keep away from Edgar Farnwell's district and don't show your face in London—you should be safe from discovery. For the time being, you will be a guest at my country estate in East Sussex and need never be seen by anyone who formerly knew you. And we can concoct a reasonable story to explain any resemblance to the late Lady Farnwell."

Still Rachel hesitated. "Can you imagine Baron Farnwell's fury if he learns of my deception? The kind of retribution he might seek?"

Skye interjected. "Lord Hawkhurst is more than able to deal with Edgar Farnwell, if it comes to that. He will protect you—and Daphne as well, I have no doubt whatsoever."

From the faint way his mouth curved, Hawk seemed amused that Skye was putting so much faith in his abilities, given that her knowledge of his role in his league of Guardians was strictly hearsay. But his tone was quite serious when he replied. "I have engaged a colleague to investigate Farnwell, and tasked the Bow Street Runners with keeping a close eye on him, but a disguise might better ensure your anonymity."

Skye studied Rachel objectively. The baroness had aged well enough that she still resembled the miniature. "What did you have in mind?"

"Perhaps she could cut her hair or dye it. Henna can notably transform appearance."

Rachel bit her lip in indecision. "You said we might not tell Daphne of her parentage at first?"

Skye was able to address that concern. "I believe we first need to sound your daughter out about her feelings toward you and avoid shocking her with the stark truth just yet. My cousin Lady Katharine Wilde lives in London and would be ideal for approaching Daphne. We can trust Kate to make any revelations at the appropriate time."

"What about . . . Lord Cornelius?" Rachel asked in a small voice.

"We need to prepare him also," Skye said, "but I should like to handle that disclosure myself, since I am best acquainted with the particulars. I think it best to invite him to stay at Hawkhurst Castle for a time. My aunt, Lady Isabella Wilde, is residing there to aide Hawkhurst in renovating his home. And I will be there as well. So it should not prove too awkward or pose an impropriety if my uncle were to join us. If you were eventually to rekindle your romance, you could pretend to have met there for the first time and fallen in love."

Rachel looked torn. "I don't want the world to know we were once lovers. I want nothing to hurt Daphne."

"I understand completely," Skye said with empathy. "We will take small steps and see how it unfolds. But the choice is yours to make."

The baroness closed her eyes and took a slow breath. "Very well. . . . I will accompany you to England."

Skye refrained from cheering, not wanting to add to Rachel's misgivings, but inwardly her elation soared at having overcome another important hurdle.

The next hour was spent planning their return journey and discussing details of their subterfuge. Even though Skye would likely continue thinking of her as Rachel or Lady Farnwell, they agreed it was best to address her as Mrs. Donnelly or Meg. By the next morning, Rachel had said a tearful farewell to the O'Briens, and they were on the road south to Wexford in Hawkhurst's coach.

Rachel's presence impacted Skye's relationship with Hawk even more than she expected. Regrettably, their interactions were restricted to formalities, so she greatly missed their intimate banter. Yet her disappointment couldn't be allowed to matter, since her primary task was supplying Rachel with support and companionship.

Skye had not anticipated, however, how difficult it would be for her to pretend indifference to Hawk now that her worst worries about Rachel were allayed. They couldn't touch, and they certainly could not share a bedchamber.

The proscribed separation created an undeniable tension between them. The first night in Wexford when Hawk made to retire alone to his own room, Skye could imagine following him, and a vision filled her mind of his magnificent body . . . of smooth, rippling muscles and sleek warm skin.

She was almost certain that Hawk felt the same tension. When his intent gray eyes fixed on her, she felt the impact like a caress, almost as if he had touched her. Her yearning was actually a physical ache, yet she knew she would have to live with the pain for the time being.

At least the journey went smoothly. The next morning, they weren't required to wait long for the ferry. And the weather was fine enough that when they reached Bristol late that afternoon, they hired a fresh team for the carriage and set out across England, making it partway to their destination before stopping at a posting inn when it grew too dark. By then another autumn storm threatened.

Skye would have been gratified to know that Hawk was having similar difficulties adjusting to the enforced segregation. His sleeping hours were still visited by tantalizing dreams of Skye lying in his arms, sharing her incredible passion, and he woke each morning hungry for her. But that evening, with the rain lashing on his bedchamber windows, sleeplessness returned with a vengeance.

The storm eventually subsided and the night sky cleared of all but a few scudding clouds, but Hawk was still wide awake hours later when a quiet rap sounded on his door. When he opened it, he could recognize the shadowy figure in the faint moonlight coming from the window at the end of the corridor. Skye stood there garbed in her traveling cloak, her pale hair falling around her shoulders in disarray.

One look at her face told him she had suffered another nightmare. Her eyes had that haunted look that couldn't be feigned.

"Please . . . may I come in?" she pleaded in a hoarse whisper.

Silently he stepped aside and let her enter. When he shut the door softly behind her, she moved directly into his arms and buried her face against his nightshirt, seeking shelter from her fears. His arms closed around her instinctively, and when he felt her trembling, he couldn't deny her comfort.

She remained there shivering for several minutes.

"I am sorry to wake you," she finally rasped. "At home, it helps to keep my nightmares at bay with warm milk and a splash of brandy. But I have neither."

"I have brandy."

She shook her head and pressed closer, wrapping her arms tightly around his waist. "I don't need liquor as long as I have you. Bad dreams never trouble me when I am with you."

It was the same with him. He could dream peacefully when she was with him. Suddenly, though, he registered that her cloak had parted enough to expose her attire beneath. Just like that he became keenly aware of the soft mounds of her breasts and the feminine warmth of her hips and thighs through the delicate fabric of her nightdress.

All thoughts of peace vanished for Hawk. He had intended only to hold her, but his feelings went from sympathetic to sexual in the space of a heartbeat, and his loins swelled and hardened.

The sudden heat sparking between them was like dry kindling catching fire. Skye felt it, too, he knew, for she slowly raised her head to gaze up at him.

In the moonlight seeping beneath the window curtains, he could make out her lovely features. Her eyes looked like dark, fathomless pools, wide and lustrous.

"Please, Hawk . . . may I stay with you?"

When he hesitated, she swallowed and licked her dry lips. "Please. Do you realize . . . this could be our last night alone together? There may never be another chance once we reach your home."

She was entirely serious, he realized. There was no teasing in her tone. No attempts to cajole or beguile him. There was only an honest solemnity that tugged at his heartstrings as well as his body.

Dropping his arms, Hawk pulled back, refusing to get lost in her eyes. Instead, he gazed up at the ceiling, striving for self-control.

But Skye went on in her quiet, imploring voice. "My family has always believed that we should make the most of our time on earth. I believe that also, Hawk. And we both know that life is too short and too precious to waste."

It was an argument that resonated strongly with him. He knew better than anyone that life and happiness could be snatched away in the blink of an eye.

"What is so wrong with comforting each other?"

"You know very well. I could get you with child if you are not already."

She pulled a small silk drawstring bag from the pocket of her cloak and held it up for him to see. "I told you I know a way to prevent conception. These sponges are designed for just that purpose."

Hawk felt himself frowning. "How did you come by those?"

"Aunt Isabella gave them to me."

He shouldn't be surprised, Hawk realized, torn between disbelief and amusement. He knew that Skye's relationship with her aunt was astonishingly frank and open about carnal matters.

Reaching up, Skye parted the lapels of her cloak completely and let it fall to the floor. Then she swallowed, as if gathering courage, and began unfastening the small buttons at the front of her nightdress. Her slow fingers were a beguiling dance that riveted his gaze as she eased the collar over her shoulders, and then that garment fell away, too.

Hawk drew a sharp breath at the sight of her. It was his most erotic fantasy: Skye nude, standing before him in the flesh, offering herself to him without inhibition or restraint. Moonlight gleamed on her white skin . . . the ripe swells of her breasts, her narrow waist, her gently flaring hips, her sleek, slender legs, the golden curls that hid her heavenly sex. . . .

She started undressing him then, clearly set on distracting him from his resolve to resist her. Calling his last reserves of willpower, Hawk caught her wrists before she could remove his nightshirt.

"You had best leave." His voice was harsh, strained.

"Best for whom? Not for me. And not for you, either, I suspect."

Gritting his teeth, he gave her one last chance to withdraw. "I warn you, Skye, I won't stop with mere caresses."

"I don't want you to stop. I want *you*, Hawk. More than I can say."

When he was as naked as she, he ground out from between his teeth, "You're a damned witch, do you know that?"

She didn't smile, didn't speak. Instead she lifted her face for a kiss. Their breath mingled as her lips brushed lightly over his.

"I know," she whispered, "but this is our final chance to be together."

The reminder settled the question for Hawk. He knew damned well that he ought to send her away, but the knowledge didn't stop him from claiming her mouth and feeding on it. He knew he should demand that she return to her own bed immediately, but he wouldn't force himself to say the words. His craving was far too strong. He wanted to fill his mouth with her taste, to fill his hands with the textures of her.

He drank of her essence while his hands roamed her smooth, bare flesh. Skye returned his kiss measure for measure, making her own craving crystal clear. Her need was as great as his own.

Hawk ceased fighting. She was utterly enchanting, and he could no more resist her than he could stop breathing. Caution vanished; resistance and uncertainty disappeared, to be replaced by hot, hungry desire.

Perhaps Skye sensed his capitulation, for her kisses shifted from his mouth to his jaw, then his throat, sipping his skin there at the hollow. She moved lower to his chest, then abdomen. Then slowly she dropped to her knees before him. In the silvery darkness, her lips traced the line of hair that led from his belly to his loins, where his erection stood at bold attention.

Every muscle in his body tensed.

"I want to please you," she murmured, her fingers closing around the thick shaft. He was already heavy and hard enough to burst, even before she cupped his balls, squeezing lightly.

"You *do* please me. . . ." His voice was husky with arousal, and then she leaned closer. Her tongue, a soft, warm touch, tasted him.

Hawk let out a faint groan. His hands tangled in her hair, and for a long moment, he held still and savored the pleasure while Skye caressed him with her mouth and hands . . . stroking, laving, suckling. And yet taking pleasure was not enough for him, so he eased her away.

"Give me the sponges," he demanded hoarsely. Allowing her no chance to protest, he reached for the silk bag.

When she handed it over, he loosened the string and drew out a small sponge, then a small vial of liquid. "Is this brandy?"

"I believe so. I have never used it before."

His gaze narrowed on her as she knelt at his feet. "You said you had no brandy."

"Not enough to drink. Not enough to ward off my nightmares. Besides, I would rather use it for this purpose."

Her answer satisfied him for the time being. Pulling Skye to her feet, he led her to the window and flung the curtains wide, the better to see her. Moonlight flooded in, filling the chamber.

Taking her hand, Hawk drew her toward the bedside table and made quick work of wetting the sponge.

Then sitting on the edge of the bed, he lifted her and settled her in his lap.

He angled his head to kiss her, this time for *her* pleasure. His lips stroked over hers as he parted her thighs with his searching hand. She was already slick to the touch from her own feminine moisture. When he pressed the sponge deep inside her woman's passage, Skye gasped softly at first, but seemed to grow accustomed to the chill of the brandy.

The heated wetness of their kiss wasn't enough, either, though. His mouth abandoning its purpose, he drew back to observe her. Her skin shimmered pale in the moonlight as his palm settled over her breast, cupping the luscious weight. His thumb passed delicately over the peak, circling her aureole, then teasing the nipple into a stiff crest.

Skye gazed back at him, her blue eyes dark and sultry with wonder. Her breath quickened when his fingers left her breasts to splay over her stomach, then lower to sift through the pale curls between her thighs. Her hips strained toward him as he stroked her, one finger within her, his thumb caressing the bud of her sex. And when he increased the pressure, she closed her eyes and shuddered.

Hawk relished the heavy passion on her face. He wanted to please her, to bring her to aching arousal as she'd done to him, just as he wanted to feel her sheath clenching around his cock.

Perhaps discerning his need, Skye wordlessly shifted in his lap and made to straddle him. He aided her, arranging her astride his thighs, her knees resting on the mattress. With his hands beneath her buttocks, he lifted her and positioned her cleft over the swollen head of his shaft.

"Slowly," he warned as she tried to lower herself onto his engorged length.

With effort, she went still and gave control over to him. He watched her face as he pressed into her, possessing her by degrees in a slow controlled thrust until he was fully embedded within her. Her body welcomed him, enclosing him in slick, silken heat.

Bringing his fingers to the thickly beating pulse at her throat, he stroked her skin. Then he slid his hand around to the base of her spine, bringing her more tightly against him, her breasts molded against his chest, her pelvis flush with his.

Her softly expelled breath wafted across his lips, and he felt her shiver around him in satisfaction.

The same satisfaction gripped Hawk. Being inside her seemed so right.

His hands grasped her hips, guiding her, encouraging her to find a rhythm. She rode him slowly at first, clutching his flanks with her thighs. But she caught on quickly. After a time, she rose without his help, then sank down again, her gaze locked on his face, her hips rocking in a surging rhythm.

In response, Hawk clenched his jaw, disciplining himself so sternly that a tremor went through his limbs. She was so hot and tight around him, so astonishingly sensual, that he let out another faint groan. When she rose again, though, he stopped her and pulled her down hard, so that he was seated to the hilt.

The pleasure sharpened for them both. Her breath coming in soft pants, Skye dug her fingers into his shoulders and arched her back, undulating to take him even deeper.

Their urgency grew. Hawk's pulse pounded wildly. Leaning closer, he kissed her again, devouring her mouth, taking all that she offered, catching the whimpers now coming from her throat.

The pleasure built between them, then spiraled out of control. Their bodies twisted feverishly together. She was liquid fire and he wanted to be burned. . . .

Her hands clenching spasmodically, she gripped him, clinging blindly. She was moaning aloud now. When he bucked, driving himself upward, Skye cried out and shattered above him, her spasms so intense Hawk felt them in every bone and sinew of his body.

A heartbeat later he followed, joining her in a wrenching climax as fierce and primitive as lightning. Sensation spiked and exploded inside him, jolting him in endless waves of pleasure.

His breathing harsh and ragged, Hawk sagged backward onto the mattress, drawing a weak, limp Skye with him. She melted over him, her face pressed into the curve of his neck, his lips against her hair, their skin dewed from their passion.

His heavy lethargy matched hers as that incredible, peaceful sensation once again washed over him. And as he lay there recovering, lightly stroking her naked back, his reflections were incoherent for the most part.

He had no regrets about making love to her fully, however; that much he knew. Skye had captured his senses, enchanting him with her vibrant warmth, firing his blood with her sensual heat.

And yet . . . as he spread his fingers over the curve of her buttocks, luxuriating in the feel of her, a vague thought teased at the back of his mind. When the quizzical notion finally occurred to him, Hawk opened his eyes and frowned up at the dark ceiling.

"You said your aunt gave you the sponges," he said in a low voice. "When?"

"I don't recall . . ." Skye answered, sounding puzzled by the question. "Some time ago."

"Did you send for them after you arrived at my home?"

She hesitated. "No."

"Then you brought them with you to Hawkhurst Castle."

Again she delayed her reply, and when Skye finally answered, her voice seemed smaller, almost apologetic. "Yes, I brought them with me."

Withdrawing his flaccid member from her body, Hawk eased Skye onto her side, then pushed up on one elbow so he could stare down at her. He wanted to see her face when he made his charge. "If so, I can only draw one conclusion, sweetheart."

She looked wary, cautious. "And what is that?"

"You planned my seduction all along."

Chapter Thirteen

She had known this moment would come. Skye studied Hawk in the silver light. His gaze was fixed intently on her face, but she couldn't make out his expression. Fearing how he might take her revelations, she was not eager to confess, yet it was past time for honesty.

Skye drew a steadying breath. "Yes, I planned your seduction."

His face closed and hardened. When she tried to reach up to touch Hawk's cheek, his fingers closed around her wrist, trapping her palm against the wall of his chest.

"That first night . . . You feigned a nightmare to lure me to your bed?"

She shook her head. "No, not at all. My nightmares are very real. Storms tend to incite them, as does sleeping in a strange place, just as I told you. That first night when you came to my room, all I wanted was comfort. The fact that we made love . . . I did not plan it that way. It just happened."

When Hawk made no reply, Skye continued on doggedly. "Don't you remember what I said then? I have horrible dreams about my parents' deaths when they drowned at sea. It started when I was ten, when I was sent away to boarding school and had to leave everyone I held dear but for my cousin Katharine." She had felt so bereft and lonely that she'd cried herself to sleep for weeks. "I cannot seem to conquer my nightmares—or at least I couldn't until I met you. I promise they are no pretense—" Skye broke off abruptly. She was babbling again, so she closed her mouth to give Hawk a chance to speak.

"You have been manipulating me from the very first," he charged.

"No, truly I have not. That would be impossible, even if I had wished to. You are not susceptible to manipulation."

"But not for your lack of trying."

"No," she agreed. "But giving you my virginity . . . that was never part of my plan, I swear it."

Skye held her breath, waiting for Hawk's response. His grim silence worried her, but not as much as when he abruptly rolled away from her side and rose from the bed.

When he lit the bedside lamp, Skye winced as sudden brightness starkly illuminated his features. His expression was cold, dispassionate, but she could sense the heat of his anger.

Feeling too vulnerable, sprawled naked on his bed, she sat up awkwardly. When Hawk tossed her nightdress at her, she put it on without protest. Her breasts tingled, feeling exquisitely sensitive, while her core was tender and throbbing—a severe contrast to the sudden ominous chill in the air.

Hawk scooped up his own nightshirt from the floor

and shrugged into it, his actions brusque. Skye bit her lip in dismay. This was hardly the scene she had dreamed of—an intimate lovers' confession where they both laid their secrets bare, whispering sweet words of desire and love.

How quickly the mood had changed. Barely five minutes ago, she'd been cradled in Hawk's arms, feeling his heated need, his hunger, the thirst in his kisses. Even in his intensity he'd been ruthlessly gentle, but now the unguarded tenderness on his face had disappeared and the mask he regularly wore had returned with a vengeance. There was nothing visible of the wonderful lover who had moved inside her with an eroticism that melted every bone and nerve in her body.

To her surprise, though, Hawk returned to the bedside and gestured for her to give him room to join her. When she complied, he arranged the pillows against the headboard, then leaned back so that he could watch her.

His smoky gaze held hers, never wavering. "You owe me an explanation."

At least he was giving her a chance to present a defense.

Skye curled her legs under her, her heart pounding at the step she was about to take. Hawk might very well end all her hopes and dreams right then, but she owed him the full truth if they were ever to move past this conflict and deepen their relationship.

"You will probably think it foolish, but my cousin has a theory about legendary lovers. . . ."

Quickly she related Kate's romantic premise about the Wildes finding their life mates based on classic romances throughout history and literature. "I thought my path to true love could follow the French fairy tale of Beauty and the Beast by Madame Le Prince de Beaumont. Have you read it?"

"I'm familiar with it, yes."

"Well, in my case you are the 'beast.' There are a number of parallels between your circumstances and Madame de Beaumont's story."

She could tell she had surprised Hawk and so hastened to add, "I don't *literally* believe in fairy tales, but I have always longed to find true love, so I thought my cousin's premise enticing. Much more important, I have admired you from afar since I first saw you when I was a mere girl. And the more I learned about you from my aunt, the more my esteem for you rose. I came to Hawkhurst Castle to answer the question of whether or not we were suited, and I concluded that you might be my ideal mate."

"Might" was too uncertain a word, Skye amended to herself. There was no doubt in her mind now that Hawk was her match.

Unfortunately, his silence this time held skepticism as well as mistrust.

"In my defense," she went on gamely, "I never meant to seduce you that night, or even invite you to my bed. Making love to you was certainly not premeditated on my part."

"What of the sponges? You clearly came prepared."

"Well . . . I had hoped that someday . . . They were mainly a precaution, just in case we ever became intimate. I suppose you have a right to be angry at me for taking my plan too far."

"Do I now?" he asked, his drawl edged with sarcasm. "Why should I be angry that you deceived and lied to me from the moment you arrived on my doorstep?"

"Perhaps I made several lies of omission," Skye countered in a small voice, "but I have rarely lied to you outright. What else could I have done? How would you have reacted if I had declared my intentions at the outset? You know you would have barred me from your castle."

"So you duped me into pursuing your uncle's lover."

"That was entirely an honest request. You were the perfect person to try to find her—which you did admirably, I must say. My faith in you was completely justified. I merely used my uncle's plight as the way to make your initial acquaintance and then my reason for staying."

When Hawk finally responded, some of the heat had gone out of his tone. "I am not your true love, wretch."

Skye was surprised he addressed that issue first. "How can you be certain?"

"The very notion is daft."

She couldn't help a faint smile. "My brother agrees with you wholeheartedly—but it isn't daft to yearn for love," she declared stubbornly.

Perhaps she *was* a bit mad for hoping for Hawk's love. This was a man who didn't share his heart easily. She would have to prove herself his match, of course—if he ever gave her the chance. She wanted to be worthy of him, an enormous feat given his past heroism. It distressed Skye that she could very well fail. Her aunt had been clear; the Guardians were his chosen calling and he wouldn't give them up readily. But she refused to consider the possibility of failure just now.

"I am not willing to give up," Skye added more softly. "I told you before, Hawk, I believe in making my own destiny. I can't bear being helpless against the whims of fate. And I think you want to make your own fate as well. Isn't that what you did by joining the Guardians? You became bent on saving lives because you were unable to save your family?"

She had struck a nerve, she could tell, for Hawk's gaze narrowed on her. Yet he must have seen some merit in her assertion, for he didn't deny it.

"That does not excuse your duplicity," he finally said.

"Perhaps not." She disliked keeping secrets from him. She didn't need her Aunt Bella's counsel to know that love could never flourish in secrecy, or that dishonesty was like poison. For that reason alone she was glad this matter had come to a head. But her secrecy was not unwarranted.

"You have your own secrets about the Guardians of the Sword," she pointed out. "In all fairness, how can you expect me to share mine when you refuse to share yours?"

Hawk looked irked by her argument. "Keeping confidences is vastly different from dishonesty and deception. I took an oath to protect the league's anonymity. There are things I can't tell anyone, certainly not a strange young lady I met barely a fortnight ago. Secrecy is not just a whim of mine. Lives are at stake."

Feeling rueful, Skye nodded her head. She fully agreed that Hawk's career not only needed to remain clandestine, it was of vital importance. Indeed, she thought it awe inspiring that he'd devoted his life to righting wrongs and had risked his life many times over.

His powerful form was now covered by his cambric nightshirt, but she remembered his ravaged flesh very well.

"I have seen your body, Hawk. I know your burns came from the castle fire, but those other scars are not burns. One looks to be a bullet wound; another a cut from a knife or sword blade."

"A scimitar," Hawk said curtly.

He was watching her through his long lashes now. His eyes were heavily guarded, his emotions like shadows, but he was considering her confession, she could tell.

His contemplation gave her hope, and made her recall the other urgent reason she had chosen to storm his castle.

"I might have tried to meet you in the normal way by seeking a proper introduction from my aunt, but you never go into society. And time was a huge factor. You were supposed to begin courting Sir Gawain Olwen's niece soon."

"I still am."

Unless she convinced him otherwise.

She needed to delay his courtship long enough for him to fall in love with her, Skye reflected. If so, she had to begin planting the seeds in his mind that he shouldn't wed Miss Olwen. After all his valiant endeavors, Hawk would be miserable with a quiet, retiring girl like Sir Gawain Olwen's niece. She, on the other hand, could be his perfect match, if only she could make him see it.

"Do you truly want to wed Miss Olwen? From all

reports, she is your complete opposite. You would not be happy married to her, I think."

"My happiness is beside the point."

"It shouldn't be. You have already made numerous sacrifices for your country. You shouldn't have to make a marriage of convenience out of duty to your mentor."

Hawk dismissed her argument abruptly. "If you know of my obligations to Sir Gawain, then you know why I must choose his great-niece for my bride."

"No, actually I don't know why."

"She is a direct descendant of the league's original founders. For me to become the new leader, I must have a blood connection to the founders, a requirement of our charter. Sir Gawain is growing too old to continue as head and wishes me to succeed him."

Skye's heart sank. "Oh." She'd thought Hawk had chosen Miss Olwen merely to please Sir Gawain. "Does that mean . . . you could never marry me?"

"Only if I want to abandon becoming Sir Gawain's successor."

"But . . . you insisted you would wed me if I am with child."

Another shadow crossed his features. "A child would change my calculations entirely."

Indeed it would, Skye thought despondently. She hadn't realized that by marrying her, Hawk would be forced to make an enormous decision—which made the obstacles to her winning his heart even greater.

She wouldn't admit defeat, though. "Regardless of our dilemma, I still think Miss Olwen is not the right bride for you."

His eyebrow rose. "Just recently you offered to help me court her."

"Yes, but I would be acting under duress. It goes against every romantic fiber in my body to aid a courtship that is so unsuitable. And much more importantly . . ." The things Skye had wanted to say for a long while spilled out of her. "You should be free to live your own life, Hawk, and not be compelled to wed for duty. Even if you never wish to marry *me*, it is time you think of yourself. Your happiness *should* matter. You cannot keep punishing yourself for the tragedy to your family."

His mouth tightened. "I am hardly punishing myself."

"Are you not? That night when I found you in the burnt wing, outside what remained of the nursery, you said you were to blame and that you should have died with them. I don't think your late wife would have wanted you to die with her. Instead, you need to try and move on with your life. You deserve to be able to live again, to know laughter and joy and love."

Evidently, the earnestness in her plea on his behalf was unexpected. For a long moment, Hawk simply stared at her.

Then his mouth twisted. "You are the most infernal, interfering busybody I have ever known."

At the reappearance of his familiar exasperation, relief flooded Skye. "Yes, but my motives are pure."

"Your motives are absurd—finding true love based on a fairy tale." His tone was part scoff, part disbelief, yet he reached out his hand to her. "Come here."

She returned his gaze warily. "What do you mean to do to me?"

His eyes were penetrating, perceptive, yet no longer cold. "To hold you. I ought to wring your pretty neck, but we both need to get some sleep."

When Skye tentatively moved toward him, Hawk drew her into his arms so that her cheek rested on his shoulder, and pulled the covers up over them both.

"You will let me stay the night with you?" she mumbled almost humbly into his nightshirt.

"For a few hours at least. You will need to return to your own room before daybreak, but for now we will comfort each other."

Skye was slightly stunned that after all her revelations, Hawk hadn't banished her or worse. If he wasn't willing to wholly forgive her pursuit of him, at least his anger seemed to have tempered. That was progress of a sort.

Hawk was nearly as surprised by his decision to let her stay. For all her brazen intrusiveness, Skye Wilde knew human nature very well. She wasn't wrong about Sir Gawain's niece. In truth, he was already having second thoughts about the sacrifices he would have to make in order to wed her. The girl would doubtless make a terrible match for him—but in some ways, that was a very good thing. He would never be at risk of loving her. A convenient marriage would suit him well enough.

Moreover, his obligations to Sir Gawain were no small matter. During his younger days, Hawk had lived the carefree life of a wealthy noble buck. His work for the Foreign Office had started more as a lark than a worthy occupation, but he quickly learned he had an aptitude for espionage, and he'd come to relish doing his small part to defeat the little French tyrant who was bent on world domination.

After Hawk's tragic loss, Sir Gawain had saved his sanity by recruiting him into the Guardians. The highly elite organization was a covert arm of the Foreign Office, dedicated to protecting England and its allies from threats and championing the cause of justice across Europe. Hawk had devoted himself wholly to the league to atone for his guilt. He hadn't saved his wife and son, so he'd turned to saving others. He'd accepted the most dangerous missions because he had nothing left to lose. He'd challenged death unafraid because his life was so very empty.

His work had become profoundly rewarding, though. And leading the Guardians after Sir Gawain's expected retirement would continue to offer a fulfilling purpose, Hawk believed, even if the need for protectors and champions had diminished somewhat after Boney's final, bloody defeat at Waterloo.

As for Skye's other arguments . . . For years he'd been a stranger to laughter and joy and happiness, so he wouldn't miss them, whether or not he deserved them.

And as for Skye herself? His anger was chiefly because she'd duped him from the first, Hawk admitted. But she hadn't tried to entrap him in marriage. Were that her intention, she could have easily forced his hand after he'd claimed her maidenhead and spent the night in her bed. But Skye had adamantly refused his grudging proposal.

Oh, she'd been very willing to give him her innocence that night. He couldn't forget how she'd clung to him when he'd wanted to withdraw, or the ardent way she had locked him to her body with her slender legs.

But he couldn't hold on to his anger now. In fact, he was strangely flattered by her desire. And how could he fault her for following her romantic ideals?

They were totally unrealistic, yet he had to admire her determination to control her own destiny. He shared that trait with her. He couldn't bear being helpless, at the mercy of capricious fate. However quixotically Skye strove to change the world to her liking, that made her deserving of his respect, even when *he* was her target.

Admittedly, he'd been hard-pressed to resist her sweet persistence. Now that he understood her chief goal, though . . . well, forewarned was forearmed. He wouldn't let her seduce him.

And he would quickly have to disabuse her of the notion that he was her life's mate. She wanted love in marriage, and he had no love to give. He'd known true love once. He'd been smitten by Elizabeth at their first encounter and had married her by the end of the Season. But their love had ended in tragedy, and he couldn't—wouldn't—endure feeling that kind of agony again. He would never let himself dream or hope for happiness, certainly not love.

On the other hand, he knew full well that he needed to move on with his life. He was resolved to overcome the pain of his loss. After ten years of wallowing in darkness, it was time.

His thoughts were interrupted just then when Skye caught his fingers and brought the back of his hand to her lips to press a soft kiss against the savage scars there.

"The burns you suffered must have been excruciating," she said quietly.

"Not as much as losing my wife and son."

"I can only imagine."

Raising her head slightly, she looked up at him and searched his face. Her eyes were full of sadness and sympathy. She'd been lying there reflecting on his tragedy, Hawk realized. She was softhearted enough that she couldn't bear to think of him in pain.

"I hope I can make the hurt feel better," she murmured, reaching up to touch his lips with her fingertips.

Deliberately, Hawk shifted his gaze to the bedside table. Reaching out, he snuffed the lamp so he wouldn't have to see those deep, soft eyes of hers, and then turned back to claim her mouth. He had planned to let her rest before taking her again, but her obvious invitation convinced him otherwise.

He would have to clearly show Skye that he couldn't love her, of course; that nothing could fill up all the dark and empty places in his soul. The key would be to shut her out emotionally. Their carnal relations would simply serve to relieve his sexual pain and hers, just as she'd suggested earlier.

As she'd also said, in all likelihood this would be the last time they would be intimate together. And Hawk calculated that there was no harm in comforting each other in the few hours they had left.

Chapter Fourteen

Upon arriving in London late the next morning, they delayed only long enough to change carriage horses and to visit a milliner's shop, where Skye purchased two fashionable turbans for Rachel to wear in public until she was able to dye her hair.

In London, they parted ways with Macky. Hawk had ordered a detailed investigation into Rachel's past, so Bow Street Runner Horace Linch had already been dispatched to Brackstone in Kent, to find out all he could from the locals about the late Baron Farnwell, William. Macky would focus on the current Baron Farnwell, Edgar, since Hawk wanted to know exactly the sort of man they would be dealing with. Edgar had not even been born until three years after Lady Farnwell had fled England, so whatever knowledge she had of him was hearsay from a long distance away.

Understanding his temperament would allow them to judge how he might react to her "return from the dead"—whether he could be reasoned with or if they could expect a battle royal.

Additionally, Macky was to deliver Skye's message to her uncle at Beauvoir, the family seat of the Marquises of Beaufort, also in Kent. Lord Cornelius had made his primary home there since assuming guardianship of the five orphaned Wilde children.

Learning of Rachel's survival would likely be a huge shock, and Skye wanted to prepare her uncle in person, rather than baldly springing the news on him in a letter. Thus, she said she had great need of him and begged him to come to Hawkhurst Castle in East Sussex to aid in restoring the earl's library to its former glory. She was certain Cornelius would comply with alacrity, since he had always put the youngsters' welfare above his own, and a library in desperate need of restoration would be an irresistible lure.

As they traveled closer to Hawk's home, however, she grew more concerned about both Rachel and Hawk. Rachel's doubts were once again rearing up, so Skye spent the remainder of the journey trying to ease her fears and giving her a wide-ranging account of how British society had changed in her long absence. Skye herself was highly sociable, with the innate ability to put others at ease, but she was looking forward to getting assistance from her Aunt Isabella, who was a champion at raising spirits.

Hawk, on the other hand, was more worrisome. Skye observed him as they drove through the iron-pillared gateway of the castle. His features were shuttered, and when the looming edifice came into view, all hint of emotion disappeared from his expression, leaving only a cold, impassive mask.

Skye searched for something to say, to distract him from the pain he must have felt each time he returned to his empty home, and wound up chattering about the nearby village of Hawkhurst, what sort of market and shops it offered. She hoped Bella would be able to help coax Hawk out of his self-imposed isolation and chip away at the granite wall of defenses he'd erected to avoid more excruciating pain.

Lady Isabella must have been watching for them, for when the coach swept up the rutted gravel drive and came to a halt in front of the castle, she ran lightly down the steps, exclaiming in delight at their arrival.

True to expectations, her warmth and easygoing nature were on display for them all. The lively half-Spanish widow was nearing middle age, but she seemed much younger than her forty-six years as she embraced Skye first. "I am so pleased to see you, my dear."

"Thank you for coming to our rescue, Aunt Bella."

"I wouldn't miss it."

Her treatment of Skye had always been motherly but in a way that fostered independence, since she ardently believed that women should not be at the mercy of men, as she had been during her first marriage to a Spanish nobleman.

Isabella turned to Hawk next and pressed a friendly kiss to his cheek. When Skye spied the silent look they exchanged, she interpreted Hawk's piercing glance to mean something like, *I intend to throttle you, Bella, for sharing so much of my past with your niece.*

Aloud, he said only, "I will speak to you later, my lady."

The moment of reckoning had to be postponed while Isabella welcomed Rachel to the castle. She caught the baroness's hands in her own, and for the sake of the servants in earshot, greeted her as Mrs. Donnelly. But once they were all inside and had handed over their outer garments, Isabella didn't delay in arranging more privacy.

After ordering tea to be brought in, she led the way to the drawing room, where a fire burned cheerily in the hearth. Immediately, she was more effusive toward Rachel and more sympathetic as well as they sat side by side on a sofa. "Please let me say that I am all admiration, my dear. After the trials you endured . . . to maintain such strength and presence of mind as to fool your tormenter and begin your life over entirely in another country . . . well, I don't know that I could ever have been as brave. I know we shall become fast friends."

Rachel flushed in gratitude and seemed well on the way to being won over.

Skye was glad her aunt would take Rachel under her wing. Not only were the two nearer in age, Bella had far more worldly experience and would be better at making a lady with such a traumatic past feel safe and cared for.

Then Hawk explained what he needed in the way of a disguise for Rachel, starting with henna dye for her hair. Isabella's dark eyes lit with mischievousness and she promptly launched into a tale about her time in the Kingdom of Algiers in northern Africa, when she'd been held captive in the harem of a Berber sheikh and learned about exotic cosmetics and beautifying agents such as henna. "Leave everything to me. I promise I can make Mrs. Donnelly look like an Irishwoman born and bred."

While her aunt was reminiscing, Skye noticed that

the drawing room had already been restored to a semblance of its former elegance. The ghostly holland covers had been banished, every wood surface gleamed with beeswax, and the air no longer smelled musty and damp.

When Skye remarked on it, Isabella beamed with pride. "I must admit, I have accomplished a great deal since my arrival last week. Wet tea leaves sprinkled on the carpets before sweeping cuts down on the dust, while incense burned daily helps drive away odors."

"You have worked wonders, Aunt."

"As you suggested, we are conquering the house room by room. It has helped that Kate started hiring staff from London—Lady Katharine Wilde is my other niece by marriage," Isabella explained to Rachel before addressing Hawk again. "A good number of the furnishings are long out of fashion, my lord. It may cost you a pretty penny to replace them, but I shall take pleasure in diminishing your purse," she teased in the bantering way of a long friendship.

Hawk did not immediately respond, for he seemed to be occupied in listening intently. Just then Skye became aware of the faint din in the distance—a din that sounded like hammering and pounding.

"The reconstruction has begun?" Hawk asked Bella.

"Not quite yet. The damaged rooms in the east wing have been razed and much of the debris hauled away. Your architect, Mr. Beald, wishes to meet with you at your earliest convenience."

"Now is a good time. If you will pray excuse me, ladies . . ."

When Hawk rose from his chair and made for the

door, Skye hurried to follow and caught him before he could leave the drawing room.

"Where are you going?"

"To confer with Beald and inspect the renovations thus far."

"May I come with you?" she asked, not wanting him to face the demolished wing alone.

He hesitated. "If I deny my permission, will you make a pest of yourself and tag along anyway?"

"Yes, of course."

The faint hint of exasperation reappeared, which relieved Skye, as did his rather mild command. "Come, then."

He led the way outside to the rear of the castle. Work had progressed significantly on the damaged wing, Skye saw at once. A gaping hole stood at the end of the east wing, and most of the evidence of the fire was gone.

The architect's crews were scurrying here and there, filling wagons with debris from the wreckage, just as Bella had said. Judging by the virtual army of workers, Skye suspected Hawk was paying a fortune for speed so he could bring his new bride home as soon as possible.

A muscle worked in Hawk's jaw, but otherwise his response was indiscernible. Skye felt his homecoming could have been much worse, though. The air of neglect and hopelessness about the castle seemed somehow diminished.

Perhaps it was partly due to the bustling atmosphere. The sun would set soon, and the laborers seemed to be striving for as much progress as possible before dusk. Or perhaps the change was due to the season and clement weather. It was a clear, crisp autumn day, and the gold and red colors of the surrounding landscape added to the pleasant aura.

Skye was immensely glad for the fair weather. Sunshine made everything brighter, and if the storms would retreat for the moment, her dreams would be more peaceful, even if Hawk would not be sleeping beside her to comfort her.

She hoped Hawk's sleep would be helped as well. He seemed to divine what she was thinking, for he drawled in a wry voice, "I won't be driven to drink or start throwing brandy decanters, if that is what worries you."

Skye smiled in relief. "In truth, it does worry me."

"Then you may stop watching me so intently. You are scrutinizing me as if I might erupt at any moment."

Actually she was more concerned that Hawk would hold all his bitterness and grief and anger inside. But rather than argue that eruptions could be healing, she noted that a tall, thin man was walking across the courtyard toward them.

When Hawk introduced him to Skye as a renowned architect, Mr. Nathanial Beald hastened to give a report.

"My lord, I am pleased to say that we are slightly ahead of schedule. The next step is to erect wooden scaffolding to begin rebuilding. And as we discussed, we will reuse the stone to make the exterior of this wing appear to match the rest. . . ."

Skye was glad to discover that the renovations would take perhaps five or six more months to complete, but the interval would do little to prevent or even delay

Hawk's expected courtship. He could still take Miss Olwen for his bride, even if he had no splendid estate to offer his countess yet.

But for just now, Skye was content that Hawk would be occupied and his dark memories overshadowed by this new purpose.

She left him conferring with the architect and poring over blueprints, and made her way back to the house. She wanted to give her aunt and Rachel time to become acquainted. Thus, rather than return to the drawing room, Skye stopped by the kitchens and spoke to the cook about dinner: where to hold it and what to prepare. Then she went to her own room to change her attire for dinner.

Isabella, bless her, had brought a trunkful of gowns, but Skye chose a simple blue kerseymere dress in deference to Rachel's lack of formal attire.

She was repinning her hair in a knot at her nape when Isabella knocked lightly and entered at Skye's invitation.

"I have given Rachel the bedchamber adjacent to mine. Poor soul. But I do like her gumption in defying her brute of a husband."

"So do I," Skye agreed.

"Tomorrow we will begin work on her disguise and shop for a proper wardrobe for her, but for now I will loan her some of my gowns. She is more my size than yours." They were of similar heights, but her aunt's figure was plumper with a thicker waist.

With those details settled, Isabella wasted no time in expressing her curiosity. "So, my dear, I am on pins and needles to hear about your romance with Hawk. What have you determined thus far?"

Skye winced. "I am convinced he is my match, Aunt Bella."

"So you are compatible in mind and body and heart?"

"In many ways, yes, I believe so. I felt sparks of lightning from the first moment we met, just as you predicted. When I am with him, I forget how to breathe. And yet we have an undeniable connection beyond the physical. He makes me yearn for something deeper."

"How far have you progressed in the physical realm?"

Skye felt her cheeks flushing at her aunt's plain speaking. "Farther than I expected. You were right. Passion with a special lover is amazing. But as for my dream of finding true love with Hawk? He is very likely wed to the Guardians, so nothing I say or do may matter." She explained his reason for choosing Miss Olwen, then sighed. "Even if I could persuade him to fall in love with me—which is questionable—we may have no future together."

"And on his part? What does Hawk believe?"

"I had to confess about Kate's theory. He thinks the notion of us being legendary lovers is absurd."

"Still, you did well to tell him the truth."

"I know. 'Honesty is imperative for love to grow.' Weren't those your exact words? If you have other secrets of seduction to share, I should very much like to hear them."

Isabella pursed her lips thoughtfully. "For now, my best advice is to strive for patience, my dear. You cannot force love, particularly with a man so emotionally scarred as Hawk. He must learn to love again, and you are the perfect woman to teach him."

"I will do my best. Perhaps I can claim some progress. Since we first met, he has become less reclusive and a trifle more open about his feelings. But it is supremely frustrating to be so helpless."

They spoke for quite a while longer, with Bella offering consolation and inspiration and Skye explaining her immediate plans, starting with the arrangements for dinner and Hawk's severe dislike of his own dining room, then catching up on the other Wilde family members and Skye's hope for Uncle Cornelius's reunion with Rachel.

The last thing Aunt Bella said before leaving to change her own attire was for Skye not to lose heart—just the encouragement Skye needed to bolster her resolve.

Following her aunt to the door, she gave Isabella a fierce hug. "I cannot tell you how glad I am to have you here, dearest auntie."

"I know, darling girl. But never fear, we will not fail."

Upon shutting her bedchamber door after her aunt, Skye marveled at how much lighter her spirits felt after their coze. In her campaign to win Hawk's heart, she had needed to call in reinforcements, and there was no better general in the war of love than Lady Isabella Wilde.

Skye had not looked forward to the evening ahead, but it turned out to be more pleasant than she'd anticipated. At her insistence, they took supper in the drawing room, with the various dishes laid out on a side table, much like a buffet supper at a ball. Skye claimed that not only was the dining room too formal for the four of them, it still needed to be cleaned and made habitable. Additionally, the warmth of the hearth fire made the drawing room more appealing.

From Hawk's sharp gaze, she knew that *he* knew what she was doing: protecting him from his dark memories. She also wanted to make his newest guest feel at home, so thankfully he refrained from chastising her and actually joined in the effort to make Rachel's first evening as comfortable as possible.

After supper they played cards. There was no music, for the pianoforte was dreadfully out of tune, and Skye decided that singing would be too effusive. But in the future, she intended to introduce music as well as charades and other parlor games and perhaps poetry readings to the evening's entertainment.

When it was time to retire to bed, Rachel's grateful-if-weary smile was all the reward Skye needed, yet Hawk also seemed more at ease than before.

In fact, the next two days proceeded better than Skye could have hoped for. She kept a close eye on Hawk, but the new aura about the castle seemed to have a positive influence. He spent most of each day out in the stables or in the meadows riding and training his new stallion to escape the noise from the construction, which at times was deafening. Skye stayed busy setting his home to rights, wearing her oldest gown and a muslin headscarf, not only supervising the servants in cleaning, but performing a myriad of other tasks. Aunt Bella and Rachel pitched in and were especially helpful in deciding whether to replace or refurbish the furniture, carpets, and wallpaper and in discussing the best fabrics and colors.

Another accomplishment was the disguise to better

conceal the baroness's former identity. The henna dye arrived from Macky by special messenger, and Isabella set to work transforming Rachel's hair from gray-streaked brown to an attractive shade of auburn, so she could abandon the turbans. Carefully applied cosmetics—particularly kohl to make her eyes appear more exotic—also created a much different look from her miniature portrait.

On the afternoon of the second day Skye had to deal with another big obstacle. She was upstairs with Rachel and the housekeeper, inventorying linen, when one of the new footmen announced that Lord Cornelius Wilde had arrived and was awaiting her in the library. Her pulse suddenly quickened in anticipation, but Rachel went rigid with fear.

Skye offered her a heartening smile. "Pray continue with the inventory, Mrs. Donnelly. I will send for you when the time is right."

If the time is ever right, Skye amended silently as she hurried downstairs. She still had a great deal of persuading to do.

She had asked for her uncle to be shown into the library for a reason. It was where the dedicated scholar was most comfortable, for one thing. Additionally, he would consider it criminal that the leather-bound tomes had been neglected and allowed to gather dust and mildew for a decade.

As expected, he had donned his spectacles and was examining the shelves closely, a disgruntled look on his lined face.

Now over sixty, Cornelius had silvering hair and heavy eyebrows. His tall, refined build and high-boned features lent him an unmistakable aristocratic elegance. Yet as a brilliant classics scholar, he had a vague, unfocused air and was uncomfortable in most social settings. To Skye, he was the dear, dear man who had given up his quiet, intellectual life to raise five rambunctious, irrepressible orphans.

After warmly embracing him, Skye removed the holland covers from a leather couch and made him sit beside her.

"As I said in my letter, you know that Aunt Bella and I are helping her good friend Lord Hawkhurst renovate his home. I have hopes that you will help save his library."

"Yes, yes," he said impatiently, "of course I will help. In truth, I am eager to begin. That is a priceless edition of Aristotle's *Nicomachean Ethics* simply rotting on the shelf."

"There is another, more important, reason I asked you here, Uncle."

"What could be more important?"

Skye took a breath. "I have some news that I think you will welcome. At least I hope you will be pleased."

As Cornelius sat waiting expectantly, she swallowed, realizing she was highly nervous herself. "The thing is, Uncle . . . I have a confession to make. Some months ago, I found your love letters to Baroness Farnwell."

His blue eyes narrowed, as if he was disappointed in her. "I thought I had those well hidden."

"You did." Skye cleared her throat, feeling once again like the child her long-suffering uncle had tried to discipline after catching her in some mischief or other. Not wanting to become sidetracked, she plowed on. "It seems that you loved her very much."

"I did."

"How do you feel about her now, after all this time?"

He looked taken aback by her question.

"I know I am prying," Skye hastened to add, "but it is not mere rudeness. I have a good reason for asking."

His eyes clouded. "I never stopped loving her."

"Then what if she didn't drown all those years ago?"

Cornelius blinked at her. "What do you mean?"

"I mean that . . . Rachel Farnwell is still . . . alive."

Disbelief warred with hope on his features as he reached out to grip her arm. "What the bloody devil are you saying?"

Unlike his charges, her mild-mannered uncle never cursed. The urgency in his tone was a measure of his shock, Skye knew, so she hurried to explain how Rachel had been so desperate to escape the abusive baron, she had staged her drowning and fled to Ireland.

When she was done, Cornelius sat there unmoving, trying to digest her revelation. He seemed stunned as if by a blow.

"Rachel is still alive, Uncle," she repeated, prodding.

"Dear God." His mouth was trembling as he worked to suppress strong emotions. "All that time . . . I never knew."

"Would you like to see her?"

He shook himself and focused his blind gaze on Skye. "See her? How is that *possible*?"

"She is here now, at Hawkhurst Castle."

"In . . . in this very house?"

"Yes. I couldn't rest until I knew what had become of her, so Hawkhurst escorted me to Ireland to try and find Lady Farnwell."

"And you actually did?" he said in wonder.

"Yes, and even better, we brought her home to England with us. She still loves you, Uncle."

"Dear God," he repeated. Shock and amazement shone in his expression. "She is truly alive?"

"Indeed. She is upstairs now, waiting for me to summon her. Would you like me to fetch her now?"

"I will need a moment to absorb . . ."

"Of course," Skye said sympathetically. She suspected he had a multitude of questions, but for now accepting the truth was the most important thing. "I will leave you alone for a while."

When she made to rise, however, Cornelius's fingers closed around her wrist again. "No, I want to see her. Now, at once."

"Then I will bring her to you."

Nodding, he released her arm. As Skye reached the door, she heard him let out a long, shuddering breath, as if still not able to believe that a fantastic, cherished dream was coming true.

When Skye returned with the baroness, she found her uncle standing frozen in the middle of the library, watching the door as if not daring to breathe.

Clutching his box of letters, Rachel stepped over the threshold tentatively and then halted, staring back at Cornelius and drinking him in.

His voice was hoarse when he finally spoke. "I could

not believe my ears when Skye told me you had not perished after all."

"I am so terribly sorry," she whispered. "Can you ever forgive me?"

"There is nothing to forgive. You acted to save your life. Can you ever forgive *me* for not knowing that brute was beating you?"

She gave a soft sob and pressed a hand to her mouth.

"Why did you never tell me, Rachel?"

"I did not want to put you in danger."

"My God, Rachel . . ." Cornelius's tone held helplessness and frustration. "You were all alone. . . ."

From her vantage point just outside the library door, Skye couldn't see Rachel's face but knew tears were streaming down her cheeks. "No, I was not alone. I had your memory."

"My dearest love . . ." He took a small step toward her, then halted as if not trusting the reception he would receive.

The same questioning caution sounded in Rachel's tone when she spoke next. "*Am* I your dearest love, Cornelius?"

"Yes, of course you are."

She shuddered with relief. "I didn't dare hope. Even when I learned you kept our rose pressed among my letters."

"I wanted a remembrance, however painful it might be. I mourned you for a long while, Rachel. In truth, I never recovered. . . ."

His own voice broke, and he brought a shaking hand to hide his eyes. He was choking on his own tears, Skye realized, her heart going out to him. Only once before had she seen her uncle so emotional, the day the terrible news came about the shipwreck that had killed his closest relatives.

Not wanting to intrude on their tender reunion any longer, Skye backed away and quietly shut the library door, intending to allow them privacy to become re-acquainted.

When she turned, wiping tears from her own eyes, she nearly ran into Hawk, who had been waiting in the corridor.

"Well?" he said, watching her.

"I think it went better than I could have hoped for." Skye gave him a watery smile. "I have dreamed about this moment since I first learned that his love was still alive." She sniffed and glanced over her shoulder at the library door, then sought his gaze again. "Thank you, Hawk. This never would have been possible without you." On impulse, Skye stepped forward and stood on tiptoes to press a kiss to his jaw in gratitude.

The gesture was simple and friendly, but his hands moved to her waist. When she recognized the sudden flash in his eyes as heat, her pulse leapt. He was looking at her as if he wanted her. . . . For a fleeting moment, she thought he might return a more passionate embrace. But then his expression shuttered, reminding her that he intended to keep their relationship strictly formal from now on.

"I'm certain you would have managed without me," Hawk said before turning away.

Skye quelled a sigh as she watched him walk down the corridor. It was frustrating, not knowing how she could persuade him to reconsider, but for now she would let herself relish the moment when her beloved uncle found the love of his life once more.

* * *

It was an hour later before Rachel sought her out. Her eyes were swollen from crying, and yet she looked happy.

"Cornelius loves me still," she effused once Skye had ushered her into the nearest empty room so they could be alone. "I cannot believe it."

"You agreed that a love as strong as yours would not easily die."

"I know, but even so . . . I want to pinch myself. Is this truly happening?"

"Yes, dearest Rachel."

"Cornelius actually wishes to marry me."

Skye felt surprise and delight at the same time. "He proposed?"

"Not in so many words. And I was glad he did not press me." Rachel's expression sobered, her smile fading. "I could never accept his offer until I tell him about his daughter, and I cannot bring myself to tell him yet. He will hate me when he learns I concealed such an enormous secret from him."

"I am certain he won't hate you, Rachel, but perhaps that knowledge would be too much, coming so swiftly after he learned you had risen from the dead. What did you say to his implication about marriage?"

"That I couldn't decide just now. That I needed time to consider." She gave a faint sob that was half laughter. "Cornelius is resolved to court me as he never could before. He says he will have to rely on you and Lady Isabella to advise him, since at his age, he knows nothing about romance."

"I think he is doing quite well on his own," Skye

said, amused at the thought of her elderly, staid, bachelor uncle seeking her advice.

Rachel's face suddenly clouded. "There is still a great need for secrecy. We have no idea how Edgar Farnwell would react if he learned of my resurrection."

"True."

"Cornelius and I mean to follow Lord Hawkhurst's suggestion. We will pretend that we have just met and that we are falling in love for the first time."

"I think that is a perfect plan. You can take your romance one day at a time."

Rachel took Skye's hands. "However can I thank you?"

"By making my uncle happy," she answered earnestly. "I promise you, that will be more than enough thanks."

Chapter Fifteen

The castle had yet another visitor that afternoon: the Bow Street Runner charged with investigating the late Baron Farnwell and his son and heir, Edgar. Hawk was closeted with Horace Linch for the better part of an hour, but by the time Skye learned the caller's identity, he had already departed.

Wanting to know what Linch had said, she went in search of Hawk and was told the earl had gone to the stables. When she reached the stable block, though, she found he had ridden out on his new stallion.

Since the noise from the renovations was louder than ever, Skye was glad to escape on her own mount. She found Hawk in the same meadow as before, putting the stallion through its paces. She spent a moment admiring the beauty of the purebred animal, whose black coat glowed richly in the sunlight, and its magnificent rider, who effortlessly controlled the creature's savage power.

Spying her, Hawk came to a halt and gave her time

to ride up to him. He didn't look particularly pleased to see her, but neither did he order her to leave.

When he raised an eyebrow expectantly, Skye explained why she had come. "Did Linch discover anything of significance from his investigation?"

"A few items of note. You may read his written report, but to summarize, William Farnwell was severely disliked by the servants and tenants in his district, and Edgar Farnwell is not much better. It seems Edgar inherited his father's temper."

Frowning, Skye bit her lower lip. "That does not bode well for Rachel. If Edgar is half the brute his father was, there may be no reasoning with him. She may always have to remain in hiding, or at least maintain a disguise."

"Perhaps, but it is too early to make that judgment yet."

"I suspect my uncle would be willing to share her exile. He is already hinting at marriage. But I would much prefer that he be free to live in England."

"You are jumping ahead of yourself, aren't you?"

Skye's smile was troubled. "I suppose so. There are still so many issues to be resolved between them. I just wish it were over and they could live happily ever after."

"You need to control your impatience."

"Aunt Bella told me something similar."

She glanced around them at the peaceful meadow. The bordering woods were shedding their leaves in a profusion of color. "This place is lovely."

Rather than agree, Hawk appeared eager to return to his training. "Do you have any other need of me?"

"Actually, I do. I wanted to warn you, we will be eating in the dining room this evening. It is only polite to offer your houseguests a table to dine on, and it will also spare the servants having to carry dishes all the way to the drawing room."

"I consider myself warned."

"Then may we count on you to join us?"

"Yes."

"Good. I realize you might prefer to eat and even sleep in the stables, but my uncle will be pleased to meet you and become better acquainted."

Hawk ignored her teasing. "If there is nothing else . . . my horse gets fractious from standing too long." As if on cue the stallion started prancing and dancing sideways. Hawk clearly wanted to return to work.

"May I stay to watch you?" Skye asked.

"Why?"

"Because I've never seen anything so fascinating—and because I want you to have company."

His mouth twisted sardonically. "You are coddling me again, wretch. I told you there is no need."

"But *I* have a need to be sure you are not moping," she declared, keeping her tone light.

The gray eyes showed a fleeting flash of amusement, which quickly disappeared. "I am not moping—and no, you may not stay to watch me."

Skye persevered. "I can understand why you flee your home every chance you get, but it is not good for you to spend so much time alone."

"Being alone suits me."

"Aren't you ever lonely?"

A shadow crossed his features. "I don't allow myself to feel loneliness. Now if you are quite done . . . ?" He closed his hands on the reins, preparing to turn away.

"I am not done trying to reform your reclusive habits, although I know it will take time. If I have learned anything from my own family, it's that men are foolishly hardheaded and stubborn sometimes, and it takes a woman to knock some sense into them."

Hawk narrowed his gaze on her. "Don't you have work to do at the castle?"

"Not at the moment."

"Then shouldn't you be keeping your uncle company?"

"He is occupied with Rachel and marveling at his good fortune at having found her alive after so long."

"Then pray go find someone else to pester," Hawk snapped.

"And to think you just told *me* to be patient."

When real vexation claimed his expression, Skye surrendered. "Very well, I am going before you growl at me any further."

She shot him her sweetest smile and turned her mount toward the castle. As Aunt Bella had advised, she would have to be patient and bide her time, but it would not be easy.

It would be even harder to reach through to the warm, human man buried beneath Hawk's enigmatic, unyielding façade, but she was not giving up, no matter how many times he sent her away.

Hawk was primarily irritated at himself for his reaction to Skye. Her smile had shot straight to his loins—and worse, made him want to smile in return. She did that to men—dazzling them with her infectious, enchanting smiles, bewitching and befuddling her unwitting victims.

Fortunately he was no longer unwitting now. Clearly

Skye was still intent on pursuing him as her ideal mate, and now that she'd accomplished her chief goal with her uncle, she was free to turn her full attention to *him*. But he was just as determined to hold on to his resolve.

Hawk resumed schooling the stallion, hoping work would serve to take his mind off Skye. Over the course of the next few days, however, the battle lines between them became more apparent. Often to his exasperation, Skye never wasted an opportunity to poke and prod him and prevent him from returning to his life as a recluse.

Her efforts in beautifying his house also continued. "A magnificent home such as this one deserves to shine again," Skye said. "Moreover, I owe you a great debt for helping my uncle. This is my way of repaying you."

When large numbers of servant staff started to arrive—the result of Lady Katharine's employment efforts—they were set to work applying beeswax and turpentine to the furnishings, polishing the lamps and chandeliers until they glistened, washing and dusting every nook and cranny, and painstakingly cleaning the lavish gilt and plaster and flocked paper of the walls and ceilings.

Skye insisted on consulting Hawk about the redecorating—her way of keeping him involved, even though he cared little for such matters. She even convinced him to accompany her around the estate grounds to solicit his opinion and preferences for changes. "*You* must make the major decisions about your estate, my lord, since your future bride is not present to do it."

Once the interior was progressing, she turned her focus to restoring the overgrown gardens to their former glory, saying, "It is a veritable jungle out there." The new chief gardener brought in crews of laborers to tackle the tangled vegetation, cutting back the haphazard growth, pruning dead limbs, and planting bulbs for the spring, but Skye enlisted Rachel to supervise the rejuvenation of the rose garden. "She knows much more about roses than I. Besides, she and Uncle Cornelius need a place to court other than your stuffy library."

By now Hawk had no trouble detecting Skye's fine hand at work, along with her sweet manner of manipulation. She did everything possible to promote her uncle's courtship and relished every tender moment the lovers shared—and freely admitted it with an edge of self-deprecating humor.

"I know I am a hopelessly incurable romantic. My cousin Kate is even worse."

"I shudder to think," Hawk drawled.

His reply sparked laughter in her eyes. "I need my attempts at matchmaking to be successful. I am obviously not a very good seductress, or I would have made more progress with you."

Hawk froze, his attention caught up in her blue eyes—so expressive, so lovely, so captivating. It was all he could do to look away.

He couldn't escape her frequent company, though. She and Isabella both greatly enjoyed riding. Intent on leaving Cornelius and Rachel alone, they regularly asked Hawk to act as their guide on excursions around the countryside.

If the days were difficult, the nights were worse, with his sexual fantasies of Skye as erotic as ever. Hawk spent many an early morning hour lying awake, his body on fire for hers.

Fortunately with all the guests living in his house, they were seldom alone. And then their numbers increased with the arrival of Skye's cousin Katharine.

"Kate wants to be part of our uncle's romantic adventure," Skye explained. "And we need to put our heads together and decide what to do about Rachel's daughter."

Lady Katharine Wilde was a striking beauty herself, with a taller, riper figure than Skye's and different coloring—auburn hair and stunning green eyes. But like Skye, Katharine possessed a sharp wit, a lively sense of humor, and the celebrated Wilde charm.

The penetrating look she gave Hawk upon meeting him seemed thoughtful and measuring, as if she were withholding judgment about him until knowing him better.

She was also unmistakably protective of Skye, and they clearly adored each other. More often than not, they could be seen laughing together. Skye seemed more content and serene with her cousin there—which she later explained in a quiet moment of candidness to Hawk. "Kate is only my distant cousin but is closer than any sister could be. We faced our parents' deaths together and afterward grew up in the same household and attended boarding school together."

Overtly, Lady Katharine had the more spirited personality, and Hawk sensed that like Skye, she preferred to rule her own fate. He could see how the two beauties together would hold sway over the ton and command the devotion of numerous suitors, which made it all the more puzzling that they were both of an age to be considered spinsters—until one recalled that their quest for true love was modeled after the world's greatest lovers.

By week's end, Hawkhurst Castle and its grounds were filled with people—guests, servants, merchants, laborers—and rang with the turmoil and noise of renovating as well as laughter and music, a stark contrast to the somber atmosphere he had faced at his arrival. His house was much warmer and livelier with the gaggle of Wildes living there, but it was Skye herself who made everything seem brighter with her energy and her appealing joie de vivre.

Hawk found himself watching her quite against his will. She found pleasure in small things, the sort of pleasure he'd deliberately shut out of his life: the freshness after rain, a romantic poem, the beauty in a golden sunset, the tang of hot cider, the scent of autumn leaves. . . .

That last revelation came about when she dumped a pile of leaves on his head on purpose, exhibiting her mischievous tendencies. She had dragged him out to the edge of the park to inspect the gardeners' progress, when, bending, she had scooped up an armful of leaves and shoved them under his nose.

"Just smell these. Isn't this scent divine?"

"Behold me in raptures."

His dry response brought a spurt of laughter from her. Before Hawk knew it, Skye threw up her arms and flung the whole lot into the air above him, raining leaves down upon them both.

"Oh, *please* forgive me, my lord," she apologized effusively for her impertinence, but her eyes fairly sparkled, and she was smiling like the devil, or a wicked angel.

Hawk felt his own mouth twitch with humor. Then Skye glanced around them surreptitiously. Assured they weren't being watched, she surprised him by stepping close and rising up on her toes to press a kiss to his mouth before he could evade her.

She delighted in keeping him off guard. As she gazed up at him, her smile was like sunlight, radiant and warm. Hawk felt a rush of desire so strong, he wanted to reach for her and haul her close. He breathed deeply of *her* scent instead of the leaves, then swore silently at the strength it took to control himself and avoid getting lost in the blue, blue depths of her eyes.

When he narrowed his own eyes at her in vexation, Skye gave another chortle and danced out of reach to escape his revenge.

That evening after dinner, Isabella caught him observing Skye and commented on his chances of resisting her. "She makes you want to please her and live up to her high expectations, doesn't she?" Bella remarked casually.

Hawk again glanced across the drawing room at Skye, who looked elegant and graceful in a dinner gown of blue silk as she played the now-tuned pianoforte in accompaniment to her cousin's singing.

When Hawk refrained from answering the obviously rhetorical question, Bella gave him a knowing look. "I have seen Skye work her magic throughout her childhood and then adulthood. Her family adores her; so do her friends. And her suitors . . . I wonder if you stand a chance against her."

"Every other poor male sod succumbs to her, so why should I be any different?"

"Yes, exactly."

It was a fair point, Hawk conceded. He longed to wring Skye's neck sometimes, but he also found himself wanting to linger in her company, making conversation or just simply *being* with her. It was not only her beauty that drew him; it was her warmth and generous nature, her undeniable charm, her liveliness, her vulnerability, her audacity, her cleverness, her optimism, and even her determination in targeting him for seduction.

"She would be very good for you, Hawk," Bella observed.

Perhaps so. She had certainly changed his home for the better, and himself as well. He no longer wanted to seek oblivion in a bottle of brandy, nor was he the ogre she had first met, either.

As Skye met his gaze across the room, Hawk recalled her earlier question about loneliness. He had never minded being alone; in truth, since losing his family, he'd embraced a solitary existence. But he was indeed lonely, even in a roomful of people. Or at least, he *had* been until Skye had landed on his doorstep, blowing into his life like an autumn gale.

It was difficult to maintain that bleak feeling of loneliness, that dark, hollow emptiness, when she was near. Her vibrancy and bright laughter was a foil for his dark moroseness. Strangely, almost miraculously, he was enjoying himself with her family also, just as she'd intended. And he enjoyed *her* enjoyment of life.

Yes, Hawk acknowledged silently. He recognized the supreme danger in letting Skye work her special magic on him. But it was becoming harder each day to remember why he was so determined to resist her.

Chapter Sixteen

If Skye was frustrated by her lack of matchmaking progress with Hawk, she could at least claim victory for her uncle. Later that evening when the guests gathered around the tea tray in the drawing room, Cornelius took Rachel's hand and led her to the mantel. Facing the company with her, he cleared his throat in order to make a special announcement.

"Ladies and gentleman, you see before you the most fortunate of men. My dearest Rachel has at last consented to become my bride."

Wondering what had caused the baroness's change of heart, Skye glanced at Rachel for confirmation and found her smiling shyly.

"I told Cornelius about his daughter," Rachel admitted, "and he has forgiven me for keeping the truth from him all these years."

Cornelius made a slight scoffing sound. "I could not understand her continued refusal to wed me, but I kept pressing and finally wore her down. Indeed, I was overjoyed to learn of my flesh-and-blood offspring."

He gazed down at Skye and Kate. "You both have been like daughters to me, but it will be good to come to know Daphne."

Both cousins leapt to their feet to embrace their uncle with delight and even a few tears of joy.

"We are elated that you are finally marrying, Uncle," Skye assured him.

Katharine chimed in. "And we will welcome Daphne into the family with open arms."

Lady Isabella seemed just as delighted. "This calls for a toast in celebration. May we raid your wine cellar, Lord Hawkhurst?"

"Certainly."

Hawk, Skye realized, had already summoned a footman and was giving orders for a particular vintage of Madeira to be brought in. Once the glasses were poured, he led a round of toasts.

Skye felt her cup of happiness running over at the tender way her uncle was gazing at his true love. Yet seeing their joy only increased her own feelings of longing. She wanted that same, wonderful happiness with Hawk—a goal that seemed just as distant as ever.

She could very well be renovating his castle for another woman, Skye reminded herself. Even so, she was sparing no effort to transform his sad house with its tragic ghosts into a home free of haunting memories. It was no small triumph that the emptiness and grief in Hawk's eyes had vanished for the most part. He seemed less grim, for certain. And that afternoon when they'd tromped through the wooded parkland, enjoying the autumn sunshine together, she had coaxed him to let down his guard yet another degree.

For a few precious moments, he'd actually looked carefree, his normally shuttered expression transformed by the smile in his gray eyes. That rare, beautiful smile had the power to enthrall her, as did the slightest physical contact. When Hawk's palm had pressed the small of her back to guide her down a different path, the simple gesture had sent a shock of awareness rocketing through Skye. She'd found herself remaining close, just to have another chance to feel his touch.

The tension was a sweet torment. For nearly half an hour, she'd fought the urge to throw her arms around him. And finally she couldn't stop herself from stealing a fleeting, impulsive kiss.

Sensation had streaked through her at that brief, forbidden taste of him. Judging from the spark of fire in Hawk's eyes, he'd felt a similar jolt.

In truth, Skye could still feel the heat of his lips now. She took another sip of wine, willing herself not to lose heart. Instead, she needed to focus on the fate of her beloved uncle.

She was glad, therefore, when Rachel's acceptance of his proposal led to an intense discussion of their daughter, Daphne, and how to reveal her parentage to her. They couldn't simply approach her with the harsh, unvarnished truth. It would be shock enough to discover that her mother was still alive without the blow of learning that William Farnwell was not her father.

Accordingly, in the past few weeks, Kate had made it a point to become better acquainted with Daphne.

"I particularly tried to probe her feelings about her family," Kate divulged to the group. "Daphne sounded highly wistful when she said she wished she had known her late mother. So I believe she would be pleased to learn the truth."

"I've given the question serious thought," Skye interjected. "I think it would be kinder if we allow Mrs. Nibbs to tell Daphne. As midwife, she birthed Daphne and helped care for her when she was a motherless baby. And they still have a sincere fondness for each other."

"Do you mean in a letter?" Rachel asked. "That seems so cold and callous."

"Not a letter," Skye agreed. "It would be best done in person."

"But Daphne lives in London, not Kent."

"Yes," Kate replied. "She prefers town to Farnwell Manor, chiefly to avoid her brother, Edgar. But there is no justification for her to visit Kent now . . . unless we were to fabricate a reason—perhaps say that Mrs. Nibbs had taken gravely ill."

"No," Rachel objected quietly. "There have been enough lies already."

"Then we must take Mrs. Nibbs to London."

Skye concurred. "Kate and I can travel to Brackstone and engage Mrs. Nibbs's help. We could leave as early as tomorrow."

Hawk spoke up. "We should courier a message to her first to prepare her for making a visit to London."

After further discussion, it was settled that Skye and Kate would leave the day after next and persuade the midwife to make a journey to London with them.

They also discussed the importance of discretion. In addition to Horace Linch's findings about both Barons Farnwell, Macky had recently sent Hawk a report. Hawk had also consulted his attorney regarding the rules of inheritance. If a nobleman remarried while his first wife was still living, the second marriage would be considered invalid and bigamous and any children illegitimate, and the title and entailed property would devolve according to the original patent of nobility. Therefore, Edgar would not be the legal heir to the Farnwell barony.

Presumably, Edgar wouldn't want a horrific scandal to taint his or his late mother's name, but undoubtedly he wouldn't want his inheritance threatened. So they must continue to keep Rachel's existence a close-held secret.

Moreover, there was no love lost between Daphne and Edgar, Kate explained with feeling. "Lord Farnwell dislikes that she achieved her financial independence from him. For years he and his solicitors controlled her purse strings and kept her under his thumb, until Daphne managed to acquire a wealthy patron who funds her research into various species of roses. She not only has won accolades for her scientific endeavors but has earned significant sums for her drawings and watercolors."

Skye was glad that they were making headway in potentially reuniting Rachel with her daughter—and hopefully, sometime in the future, Daphne with Cornelius. But another event of note occurred that night that dimmed the glow of success for Skye: her courses came. They were a bit late, enough that she'd begun to wonder if she might be enceinte.

The loss she felt was foolish and inexplicable. She should have been relieved that she wasn't carrying Hawk's child outside of wedlock. She didn't want him to be forced to marry her because of a sense of responsibility or a guilty conscience. But her failure to conceive could instantly end their future together.

Not surprisingly, her cousin immediately detected her despondency and demanded to know what was wrong, and Skye was forced to prevaricate.

"I am perfectly fine, dearest Kate. It is merely pain from my monthly time."

Quite naturally, Kate was avidly curious about Skye's romance with Hawk, but while they had always shared most confidences, this one matter seemed too intimate to discuss even with her closest friend.

The need to fib disturbed Skye yet confirmed what she had long suspected: She had fallen deeply in love with Hawk.

Madly, irrevocably in love.

He owned her heart, now and forever. Her yearning for him was a physical ache in her chest—as was her fear. In all likelihood, Hawk might never open his heart to her. He'd suffered the cruelest pain imaginable, and he would not overcome his loss easily, no matter how much she willed it.

For an instant, Skye considered holding off telling him about her condition in order to gain more time with him. But if she had learned anything at all in the past weeks, it was that Hawk wanted honesty from her. And if she ever hoped to win his love, she would have to employ honorable means, which meant abandoning her usual reliance on feminine wiles and giving him the unvarnished truth.

Therefore, she quietly asked for a private word with Hawk, and when they met in his study, Skye told him in very few words about her courses, searching his face all the while.

His expression remained as enigmatic as ever as he replied. "That is good then."

And somehow his dispassionate response hurt more than she ever dreamed it would.

Skye's news, however, was not nearly as welcome as Hawk had expected. As soon as she left his study, the realization struck him with startling force: He would have liked having another child.

His mind went back to an image of Lucas as a newborn baby, how proud and joyous he'd been at becoming a father, the adoration he'd felt upon holding his tiny squalling son for the first time. And then Lucas as a toddler in leading strings, the fierce love he'd felt . . .

Strangely, the agony of remembering was gone, the recollection more bittersweet and poignant than gutwrenching.

He was letting go of the pain, Hawk realized, in large part because of Skye. She was vibrant and warm, like sunlight, and, like sunlight, she had healing powers. For a decade, the hollowness inside him had been like a dark, empty pit, but he could slowly feel himself coming alive again, much like his house.

And once she'd departed for Kent with her cousin, it became starkly evident how she had changed his home for the better. Skye's absence didn't keep him from thinking about her often, either, or—worse—realizing how badly he missed her.

It was amazing to long for someone who had entered his life only recently, Hawk conceded. But he missed her liveliness and optimism. He missed the warm light in her eyes.

In short, he simply missed *her*.

Skye missed Hawk greatly as well, but she forced herself to concentrate on informing Daphne Farnwell about her mother's survival in the kindest way possible.

Mrs. Nibbs was ecstatic to learn that her beloved mistress had made it safely to Ireland and was now back in England once more. And despite the increasing fragility of her body and mind, the midwife was eager to help.

Skye and Kate both thought it best to break the news in gentle stages and judge Miss Farnwell's reaction at each step, beginning with the fact that Rachel hadn't drowned but had taken refuge in another country, and then her reason for fleeing. If Daphne showed anger at her mother, or unwarranted sympathy for her late father, they would divulge nothing further just then.

But Skye hoped Daphne would be eager to make her mother's acquaintance, and, if so, she would be invited to Hawkhurst Castle.

When they arrived in London, it was late afternoon, but they chanced calling then rather than waiting another day at a more proper time. Daphne lodged in an elegant town house belonging to her wealthy patron, the Countess of Gowing.

Daphne's features bore a certain resemblance to Rachel's, Skye noted when a footman showed them to the library where Miss Farnwell was reading. But her golden brown hair and her light blue eyes, combined with the twenty-five-year difference in their ages, made their likeness much less obvious.

Daphne looked surprised and troubled when Mrs. Nibbs appeared unexpectedly on her doorstep and was very solicitous of the old woman's health, settling her before the hearth fire and ordering hot tea and a warm shawl to be brought in immediately.

Daphne also claimed to be honored by a personal visit from the Wilde ladies. At her quizzical look, Kate deferred any explanation by saying they would let Mrs. Nibbs tell the story.

When the midwife was situated comfortably, Skye watched closely and was unsurprised when Daphne initially reacted much as Lord Cornelius had done.

Shock came first. "My mother did *not* die?" she rasped.

"Nay, her ladyship was only forced to pretend so," Mrs. Nibbs answered.

"Whatever do you mean? Why would she *pretend* her death?"

"You see, it was like this, Miss Daphne. . . ." The midwife gave a curt summary of William Farnwell's cruelty to his lady wife, making it clear that Rachel's very life had been threatened.

The horror Daphne clearly felt was written on her face. After absorbing those revelations in silence for a moment, she pressed her lips together tightly. "That does not astonish me as it ought. Papa could be brutish. It was shameful, how he treated some of our servants."

"Aye, it was indeed," Mrs. Nibbs agreed.

Another moment passed before Daphne's revulsion

and anger was overtaken by bewilderment. "Then what happened to my mother if she didn't drown?"

"She took refuge with a cousin in Ireland."

Confusion and hurt swiftly followed. "But why did she leave me here with my father? If she was alive, why did she never attempt to see me?"

"Because she felt she had no choice," Mrs. Nibbs explained quietly. "Under the law, she had no right to take you away. You were but a babe, and your safety would have been endangered also had she absconded with you. Moreover, she felt his lordship could offer you a much better life of privilege and comfort."

"What kind of life did I have without a mother?" Daphne murmured, unable to hide her resentment. Then abruptly she shook her head. "Forgive me, that was uncharitable and childish of me, to be only thinking of myself. Especially when you say my father drove her to it. . . ."

Her words trailed off as she glanced down at her clasped hands, her mind obviously leaping from one thought to the next, the play of emotions on her face changing in quick succession. "My God . . . then she did not kill herself after all."

The next moment her eyes filled with tears. "As a suicide, she was never buried on consecrated ground. And to think . . . all those years I blamed her for selfishly leaving me without a mother."

Wiping her eyes, she glanced back up and searched the midwife's lined face. "And then what?" Daphne took a deep breath, as if bracing herself for sad news. "It has been so long, she cannot possibly still be alive . . . could she?"

Looking puzzled, she shifted her gaze to Kate, then

Skye. Suddenly, there was wonder and hope in her eyes along with wariness. "You have knowledge of my mother, don't you, Lady Katharine? Why else would you have brought Mrs. Nibbs to see me?"

Without replying, both Kate and Mrs. Nibbs glanced at Skye, since they'd agreed the choice to proceed would be hers.

"Yes, Miss Farnwell," Skye said gently, coming to a decision. "We have knowledge of your mother—and she is very much alive."

Chapter Seventeen

Daphne made a strangled sound that was half gasp, half sob, and brought her hand up to cover her trembling mouth. Briefly she shut her eyes, then opened them and threw Skye a pleading look. "I am not dreaming, am I?"

"No, you are definitely not dreaming," Skye said tenderly.

"Dear God," Daphne repeated in a hoarse whisper. "Please . . . tell me, where is she?"

"She is here in England now."

Daphne shook herself. "This is unbelievable. May I see her? Does she want to see me? How is she?"

Looking dazed, Daphne rose to her feet and took two steps toward Skye, then stopped. "Forgive me, I am behaving like a madwoman."

Skye smiled briefly. "Not at all. It is only natural that your thoughts are scattered after such an enormous revelation caught you off guard."

Inhaling again, Daphne forced herself to resume her

seat. "I have innumerable questions, but perhaps I should allow you to speak, Lady Skye."

"To begin with, your mother is well, and she longs to meet you. The story of how she came to leave you is dreadfully painful for her, and she wishes to explain her reasoning herself in more detail and beg your forgiveness."

Daphne nodded, her expression becoming more subdued. "How did you and Lady Katharine come to be involved with my mother?"

"I happened across some of her correspondence to my Uncle Cornelius before her marriage and realized she had once been a friend of his. When Mrs. Nibbs confided the circumstances of her escape, I went to Ireland to find her. She has been living there under an assumed name. This is her likeness when she was much younger."

Skye withdrew the miniature from her reticule and passed it to Miss Farnwell, who sat there staring avidly.

"I look a good deal like her at that age."

"Yes, but we have been at pains to disguise her appearance in order to maintain the fiction of her death."

Daphne's brow furrowed, then cleared. "Because of my brother? Edgar doesn't know, does he?"

"No. The consequences could be dire for Lord Farnwell. The succession would be in question if it were proven that his own mother's marriage to your father was invalid."

Evidently Daphne had no desire to dwell on her brother, for she returned to the former subject. "When may I see my mother?"

"Very shortly, if you wish," Skye said. "For now she is staying with a friend of my family's in East Sussex. Katharine and I thought we should devise a natural pretext for you to accompany me to the country. Perhaps I could commission you to paint some watercolors of a lovely old rose garden."

"That seems ideal," Daphne mused aloud, her thoughts racing ahead. "I could easily leave tonight. Lady Gowing will not mind making do without me for a time. I only need to cancel some engagements first. . . ."

Kate interjected her own opinion. "There is no need for such haste, Miss Farnwell. Tomorrow will be soon enough, or even the day after. We don't want to raise any undue suspicions with your unexplained actions."

Daphne frowned at her choice of words. "No, of course not. Even if Edgar were completely unaffected by my mother's return, I don't want him to know of it. He is spiteful enough to thwart my happiness on general principle. We have long been at loggerheads."

"So you can understand why we must maintain secrecy for now."

"Indeed I do."

The discussion turned to formulating plans then, and they agreed to wait another day and a half before Skye escorted Daphne to Hawkhurst Castle. Kate planned to remain in London rather than accompany them. Her carriage would return Mrs. Nibbs to Brackstone the next day and then be at Skye's disposal.

That night Skye slept in her own bed for the first time in weeks. It was good to be home, she decided, even if the magnificent town house belonging to the Earl of Traherne seemed strangely empty.

Quinn was still away at points unknown, having become obsessed with his own version of changing fate. Their parents had died at sea off the coast of France—a tragedy that might have been prevented in a vessel that could outrun a storm. Thus, Quinn was set on funding the design of an enormous steam engine that could power sailing ships.

He had disappeared on his quest over a month before, but Skye was glad for his absence, since she hadn't wanted him interfering with her attempted romance with Hawk. She spent the next day catching up on correspondence with her friends and dispatching social obligations. And the morning after that, she set out for East Sussex with Daphne in Kate's carriage.

Daphne was alternately excited, anxious, nervous, and hopeful. As they neared Hawk's castle, she asked Skye to remain with her when she met her mother for the first time. Skye did her best to put Daphne at ease and prepare her for what to expect, particularly for what her mother was like. And then Skye listened while Daphne shared her concerns.

When they arrived, it was near midday and a chill rain was falling. The renovations for the family wing were not as obvious upon their approach, but the gravel drive seemed less rutted and the overgrowth of the park had been significantly pared back. Rachel must have been watching anxiously from a window, for as soon as their carriage drew to a halt, she appeared on the front steps above them.

Clearly, Daphne hardly dared to breathe as a footman opened the carriage door for her. Rachel looked just as nervous as she slowly descended the stone stairway.

When she reached Daphne, they stood there in the rain, drinking each other in. Lord Cornelius had followed at a discreet distance and stood watching the two of them. It was left to Skye to make the introductions, then move the encounter inside, where liveried footmen accepted their wet outer garments and bonnets.

They couldn't hold a tender reunion in front of all the servants, yet once they made it to the parlor, the searching glances resumed. Mother and daughter were both weeping silently, tears of happiness running down their faces.

Then Rachel took Daphne's hands and murmured in a hoarse voice, "Can you ever forgive me?"

Daphne gave a watery laugh. "Of course I can, Mama." Then she winced. "I ought not call you that, oughtn't I?"

"I fear not, my dearest girl. You must address me as Mrs. Donnelly or Meg."

"It doesn't matter. It only matters that I have found you. I always dreamed of knowing my mother, but it seems impossible that my dream has come true."

"I feared you would hate me," Rachel said in a choked voice.

Daphne's expression remained solemn. "When I first learned of your existence, I felt a bit resentful that you had left me."

"I could not take you with me, Daphne, no matter how agonizing the choice. You were so very young— just a tiny baby. Your father would never have ceased looking for us if I had stolen you away. It was difficult leaving my family and friends, but abandoning you was like ripping out my heart."

Daphne's slow nod suggested understanding. "I realize why you felt it necessary to fabricate your death. Papa was not only cold and heartless but physically brutal. But it is harder to accept why you kept the secret from me after he was gone."

"I was frightened by the possible ramifications. The truth could alter your life so drastically. I didn't dare expose you to your half brother's wrath, for one thing. He inherited your father's temperament, from what I can gather."

"Yes, Edgar is much like Papa."

"So perhaps you can see why I thought it best for your sake to maintain the lie that I had lived for twenty-five years. Moreover, I had no confidence that you would welcome the news, until Lady Skye persuaded me to take the risk."

Daphne cast Skye a thankful look. "I am enormously grateful that she did."

Rachel hesitated. "I must ask, Daphne . . . did your father ever raise a hand to you?"

"No. He was mostly indifferent. I think because I was a daughter, not a son."

Rachel shut her eyes briefly in relief. "Thank God. That was my worst fear—that he might hurt you, but I gambled that he would provide you a far better life than I ever could. And later . . . I learned that his new wife was a quiet-spoken gentlewoman from an impeccable family and hoped she could raise you to become a genteel young lady. I see I was not wrong."

Daphne smiled at the compliment. "My stepmother was not unkind, simply frivolous and shallow. She had a great eye for fashion and style, though, and she encouraged my interest in roses and watercolor painting, even though she disliked being out of doors herself and had no fondness for art or science. I think I must have acquired my attachment to roses from you. I know that you loved roses. . . . Painting in your rose garden at Farnwell Manor always comforted me. Somehow I felt close to you when I was there."

Suddenly, Rachel buried her face in her hands and heaved a great sob. Groping blindly, she sank into the nearest chair and continued to weep.

Daphne's concern was evident in the way she hovered over her mother. Cornelius, too, was visibly anxious at her distress, but Skye felt certain the tremendous emotion Rachel was feeling was relief and joy rather than sadness, and so she passed over a handkerchief from her reticule.

A short while later Rachel quieted and wiped her eyes. Still sniffing, she looked up. She was smiling broadly. Beaming, in fact. "I am perfectly fine, my dear. I am crying from sheer joy. You cannot know how I have longed for this moment."

Daphne's features softened. "Indeed, I can, for I have felt the same longing all my life."

At the touching exchange, Skye let out her breath in relief, her own fears allayed. This promising, heartwarming beginning boded well for their reunion.

After Rachel's outburst, they all took seats and initiated the process of becoming acquainted. They were strangers, after all, and had a quarter century of catching up to do. Emotions and feelings and thoughts came pouring out in fits and starts. One comment led to another tangent, which diverged to a different subject altogether, before circling back again as they explored each other's lives and characters and history.

Most surprising to Skye was Daphne's familiarity

with Cornelius's scholarly works. She had read his treatise on Ovid numerous times and professed to be a great admirer. Skye's biggest regret was that her uncle and Rachel had to hide their love. Cornelius was merely introduced as the patriarch of the Wilde family and a longtime friend of Rachel's.

Skye badly wanted Daphne to know about her parentage, but the truth could only hurt her. As the daughter of a baron, she might be able to weather a scandal involving her stepmother and stepbrother. But if it was discovered that she was the child of her mother's illicit lover, she would be ruined in society, no matter her illustrious patrons or connections.

Even so, their reunion was a joyous occasion, and Skye was resolved to enjoy it. At dinner that evening, Daphne met Lady Isabella, who contributed to the congenial, lively atmosphere.

Hawk was also present, to Skye's mixed relief and dismay. She hadn't encountered him the entire day, whether because he was busy or purposely avoiding her, she couldn't tell. She couldn't read his expression, either, but the impact of seeing him again was just as powerful as always: Her heart lurched and warmed at the same time, while her body was jolted with sexual awareness.

She had no opportunity to speak to Hawk alone, a circumstance she was certain he had contrived. It was the following afternoon and nearly teatime when Aunt Bella found Skye to say that she was worried about Hawk after just witnessing a disturbing episode: A gardener had found a metal box of toys buried beneath a bush that likely had belonged to his lordship's son. Upon opening it, Hawk had stiffened grimly, then stormed away.

Aunt Bella thought he might have taken refuge in his study. "I think you should go to him, Skye."

"Yes, of course," she answered, knowing the find would have brought up more agonizing memories for him.

Skye went directly to the study. The door was not locked, so she pushed it open slowly and peered inside the room. Hawk was seated at his desk, a sheaf of papers before him, but he was neither reading nor writing. Instead, he was staring down at a small, bronzed toy horse that stood on his desktop.

Quite obviously, he'd been raking his hands through his hair. And when he glanced up at the intrusion, the bleakness in his eyes was unmistakable.

Fierce compassion swamped Skye. She desperately wanted to go to Hawk. She longed to smooth back the disheveled locks falling over his forehead and ease away the lines of pain on his face. She yearned to wrap her arms around him and comfort him and drench him in tenderness and love.

But she did none of those things. Rather, she flashed him a bright smile and exclaimed cheerfully, "Good, I found you. Don't go away, my lord. I shall return posthaste."

With that, Skye closed the door softly and hurried upstairs to her bedchamber, all the while praying she could soon provide Hawk with at least a temporary balm for his despair.

Chapter Eighteen

Skye returned to the study with her notebook listing her planned renovations and refurbishments for Hawk's castle. The toy horse was gone from his desk, as was his look of bleakness, but his desolate expression had been replaced by no emotion at all—which was almost worse, in Skye's opinion. She couldn't bear for him to shut her out.

"Please, will you come with me, Hawk?" she asked. "I want your opinion about what to do with the west tower."

"Now?"

"Yes, this very moment. It cannot wait."

His gaze narrowed on her, taking in her attire. The serviceable apron she wore over her gown was meant to reassure him of her businesslike focus. Skye hoped she looked more housekeeper or chatelaine of the manor than seductress.

Not giving him time to send her away, she confiscated his quill pen and returned it to the stand, then pulled Hawk to his feet and preceded him from the study. They passed several servants as they negotiated the corridors, but met no one else as they climbed a winding staircase to the circular west tower room. Upon reaching the landing, Skye led Hawk inside and closed the door for privacy.

From the high mullioned windows, one could see across the fields and meadows and woodlands of the vast Hawkhurst estate. The tower was chilly, although pale autumn sunlight gave the illusion of warmth and illuminated dust motes dancing in the air. Unlike the rest of the castle, which had been scoured and scrubbed within a proverbial inch, this particular room had been left untouched for a decade.

A set of armchairs and a side table, all swathed in holland covers, occupied one side of the floor—for reading or daydreaming or watching the sun set, she suspected. Otherwise, there was no other furniture.

Skye locked the door and turned to face Hawk, prepared to explain her ulterior motive. It distressed her to think his tragic loss might always come between them, but her own romantic dreams were nothing compared to his pain. Nothing would erase that terrible experience for him, but she could try to heal him and take the bleakness from his eyes.

Those eyes had filled with gathering suspicion as he studied her.

"I am worried that the beast has returned," she confessed honestly. "And I hoped lovemaking would serve to lighten your mood."

"You lured me up here to have sex?"

"Well, yes."

She held her breath as Hawk stared at her.

His handsome features suddenly relaxed. Rather

than showing anger or vexation, he looked amused. Apparently he had forced himself to shake off the grim remembrance of his son's toy. Skye felt so relieved, her knees went weak—yet Hawk was not ready to capitulate, she realized at his next words.

"I'm not so fragile as you seem to think, angel. I don't need you to comfort me every time I must face a difficult memory."

"I know. But I am not thinking only of you. I want comfort, too. I have missed you dreadfully. Haven't you missed me?"

"That is beside the point."

He moved toward the door, eying the handle behind her, as if intending to leave.

Skye quickly slipped the key into her apron pocket, along with her notebook. Pressing her back against the door, she spread her arms wide, creating a barricade with her body.

"Skye . . ." he said warningly.

"Please don't go, Hawk."

"You know making love is foolhardy."

"Yes, I do. You are concerned you will get me with child. But *you* know the sponges have been effective in preventing pregnancy. I am wearing a sponge, Hawk."

"*Now?*" he repeated, his eyebrows rising.

"I inserted one when I went to my rooms a moment ago."

His chuckle of disbelief was followed by a penetrating scrutiny. "Do you know your trouble? You are too damn manipulating."

"Usually that is true, but not in this case, I swear. I truly need your opinion on restoring this room. And my notebook and apron were not a ruse to fool you but the servants. I needed a legitimate reason for us to be here, and I could think of no other way we could be together, or any other place in the house where we could have privacy, and I was afraid you wouldn't come with me if I simply invited you. . . . You are stubbornly unyielding, Hawk, and it is infuriating, really—"

"Be quiet, sweeting. You are babbling."

Skye obeyed, in part because she was running out of breath. When he hesitated, she peered up at him through her lashes. "Kissing me would be an excellent way to silence me."

He still looked unconvinced.

"I won't let you go," she declared.

"How do you plan to stop me?"

"Physically. You will have to wrestle the key from me. I dare you to try."

She felt giddy with the dawning laughter in his eyes.

"I cannot believe such a big, strong hero is afraid to make love to me," she prodded.

At the exasperation written on his face, a bubble of laughter rose in her throat and escaped her. "I want you, Hawk. Don't you want me the least little bit?"

When she was unable to elicit an answer from him, she left off teasing him. "Please stay with me," she pleaded.

He took a step closer, glancing down at her bosom that was covered by her apron and gown bodice. She felt the look as if he'd touched her, her nipples peaking against her chemise.

A ripple of sexual awareness ran through her as Hawk closed the final distance. She wanted to sink into his embrace and hold him against her. She wanted his mouth on hers. . . .

As Hawk's face lowered toward hers, Skye sighed in anticipation, yet he didn't kiss her. Instead, he pressed his lower body against hers, wedging her firmly between the door and his rock-hard thighs.

She couldn't be disappointed, though. Not when she could feel the hard jut of his arousal through her skirts.

"You *do* want me," she breathed.

"Of course I do, witch. How could I not?"

"Then show me."

His hand slid between her thighs, his fingers curving over her sensitive woman's mound beneath the layers of fabric and pressing firmly. Instantly aroused, she let out a soft moan.

"Hush, don't make a sound," Hawk cautioned. "You don't want a servant coming to investigate, only to find me tupping you against the wall."

"Is that what you mean to do?" she asked, intrigued.

"Eventually."

A dart of pleasure shot through her at his words. "Then what are you waiting for?"

He made at tsk-tsking sound. "So impatient."

"I can't help it. You make me feel frenzied."

"Let's see if we can increase your frenzy."

Easing back a step, he unbuttoned the front placket of his breeches to free his swollen erection. A shiver swept through her at seeing that masculine flesh that could give her such wild pleasure.

Wanting to touch him, Skye reached down to curl her fingers around his shaft, but Hawk wouldn't allow it. Taking control, he lifted the hem of her apron, then caught a handful of her gown.

"Hold up your skirts," he ordered.

Heat pooled in her lower belly. He didn't mean to undress her, she realized. He planned to take her there against the door, fully dressed.

Her heart racing, she obeyed, baring her sex to the coolness of the tower air.

"What now?"

In answer, his fingers caressed her curls, probing until he found the bud hidden by her feminine folds. "I need to make you ready for me."

Skye felt a tightening of her body, a rush of heat. He kept his caresses delicate and unhurried as he circled and stroked until her flesh was wet with her own juices.

"I am ready for you now," Skye insisted breathlessly. The tingling heat of his touch only magnifying the surge of want, the delicious sensation of weakness flooding her.

"Not yet," he pronounced.

Staring into her eyes, he slid a finger inside her and stroked her inner walls. Skye inhaled sharply. She was melting. Her breasts felt hot and tight while her sex swelled and throbbed.

"Hawk, please. . . ."

His eyes gleamed with little sparks of amusement. He was set on teasing her, making her wait, and judging from the sensual glimmer there, he was reveling in her helpless response.

She reached down for him again, wanting desperately to feel him inside her.

"No, not yet."

"You are a devil."

Hawk flashed her a slow smile full of wicked promise. He used his fingers to play her, to please her, until she was panting softly. She could tell, however, that he was not as unaffected as he pretended. The humor in his eyes had changed to a different light. Desire smoldered and flared in the gray depths.

Skye felt a certain sense of triumph. Her heartbeat hammered in her throat as she stared back at this utterly beguiling man with the hot-silver eyes. She wanted Hawk to want her till he ached, just as he was making her ache.

Releasing her skirts, she threaded her fingers in his tousled ebony hair, trying to bring his mouth to hers, her lips burning, ready to be soothed. But still he wouldn't kiss her. He merely lowered his mouth to her neck and pressed his lips to her pulse there, his tongue tasting her skin, sipping lightly.

At the same time, he slid another finger inside her while rubbing the nub with his thumb, stoking the restless hunger simmering in her veins.

Skye nearly groaned. Her senses were knife-sharp and almost as painful. When her knees buckled, she altered her grasp once more and gripped his shoulders to maintain her balance.

"Hawk—*now*," she demanded in a rasping whisper.

Finally, at last, he obliged. Raising his head, he shifted his hands to her buttocks and lifted her up. Spreading her thighs to position his arousal at her opening, he began to enter her, the engorged crest pressing inside her slowly. He was full and hot and hard . . . iron hard.

Watching her intently, he glided into her waiting warmth, stretching her, searing her. Skye gave a soft whimper at the blissful fullness.

His fascinating eyes riveted her as he inched back out again. The friction against her slick flesh made her inner muscles clench around him. Instinctively she wrapped her legs around Hawk's hips. She was enraptured, filled with a strangled pleasure.

Hawk held her gaze as he moved slowly inside her, his languorous thrusts deep and sure. Skye moaned again at the primal delight he was giving her, heedless of his earlier warning.

"Hush," he reminded her. "Someone might hear and then the game would be up."

It was somehow titillating to think their illicit rendezvous might be discovered. The threat only increased the quaking excitement he was kindling in her. Hawk was driving her mad, pushing her to the brink but not carrying her over.

His eyes were storm-dark now, his features tight. When he clamped his hands on her buttocks to hold her in place, Skye arched her back and tilted her hips to give him better access. The naked hunger on his face burned through her senses, setting her nerve endings on fire.

Another moan vibrated in her throat. Her eyes drifted closed as his rhythm increased. She could feel herself trembling, shaking against him as he rocked her against the door. Each time he thrust, another bolt of dark fire shot through her and she gasped at the bright flare of sensation. And then she was caught up fully in the conflagration. Hawk ground himself against her as she convulsed, her body throbbing around his in shattering, fiery bursts. She shook and quaked, her response wild and abandoned.

Only then did he capture her mouth with his. In one part of her dazed mind, Skye reveled in the ravenous way he kissed her, as if he could never have enough. He claimed and stole her will while he took her body, no longer calm and controlled, driving into her, his hard thrusts primitive and powerful and urgent, every muscle taut.

Her climax still pulsed around him as he plunged in and out of her, surging with raw passion. His name was a cry on her lips when he plunged himself to the hilt one last time, impaling her. Buried deep, deep inside her, he found his own explosive release. Hawk shuddered, his own harsh groans loud in her ear as he collapsed against her. When it was over, he pressed his face into her neck, panting for breath.

Still gasping herself, Skye clung to him. She wanted this moment to last forever and for this man to love her. Her heart had craved him her whole life, and she never wanted him to leave.

To her immense gratification, he remained still for a long time afterward. . . . And yet reality intruded all too soon, along with common sense. Her cries of ecstasy could have gotten them in big trouble, Skye realized, not withstanding that her position was rather awkward and uncomfortable, being pinned against the door by his powerful body.

Skye gave a muffled, breathless laugh into his shoulder. "You said we needed to be quiet. I would say we failed miserably."

When Hawk weakly pulled away from her, his heavy lashes lifted enough to look into her eyes. When she smiled teasingly at him, he smiled in return.

His response lifted her heart, as did the unexpected softness in his eyes. Skye felt herself go still with the impact of his gaze. He had just ravished her thoroughly, but she still felt lightning sparks when he merely looked at her.

He didn't seem aware of how much he captivated her, though—which perhaps was a blessing. With care, he withdrew from her body, holding her until her feet found the floor, then steadying her as she tried to stand on shaken, uncertain legs.

"I suppose we ought to go below," she said with reluctance. "By now the others will likely be gathered in the drawing room for tea and will be expecting us."

Hawk grimaced, clearly not eager to comply, although he nodded in agreement.

Just then Skye felt the wet gush of his seed down the inside of her thighs. "On second thought, I cannot take tea like this," she amended. "I had best return to my bedchamber and clean myself."

"I will wait a few moments before following you."

"That is wise. We shouldn't go down together. One look at us and everyone will know what we have done."

She started to move but then decided against it. "I think I need a handkerchief."

She fumbled in her apron pocket for one, but Hawk took it from her. "Allow me."

Reaching beneath her skirts, he deliberately stroked her still sensitive flesh with the delicate cloth. His attentions were highly erotic and sensual, making heat race down her spine again and spread through her, before wedging the handkerchief between her thighs.

"Are you punishing me for teasing you?"

"However did you guess?"

"Like I said, you are a devil," she murmured with another laugh.

Passion still throbbed between them, but she forced herself to retrieve the key from her pocket and unlock the door. Then giving Hawk one last lingering kiss, she slipped from the room.

When she was gone, Hawk used his own handkerchief to dry his loins and then rearranged his clothing, but his mind was on Skye rather than his task. Her scent lingered, filling his senses, but it was her last image that filled his mind. She had been laughing at him with her eyes, a sparkling, tender kind of laughter that was innocent and full of deviltry at the same time.

He found himself grateful for her light touch. She'd provided just the distraction he needed after finding that bronzed figure of a horse, a gift to Lucas on his first birthday. The memory was churning in his gut when Skye pulled him out of his study, his chest aching with grief and guilt and anger at fate.

The ache had slowly settled as he climbed the tower stairs with her, but her seduction was not at all what he'd expected—dragging him up here to have her way with him, literally daring him to make love to her.

Then again, she was constantly surprising him. At her offer, lust and need and want had hit him with brutal force. And faced with the chance to lose himself in the sweetness of her body, he'd had only one choice.

In truth, she'd never given him much choice in their entire relationship, Hawk acknowledged. She kept reaching through his defenses, even when he'd fought her.

Hawk glanced around the tower. In every room, there were haunting shadows that Skye was systematically vanquishing. The dark dreams that plagued his sleep were less frequent as well, and he no longer craved solitude. During her recent journey to London, he'd realized how cold and empty his house had felt without her lively presence . . . which raised a question. What would he do without her when she left for good? When he courted and wed Sir Gawain's niece and brought her home to his bed?

A frown claimed Hawk's mouth. He didn't like contemplating the answers. On the other hand, he could easily become accustomed to having Skye in his bed, in his life, always. . . .

He froze as a jolting thought occurred to him: He wanted Skye as his bride.

After a startled moment, Hawk tested the theory in his mind by picturing her recent look, remembering the warmth that filled him as he'd gazed into her laughing eyes. He felt a peculiar lightness in his chest when he could swear he wasn't capable of any light feelings at all. He was able to recognize the sensation as affection—

And perhaps something stronger?

It was too soon to tell, Hawk decided. But his insistence that Skye meant nothing to him was laughable, really. And his plan to resist her had failed dramatically.

He'd intended to show her that he no longer had a heart to give her, that tragedy had destroyed that particular organ. But like the seemingly dead rosebushes in his garden, he was beginning to think his heart might not be completely dead after all, just lying dormant.

And if there was life there beneath all the dead undergrowth, he might conceivably be able to love again.

Hawk shook his head in disbelief. Never in his wildest dreams had he believed he would come to that point. But for the first time in a decade he wondered if it might be possible.

At the thought, he waited for the expected guilt to

strike him. *How can you open yourself to happiness with another woman when Elizabeth is gone?*

Yet ten years was a very long time to mourn his late wife. Skye was right when she'd said Elizabeth wouldn't want him to die with her. And living half a life would not bring her back. Moreover, he was beginning to question whether he should let the fear of losing his loved ones keep him mired in emptiness forever.

So what if you were to give yourself permission to love again?

It was then that Hawk recalled his obligations once more. By now he should have been well along in courting Sir Gawain's niece, a plan he'd delayed in order to aide Skye's quixotic romantic cause with her uncle.

Hawk's jaw tightened. He couldn't put off his courtship much longer. Not when wedding Miss Olwen was the only way he could lead the Guardians.

No, your future is settled.

Unless . . .

Unless you elect against a marriage of convenience.

The notion held more appeal than it should have.

Trying to change his fate, however, would present a profound dilemma. He would be pitting honor and obligation against desire, professional fulfillment against personal happiness, loyalty to Sir Gawain against his own private longings.

But perhaps the choice was not so difficult after all, Hawk conceded. He might regret opening his heart further and letting Skye in, but he would likely regret more not pursuing the possibility of a future with her.

Chapter Nineteen

Once the notion to wed Skye took root in Hawk's mind, he couldn't shake it. He had never desired Miss Olwen for his bride, and by postponing his courtship these past few weeks, he knew he'd been seeking an escape from an unsuitable match. Yet only now did he acknowledge that their union might be an actual mistake.

Convincing a shy young lady more than a dozen years his junior to serve as a broodmare so he could sire an heir of Guardian lineage was the height of calculating cynicism, despite the virtue of his motives.

The more Hawk considered his course, the stronger his temptation became to devise a way out of his obligations. He would have to withdraw his candidacy for the league's leadership, but the thought of heading the Guardians was not as fulfilling as it once was. Regardless, before contemplating such a drastic step, he needed to speak with Sir Gawain directly.

The baronet's latest communiqué had declared Sir Gawain's intentions of arriving in London the past week. Without a doubt, he would be keenly disappointed if Hawk suddenly made a drastic about-face in his nuptial plans—and disappointing his friend and mentor weighed heavily on Hawk's conscience. But he needed to at least broach the possibility. Thus, Hawk wrote to the baronet and requested an interview in London for the following afternoon.

Instead of sending a written reply, however, Sir Gawain appeared in person late the next morning—unsurprising, since resolving the issue of leadership after his impending retirement was understandably his chief priority just now.

Upon gaining entrance to the castle, Sir Gawain was shown into Hawk's study at once. By odd coincidence, the elderly baronet somewhat resembled Lord Cornelius. Both were tall, lean, elegant gentlemen with silver hair. But Sir Gawain's features were lined with worry and fatigue—the consequence of three decades of commanding the Guardians—and his penetrating, pale blue eyes were always gravely serious. He was also fifteen years older than Cornelius and walked with a slight limp, the result of a still-painful injury incurred during a mission long ago.

After issuing warm greetings and settling on a couch, Sir Gawain adopted a pensive frown. He listened intently as Hawk explained his reservations, but looked dismayed as he responded.

"I feared you might be wavering when my greatniece heard no word from you since your arrival in England, Hawk. May I remind you of the stakes? The very future of our league is in jeopardy."

"I need no reminder, sir."

The chivalric order had been formed more than a

thousand years before by a handful of Britain's most legendary warriors—outcasts who had sought exile on the Mediterranean island of Cyrene—with the purpose of performing valiant deeds, righting wrongs, and protecting the weak and vulnerable. Only within the past half century had the long wars with France necessitated the expansion of their reach. Currently the Guardians operated chiefly in Europe as a secret arm of the Foreign Office. There were a dozen or so members living on Cyrene, fifty others scattered across Europe and England, and even several Americans.

"I am fully aware the league cannot be left rudderless," Hawk replied, "but there are others who could serve in my place."

"But none who are willing to wed in order to secure the succession and fulfill the terms of our charter, as you are, Hawk."

That was the rub, Hawk knew. The charter required leadership to be passed down through the descendent families of the original knights, to which Miss Olwen belonged. Nominally, she would be the acting head of the Guardians and Hawk would lead on her behalf. And if he sired sons or daughters, he would lead in his children's name.

The thought of siring another son was brutally painful, unless it was with Skye, Hawk had decided. But that was not a subject he wished to discuss with his mentor.

"Moreover," Sir Gawain continued in a pleading tone, "few leaders would be as effective as you, Hawk. You are able to inspire loyalty and devotion. You well know that quality is invaluable."

The league's agents usually had specialties. Hawk's

prime skill was gathering intelligence, but his most valuable asset was his ability to lead men.

"Your services are *needed*, Hawk. As my successor you will do a vast deal of good. Saving lives and meting out justice are supremely worthy causes."

"I agree." His original desire to assume the reins from Sir Gawain had never been a lust for power, but a conviction that he could make a difference. Additionally, Hawk felt an ardent personal obligation to the baronet. "But our work is not as crucial now that Boney has been defeated."

"It is still critical, however. And we cannot afford to be without a strong leader."

Sir Gawain was right, certainly. And Hawk couldn't—wouldn't—leave the Guardians without a leader. But perhaps the criteria for leadership could be revised. . . .

"What if we could amend the charter to reflect how greatly our circumstances have changed over the years? What would that require? A vote of the entire membership?"

The baronet frowned thoughtfully. "I fail to see how an amendment is possible. And even if it were, you are best prepared to shoulder the mantle of leadership." His expression turned imploring. "You and I are different from normal men, Hawk. You have never flinched from making sacrifices. What has caused this hesitancy now? For the past year or more, you have wholly supported my plan for the succession."

I returned home to terrible memories, he thought. Aloud, he said, "The closer I came to making a marriage of convenience with your great-niece, the more I disliked using her as a pawn."

"Amelia is a dutiful girl who accepts her historic obligations. There will be no objection from her or her family."

At Hawk's hesitation, Sir Gawain went on pressing his case, his tone revealing his growing anxiety. "It is only natural for you to have second thoughts about entering into another marriage, Hawk, but I am certain you see this opportunity as your duty."

"I do." Until now he'd never before questioned his devotion or commitment to the Guardians or his loyalty to their leader.

And duty was paramount to Sir Gawain. The baronet had long fostered his agents' sense of honor and obligation to a cause greater than their own. His determination to put the league first was one of the traits that made his leadership so admirable and effective.

It was then that Sir Gawain returned to his personal plea. "Please, I beg of you, Hawk, do not withdraw now. You are like a son to me. I promise, this will be my last significant request of you."

At those simple words, reality returned with a vengeance for Hawk. He'd let himself forget how important the succession was to Sir Gawain.

How could he forsake the man who had been like a father to him, the man who had saved his sanity? Furthermore, did he have a right to put his personal happiness above his sworn oath to the Guardians?

Hawk slowly nodded, reluctantly accepting the inevitable. His life was dedicated to the Guardians. And he had given his word to Sir Gawain. It was too late now to renege.

"Very well. I won't withdraw."

The relief on Sir Gawain's face was palpable. "*Thank*

you, Hawk." He exhaled quietly, then moved on to another matter. "I fear I must return to London directly since there is an urgent situation requiring my attention. I would be much obliged if you could accompany me there this afternoon. We have much to discuss about the situation in Calais, and you could renew your acquaintance with my niece while you are in town. She has been expecting your attentions for weeks now."

Hawk managed to hide his grimace. "Yes, I will accompany you to London. But I have several affairs I must attend to first. I will need an hour or so."

"Of course, but I hope to leave as soon as you are able."

"Yes, sir," Hawk replied politely, his thoughts leaping ahead.

He needed to speak to Skye and put an end to any romantic aspirations she had of being his ideal match. He couldn't lead her on when he wasn't free. The simple fact was, he couldn't both wed her and command the Guardians, and the league had to come first for him.

He wanted to let her down gently, though, before she became more deeply involved. Before *he* became more deeply involved. He was loath to hurt Skye, but he wasn't the right mate for her. She had brought passion and pleasure into his life again, even happiness, yet pleasure was a far cry from love. She'd been a refuge, a haven, but a temporary one. And her continued presence in his life would only be a torture.

The trouble was, Hawk realized as he left Sir Gawain and went in search of Skye, he kept recalling recent images of her. Most particularly, his mind kept flashing back to the previous day's encounter in the tower room . . . the tenderness in her voice, her beautiful smile, her sweet laughter.

But with a new grimace, Hawk girded his loins, so to speak. Until recently he'd been content with the cold, gray emptiness of his life, and he could be so again.

It would be kinder to Skye to terminate their affair now before he gave her any more pain—and kinder to himself before she became any more vital to him.

Upon finding Skye conferring with the staff in the kitchens, he asked for a moment of her time and drew her into the nearest private room, which happened to be the housekeeper's office. When she gave a small laugh at his choice of a meeting place, Hawk realized how much he would miss that sound.

His silence must have puzzled Skye for her expectant smile dimmed as she gazed up at him. "Why are you wearing such a grim look? Has something happened?"

In the end, Hawk chose the cleanest method of breaking his news: swiftly and dispassionately. "I wanted to inform you that I am leaving this afternoon. Sir Gawain Olwen called a short while ago, and I mean to return to London with him. It is long past time that I begin courting his great-niece."

Skye's smile faded altogether. "Do you truly wish to marry her, Hawk?"

"Yes," he said after only the slightest hesitation.

Her skepticism showed. "I cannot believe it."

Hawk purposely kept his reply clipped. "You've known from the first that I have obligations and what my plan was."

"Yes, but I hoped . . . expected that I could change your mind."

"That isn't possible. In order to lead the Guardians, I must wed Miss Olwen."

"And you mean to accept such a cold fate?" Skye's blue eyes were suddenly hot and bright with unshed tears. "If you don't wish to marry her, why would you torture yourself that way?"

Hawk's own chest grew tight. Pushing Skye away was the right step, the honorable step, but that didn't keep him from wanting to haul her close and tangle his fingers in her hair while kissing her to offer her comfort.

His silence was damning, however.

"Hawk, *please* . . . consider what you are doing." There was real despair in her tone now.

He hated the hurt in her voice. Wanting to ease it, he stepped closer and reached up to trace a fingertip over her cheekbone.

A mistake, he realized when she closed her hand over his with an almost desperate tightness. "Hawk . . . I know you want to please your mentor, but isn't it time that you think of yourself? That you live your own life instead of a life dedicated to others? Haven't you punished yourself enough for failing to save your family?"

"I don't intend to argue with you, sweetheart," he said gently.

"Then don't argue, just *listen*. I can understand if you don't want to marry *me* . . . if you could never love me—"

"My decision has nothing to do with love."

"But shouldn't it? Love should be an important consideration when you marry."

"Not in this case."

She took a deep breath, obviously struggling for composure. "I realize how difficult it would be to let yourself love again. I felt the same fear after my parents died. But how much worse is it to deny yourself the chance for love? Look at my uncle and Rachel, how much time and happiness they lost. What happened to them was a tragedy."

The parallels were unmistakable but made no difference to his future. Carefully but firmly, he withdrew his hand from her grasp.

Her eyes were filled with despairing futility, but in typical Skye fashion, she was unwilling to give up. "We both know that life is too short and precious to waste, Hawk. I wish I could make you see that—"

A soft rap on the door interrupted her passionate argument. Skye look startled for a moment, then clamped her lips together to hold back what might have been a scream of frustration.

When Hawk curtly bid entrance, the door opened and the housekeeper thrust her head inside the room.

"Begging you pardon, m'lord, but you said you wished to know if Lord Farnwell ever called. He has, and he insists on speaking to Miss Farnwell."

"Where is he now?"

"He was shown into the drawing room, m'lord."

"You did well to tell me, Mrs. Yeats. I shall be along shortly."

When the door shut softly after the housekeeper, Hawk glanced at Skye, whose look had changed from frustration to worry. "Why ever would Farnwell call here?" she asked.

"I intend to find out."

"Whatever he means to say to Daphne, I want to be present."

"As you wish."

Skye's brows grew together. "What do you mean to say to him?"

"That depends on what he wants," Hawk replied as he escorted Skye from the room, feeling a similar frustration but also relief.

By no means were they finished with their argument over his marriage plans, but for the moment they had to postpone their discussion while they dealt with Daphne's brother, Edgar.

Chapter Twenty

To *Skye's mind*, the timing of Baron Farnwell's interruption could not have been worse. She made a valiant effort, however, to swallow her despair and frustration. Most certainly she wasn't done trying to persuade Hawk of his folly in deciding to wed Miss Olwen, but she pushed her feelings aside since she wanted to be present in case Daphne needed defending.

Skye and Hawk reached the drawing room in time to overhear a grating male voice uttering an accusatory expletive. Upon entering, they found Daphne standing her ground against a young gentleman of medium height and rather portly build who was dressed like a tulip of fashion. His coat was rose-colored satin, his waistcoat made of gold brocade, and his shirt points so high they reached above his ears. Yet his pugnacious demeanor belied his effeminate attire.

"Lord Farnwell, I presume," Hawk said in a chilly tone.

Breaking off in vexation, the resplendent visitor snapped as he turned, "Yes, what is it to you?"

"I am Hawkhurst. You dare to swear at a lady in my home?"

Farnwell swallowed, looking somewhat intimidated by Hawk's tall, imposing form. "Beg your pardon, Hawkhurst," he said grudgingly.

"Pray state your business," Hawk ordered.

"I have a personal matter to discuss with my sister."

Although lavishly garbed, Baron Farnwell boasted nondescript features with dull brown hair and eyes. He was certainly no match for the aristocratic aura of power emanating from Hawk. Indeed, despite his peacock feathers, Farnwell seemed like a wren opposing a fierce bird of prey.

When Hawk repeated his command, the baron grimaced. "I wish to speak to Daphne *alone*."

Daphne replied calmly, "But I don't wish to be alone with you, Edgar. Lord Hawkhurst may hear whatever you have to say, as may Lady Skye. I have no secrets to hide from them."

Disconcerted and annoyed, Farnwell moderated his belligerent manner only somewhat when he spoke. "I have no intention of airing our intimate affairs, Daphne."

"Then you may take yourself off."

He gritted his teeth at his sister. "You know more than you are letting on, I am sure of it."

"Why would you think so?"

"Because you have always been thick as thieves with Nibbs. As I was saying before we were interrupted"—he shot a derisive glance at Hawk and Skye—"all the fancy carriages at her cottage aroused my suspicions. I wondered why so many noble ladies were visiting Nibbs when she is naught more than an old peasant."

Daphne pursed her lips in distaste at his description. "Mrs. Nibbs is a very skilled midwife who brought you into the world, Edgar. There is no need to disparage her."

Skye had been concerned for Daphne, but she was holding her own quite well with her domineering younger brother and resisting his bullying tactics. But his frustration was obviously growing.

"Nibbs claimed your mother did not drown all those years ago."

Daphne hesitated, as if deciding how to reply. "Did she?"

"Yes, but she refused to say more, no matter how strongly I urged."

"You mean how much you threatened her."

It surprised Skye that the midwife would divulge the baroness's secret, but perhaps she'd been driven to blurting it out by Lord Farnwell's aggressive manner. He seemed perfectly capable of frightening an old woman. Or perhaps Mrs. Nibbs had let it slip in a moment of confusion or forgetfulness.

Regardless, Farnwell was intent on putting the tale to rest. "Such a scurrilous lie cannot be allowed to stand. Naturally I demanded that Nibbs recant, and when she refused, I immediately traveled to London to find you and discover what you know—but your servants said you were a guest here at Hawkhurst Castle. I thought it exceedingly odd. I wasn't aware you were acquainted with the earl," Farnwell added with another glance at Hawk.

"We only recently became acquaintances," Daphne explained.

"Well, that is neither here nor there. I wish you to

return home with me and speak to Nibbs directly. You must insist that she retract her outrageous nonsense."

"If you believe it to be nonsense, why would you give it any credence?"

He sucked in a ragged breath, clearly struggling for control. "Blast you, Daphne! You are trying my patience."

"I am sorry, Edgar," she replied congenially, "but you must admit, your patience is easily tried."

"Just tell me if there is any truth to her allegation!"

"Very well, if you wish to know . . . Yes, there is."

Farnwell stared, his expression one of consternation. "That cannot be."

"I regret that it is. The ugly truth is that our father was so abusive that he drove my mother to falsify her own death in order to escape his brutality."

His anxiety shifted to cold fury. "*You* are now the one disparaging our father."

"Am I? You cannot deny that Father was a brute to our servants. Why would you think him incapable of cruelty toward my mother?"

His gaze bored into hers, but clearly his thoughts were racing. "When did you learn of this?"

"Only this past week."

"How could you have kept this from me?" he demanded, his voice rising again but this time with an edge of panic.

"In part because I knew you would be upset and feared you would react exactly this way." Daphne was trying to soothe him now. She must have had experience placating his contentious manner. "But mostly because I wished to meet my mother for the first time in private."

Farnwell now looked both shocked and fearful. "Dear God," he rasped. "She is still alive?"

"Yes, quite alive."

"She is *here*? In this very house?"

"Yes."

"Dear God," he repeated, the words no more than a hoarse whisper.

Skye could understand his alarm, for he had realized the possible consequences. Rachel Farnwell's existence not only put his nobility in question but his very legitimacy. The impact to his birthright would dwarf any scandal from his father's bigamy and abuse, which was doubtless why he'd felt the urgency to make Nibbs retract the story of Lady Farnwell's drowning.

The baron looked so thunderstruck that Skye almost felt sorry for him, except that she knew Daphne didn't consider her brother overly deserving of sympathy. Edgar was a selfish prig, with a streak of meanness he had likely inherited from his father.

As if on cue, his combativeness rallied in short order. "No, I shan't believe it," Farnwell declared. "You have been utterly deceived, Daphne. Someone is impersonating your late mother and spinning lies."

"You are entitled to your opinion, Edgar, but you are wrong."

"How could you possibly know? You were but an infant at the time of her death. What proof do you have that she is your mother?"

"I need no proof. It is a *feeling*."

Farnwell seemed to gain confidence the more he thought about it. His panicked air receding, he squared his shoulders in a more belligerent frame. "I demand to see this imposter for myself."

"You needn't be concerned, Edgar. She has no intention of making our father's sordid history known or resuming her former life."

He might have replied, but just then Rachel entered the drawing room, accompanied by Cornelius and Isabella. Reaching back, Rachel shut the door carefully behind her, no doubt to keep their conversation from the servants.

"We heard shouting," she murmured with concern. "Are you all right, my dear?" she asked Daphne.

"I am quite well, thank you, Mrs. Donnelly," Daphne assured her.

Edgar had frozen and was scrutinizing Rachel as if she were some sort of strange mythical creature.

"Allow me to introduce myself, Lord Farnwell," Rachel said with composure. "I was wed to your father in another lifetime."

He responded with an angry sneer. "You cannot deceive me, madam."

Rachel moved toward him. "Why would I even attempt a deception?"

"Because you covet my fortune for yourself and your daughter."

"You are mistaken, my lord—"

Farnwell cut her off with a scoffing sound. "I warn you, if you dare try to claim my inheritance, I will bring criminal charges against you."

Rachel tilted her head serenely. "On what grounds? Lord Hawkhurst's solicitor has advised us on the law regarding deceased spouses. My case against you would be good. I would first have to prove that I am

Lady Farnwell, but that could be achieved by finding reputable witnesses who once knew me."

Her assertion made Farnwell clamp his lips shut in outrage.

Rachel smiled politely. "But please, rest assured I have no intention of mounting a legal challenge. I won't contest your legitimacy."

"Why the bloody hell not?" he ground out through his teeth, earning a sharp glance from Hawk.

"Because as I said, that was another lifetime ago."

Of course there was a paramount reason she would not seek to elevate her daughter in Edgar's place, Skye knew. Daphne was not actually William Farnwell's daughter, so morally the inheritance didn't belong to her, even if legally a case could be made. They couldn't risk the truth coming out, however. Not only would an explosive scandal result, but Daphne would forever be shunned by polite society.

Moreover, Daphne had no idea of her true parentage yet—and certainly her brother could never be allowed to learn of it.

Fortunately Farnwell was focused on his own complaints. "There should not even *be* a question of my legitimacy. You were thought to be dead when my father remarried. The validity of his second marriage should be unassailable."

"But it is not."

"Then the law is monstrously unfair."

"Perhaps, but you have nothing to fear from me. Daphne and I have discussed the matter. We believe it is best to let sleeping dogs lie."

When suspicion suffused his features, Daphne voiced her agreement. "Mrs. Donnelly had to persuade me to go along, but not for the reason you think." She gazed at her mother solemnly. "What disturbed me most was that you never received a proper burial. I wanted the world to know that you did not kill yourself, so the stain on your memory would be erased."

Rachel returned a poignant smile. "My reputation isn't important, my dear."

Farnwell broke in again. "If you bring me down, Daphne will be mired in scandal as well. I will make certain of that."

"Which is why I intend to keep the secret."

"There will be no possible way to conceal your existence," Farnwell refuted, his voice rising an octave in frustration.

"I beg to differ, my lord. I assumed the name of an Irish relative years ago, and I shall continue the pretense for my remaining lifetime. Any resemblance to Daphne can be brushed off as a family similarity. Even if, by an unlucky chance, someone happens to recognize me as Baroness Farnwell, I will deny it and laugh it off. My identity will remain a strict secret— unless you choose to advertise it by shouting to Lord Hawkhurst's entire household."

"What about Nibbs?"

"Who," Daphne countered, "would believe the ravings of 'an old peasant,' as you just termed her?"

"Even so, I do not *trust* you, madam," he almost hissed.

At his savage tone, both Cornelius and Isabella moved closer to Rachel's side, hovering protectively, as if to show strength in numbers. Skye found herself instinctively closing ranks as well.

But Daphne, who knew her brother best, chimed

in. "Please believe me, Edgar, I am not after your fortune, even if you have always been a nipcheese with mine."

From Edgar's perspective, his worry was understandable, Skye thought. Daphne had been left a modest dowry and portion by her father, but Edgar controlled the purse strings and was exceedingly stingy.

"I will *never* believe you," he insisted.

Rachel intervened with a rational explanation. "Lord Farnwell, I will not need your fortune. I have been living very simply in a cottage all these years and have very modest needs."

"Now you claim you have no desire to improve your station? You are living in a virtual palace"—he glanced around the elegantly refurbished drawing room—"and you prefer a cottage to this luxury?"

The sneer was back in his tone, but this time it held a tinge of jealousy of Hawk's inherited wealth. Briefly Skye met Hawk's gaze and saw his gray eyes glittering with irony. Farnwell had no idea of the trials Hawk had suffered and was still facing.

Then Rachel continued in a milder voice, "Cottage or palace makes no difference. And even if it did, I am now engaged to wed Lord Cornelius Wilde. He has fortune enough to keep me in luxury should I crave it."

After a start at her mother's sudden announcement, Daphne looked only faintly surprised. Perhaps she had guessed at Rachel's affection for Cornelius after witnessing them together for the past sennight, although they had maintained their pretense of being merely old friends until they considered her ready to accept the news.

Rather than be comforted, Farnwell resorted to genuine hostility. "I have a better solution. You should stay dead!"

Rachel looked startled herself. "Wh-what do you mean?"

"Your vow to keep quiet is not good enough. You need to leave England and return to wherever you have been hiding."

Skye felt herself bristling. Daphne had said her brother tended to become abusive and threatening when he didn't get his own way, and his tone as he berated Rachel bore that out.

Surprisingly, however, his demeanor only stiffened Rachel's spine. "I will not be forced to leave England again," she said quietly.

When Farnwell took a step toward her, Cornelius let out a low growl and moved between them, his stance rigid, his hands curled into fists warningly as he faced down the baron. Skye was taken aback to see her mild-mannered, scholarly uncle prepared to employ physical violence. But he had also waited twenty-five years to defend the love of his life, and that failure would have grated on his soul as a man.

"She has suffered inexcusably at your vile father's hand," Cornelius bit out before Rachel laid a calming hand on his arm.

"Thank you, my dear, but I have quailed for too long and am determined to stand up for myself." With consummate dignity, she addressed Farnwell. "I have already wasted over half my life living in fear, my lord. I will not do so any longer."

Skye silently applauded Rachel's refusal to leave timidly or quietly. But there was no need for her to fear an abusive bully anymore, either. She now had wealthy, powerful supporters—Lord Cornelius and the entire Wilde family, as well as the Earl of Hawkhurst.

His complexion flushing red, Farnwell stared at the company, but when he brandished his own fists at Cornelius, Hawk stepped in.

"I don't advise it," he warned softly.

Farnwell was livid by now, but evidently he thought better of starting a brawl.

"My majordomo will escort you from the premises," Hawk added in a silken drawl.

The baron not only looked outraged but flabbergasted. "You are ordering me off your property? *Me?*"

"Indeed. And I will advise my servants to keep you off permanently. You return at your own peril."

Hawk's eyes were like slate as he stared down the baron. Farnwell was clearly furious but helpless.

With a strangled sound, he abruptly capitulated. Brushing past the others, he stalked across the drawing room and flung open the door. With a final seething glance behind him, he quit the room.

"Pray excuse me a moment," Hawk murmured before following Farnwell, no doubt to instruct the castle servants to make certain he left the premises. Skye highly approved of the precaution. Hawk was taking no chances that the baron would take his anger out on Rachel.

Although no one was ready to say the issue was resolved, there was a visible relief of tension at his retreat. Rachel exhaled a long breath while Cornelius's stance relaxed.

Daphne recovered most quickly, however, and proceeded to marvel at her mother's betrothal announcement. "I shouldn't be surprised that you and Lord Cornelius intend to marry. It has been fairly obvious that you are in love."

Rachel cautiously studied Daphne's face. "We would like your blessing, my dear."

"Of course you have it. I am very glad that you love each other."

Cornelius clasped Rachel's hand in his. "Your mother is correct, Miss Farnwell. I have an ample fortune and can provide for her and for you as well. You will not lack for fortune, even though you are unable to claim Farnwell's."

As much as Skye would have liked to hear the remainder of the conversation, she was more eager to speak to Hawk alone, and so quietly slipped from the room in pursuit of him.

Farther along the corridor she spied an elegant, silver-haired gentleman. He had stepped out of Hawk's study, she suspected, because he was curious about all the commotion. It had to be Sir Gawain Olwen, Skye thought as he momentarily waylaid Hawk.

When she halted, debating what to do, she realized that Aunt Bella had followed her into the corridor.

Her aunt took one look at her dismal expression and instantly grew concerned. "What is it, my love? Something is amiss, I can tell."

Not for the first time did Skye wish her aunt was not quite so perceptive.

Determinedly she swallowed the ache in her throat. Hawk was fully occupied at the moment, but she would not allow him to leave for London without another attempt to renew her arguments about his impending courtship and marriage. By forcing a confrontation, she would be fighting for him—for *them*, Skye told herself. But perhaps she needed Isabella's wise counsel beforehand. . . .

With a final glance at Hawk, she turned back to her aunt. "Now that you mention it . . . You are an expert on romantic matters, and I could use your advice. My own arsenal of tricks is entirely depleted."

"Of course, my dear," Bella said gently as she slipped her arm in Skye's. "Come with me to my rooms and we will have a quiet coze."

Chapter Twenty-one

It went against Skye's very nature to give up, but relinquishing hope for Hawk's love was precisely what her aunt recommended.

In fact, when told of his plans, Isabella seemed more torn by *his* dilemma than Skye's. "I understand why Hawk feels obligated to fill Sir Gawain's shoes. He would not want to betray the man who has been like a father to him."

"Oh, I understand," Skye agreed. "But what can I *do* about it, Aunt? I have tried my utmost to make him love me, to no avail."

"Do you love him?"

"Yes. More than anything. But clearly he doesn't return my feelings. And even if he did, we have no future together. Not when he insists on wedding Sir Gawain's niece so he can lead the Guardians."

Isabella pursed her lips thoughtfully. "I believe you have done all you can, Skye. As I have told you before, one cannot force love. If you are meant to be together, then you will be."

Skye badly wanted to refute her aunt's assertion. All her instincts were clamoring for her to persevere. She wanted to *fight* for Hawk's love and win.

But Aunt Bella interjected more guidance using the voice of reason. "You know that arguing and demanding will only push Hawk away. You must let love come to you, Skye."

"You are saying that he must make the choice himself?"

"Yes, exactly."

No matter how sage the advice, Skye's natural impulses continued to rebel. She had always been driven to control her own fate. She didn't want to leave the decision to Hawk, unable to manage the outcome. But for once in her life she might be unable to get what she wanted.

"The Guardians are his life," Isabella added in a somber tone. "Forcing him to choose between you will only cause him pain. Is that what you want for him? More pain?"

"No, of course not."

"But that is what will happen if you continue pressing him."

Skye's throat grew tight. She'd been proceeding blithely these past few days, her heart filled with love and dreams. But now her dreams were about to be shattered.

"Sir Gawain wants Hawk because he is a born leader," Aunt Bella went on. "Although some other Guardians are as brave and skilled as he is, few could fill that particular role as well as he."

Skye swallowed the hard lump of emotion in her throat, attempting to see the decision from Hawk's perspective. The Guardians were his calling. They had made him the man he is today. Did she have the right to ask him to give them up?

The reminder led her to question her own motives—and a dozen thoughts crowded into her mind as a result: How selfish of her even to try to persuade him. Hawk was a hero, a man of action. He had dedicated the previous ten years of his life to righting wrongs and saving lives. He did what was right, despite his own self-interest. Could she do any less?

He was making the sacrifice to serve his country. Could she make the same sacrifice? Love meant sacrificing sometimes. And she wanted to prove worthy of his love.

The noble thing would be to let him go. If she loved him, she had to let him go.

With extreme reluctance, Skye nodded at her aunt's unwelcome counsel. Feeling a hollow, aching need rise up within her, she wondered if she'd made a grave mistake from the very beginning. Why had she let herself fall in love with Hawk? If she had known it would hurt this much, would she still have pursued him?

But yes. Following her heart was in her very blood. Her family loved with a bone-deep fierceness, and she was no exception.

Skye blinked away the sudden sting of tears. She would have to be stoic when she faced Hawk, just as she would have to control any display of painful emotions. She often wore her heart on her sleeve, but she certainly couldn't tell him of her love, for that would only add to his burden of guilt.

No doubt her aunt was right. She had done all she could. The rest was up to Hawk.

A quarter hour later, when she found Hawk in the corridor outside his study, he halted upon seeing her.

"May I have a moment of your time?" Skye asked quietly.

His gray eyes were wary, before his dark lashes lowered to hide any hint of emotion.

"You needn't worry," she hastened to add. "I haven't come to repeat my entreaties. I only want to bid you farewell."

"Indeed?" he said politely, distantly.

Skye felt her stomach sink further with dread. Hawk's expression was impassive, as detached as ever, as it had been in the early days of their relationship.

He ushered her inside the study and went to stand by the window, his profile stark and stunning in the gray afternoon light. It frightened her to think that her greatest fear was coming to pass, but she forced herself to launch into her short, prepared speech.

"I won't implore you to reconsider, Hawk. Of course I don't want you to wed Miss Olwen, but I understand why you must put your league first. Your duty is more important than any personal contentment. You must do what you must."

"Yes, I must."

His concise response brought the ache back to her chest. She desperately wanted this man to love her, but her hope was futile. Hawk would never open his heart to her. He wouldn't permit himself. There was no answering fire in his eyes, no feeling at all.

Skye willed herself not to show her despair. "I agree,

you should lead the Guardians. You save lives, Hawk. You shouldn't be compelled to give that up."

Even though it means I must give you *up.*

She felt the ache cut through her heart. Her chest tight, her eyes burning, she offered him a tremulous smile and moved to stand directly before him.

She hesitated a moment memorizing his beloved face, the proud curves of cheekbones and chin and forehead, before saying simply, "If this is farewell . . . I want you to remember me."

"I could never forget you, sweeting."

He lifted his hand, touching his fingertips along the rise of her cheek. "Your name should be Sunshine. . . ."

His tenderness was like a nail to her heart.

Forcibly she swallowed a sob. "Before I go . . . will you allow me one last kiss? That is all I ask."

Resistance was etched in the chiseled planes of his face, but Hawk complied and lowered his head so their mouths could meet.

His lips were warm but not welcoming. Determinedly, Skye slid her arms around his neck to pull him closer, and for a fleeting instant, their kiss turned hard, with a hint of the glorious passion they had always shared. She tried to press herself deeper into the hard, muscular shelter of his body . . . but almost as suddenly, Hawk broke off their embrace. His hands on her shoulders, he deliberately set her away.

As he drew back, Skye glimpsed something in his eyes . . . the hot need burning just below the surface. But then his heavy black lashes veiled his gaze.

The implacable lines of his face were like a knife twisting in her heart.

"Godspeed on your journey, Hawk," she whispered.

Then, before her voice could break entirely, she turned and ran from the room.

Scalding tears filled her eyes, blinding her, but she didn't stop until she reached her own bedchamber and shut herself inside. Squeezing her eyes shut, Skye stood with her back pressed against the door, tears spilling helplessly down her cheeks.

All her hopes for happiness had gone up in flames. Yet she was crying not only for herself but for the man who would go on living without love.

Chapter Twenty-two

London was as cold and gray as Hawk felt. Inside Sir Gawain's overcrowded town house, however, the heat from numerous chandeliers and perfumed bodies masked the chill.

Hawk gazed out over a sea of colorful gowns and elegant coiffures, fighting a cloying sense of oppression. This was the second major event of his courtship—a dinner and ball hosted by the baronet. Sir Gawain's great-niece and her parents had stayed at his London home for several weeks now and seemed anxious for Hawk's appearance.

Their initial meeting had gone awkwardly, though. Miss Amelia Olwen was pretty and gentle and sweet in nature, but utterly, mind-numbingly bland.

She also looked as if she might swoon at the first hint of danger. She clearly found Hawk intimidating, and she was appalled by his scars.

Unlike Skye, who sees your scars as a badge of courage.

For an instant, Hawk let himself dwell on his last

memory of Skye when she'd kissed him farewell at Hawkhurst. Her eyes had been luminous with sadness, and when she smiled that tremulous heartbreaking smile, he wanted to call off his entire plan.

He'd spent the three nights since arriving in London alternately suffering a restless, dream-tossed sleep or lying awake with a hole in his gut. Not because of the ghosts of his dead family—those he had managed to conquer with Skye's help—but from haunting regrets at being forced to leave her.

His heart sat in his chest like stone at the thought of cutting her out of his life, never touching, never laughing with her, never seeing her radiant smile. . . .

Hawk muffled an annoyed oath at himself. He bloody well had only himself to blame for letting Skye's captivating charm work an enchantment on him. Besides, he was resigned to his unpalatable future. Eventually, in time, his life would be restored to the same place it was before she came into it . . . cold, gray, empty, joyless.

Shaking off his grim thoughts, Hawk instead focused on watching his future bride dance with her current partner. When the orchestra music came to a close, Miss Olwen cast him a timid glance, as if reluctant to return to his side.

At the sight of her timidity, an unwanted image of Skye slipped into his mind again. She was so alive and vibrant and fearless—so vastly different from the insipid girl he was supposed to wed.

Also unlike Skye, Miss Olwen seemed noticeably reluctant to marry him or even to entertain his courtship, a stance that only added to his internal conflict. For Hawk, their first dance tonight had confirmed that their union would be a grave mistake. But the untenable problem still remained of how to extricate himself from his obligations—

Just then, he felt a light slap on his back and heard an amused drawl commenting on the irony of seeing a confirmed recluse at a crowded ball.

Turning, Hawk welcomed the unexpected appearance of one of his closest friends and fellow Guardians, Sir Alex Ryder. Ryder was tall and dark-haired like Hawk, but his build was more lean and muscular and his face more darkly tanned by the Mediterranean sun. Ryder had begun his career as a hired mercenary and was an expert in arms and munitions.

He must have just arrived in England from Cyrene, Hawk thought as they shook hands. "I didn't expect to see you so soon, Ryder. Aren't you supposed to be enjoying your wedding trip?"

"You know one doesn't ignore a summons from Sir Gawain, even for nuptial bliss. He bade me return for *your* wedding—but it seems your courtship has not progressed so far."

Hawk sidestepped the issue. "Did your new wife accompany you here?"

"Yes. Eve didn't relish us being apart for so long, and she wanted to see Claire."

Ryder had recently wed the love of his life, the widowed Countess of Hayden, whose younger sister Claire had surprisingly married Macky and settled in London with the former actor.

In fact, there had been a rash of happy marriages among their colleagues in recent years and some births as well. Ryder and Eve were anticipating their first child next spring. Of all their members, though, Ryder was one of the few who originally hailed from the island.

"You plan to settle on Cyrene, don't you, Ryder?"

"Eventually, yes. Why do you ask?"

Because he couldn't conquer the desire to ward off his current fate.

"Because I would need to find a replacement if I were to withdraw as candidate for leader."

Ryder's gaze narrowed in surprise. "The Olwen chit is that bad, is she?"

"She is not repulsive, if that is what you mean."

"But you are having second thoughts."

"You might say so." *And fourth and fifth thoughts as well.*

A measure of guilt and regret accompanied Hawk's subversive admission. The last thing he wanted was to disappoint and betray Sir Gawain's hopes for him. Even so . . .

Ryder chuckled. "I confess I am not surprised. I never thought you two were suited in the least."

"I am beginning to agree," Hawk said with a grimace.

He had also concluded that he would need Ryder's support to find an answer to his dilemma—or perhaps Ryder in conjunction with another of the elite Guardians.

"Where are the rest of our cadre at the moment?"

"I left Caro and Max on Cyrene, enjoying their newborn son. Thorne and Diana are here in England visiting his father, the duke. And Deverill and Antonia are planning a voyage to America to see his cousin Brandon."

Hawk was about to reply when a flash of color above his head caught his eye. Both he and Ryder tensed as they looked up, automatically reaching for weapons they weren't carrying, given their formal attire.

But there was no need to defend themselves from the lad up in the gallery sitting astride the railing. The boy was garbed as a pirate with eye patch and sash, but the short sword he carried was painted wood, and he looked to be perhaps twelve or thirteen.

"Isn't that Sir Gawain's great-nephew?" Hawk asked curiously.

"Yes, Timothy is his name."

The boy didn't seem related to his shy older sister, Amelia. Even as they watched, Timothy carefully got to his feet and balanced on the railing with his arms held out—playing at walking the plank of a pirate ship, Hawk surmised.

The incident brought to mind another scene from years earlier, of Skye when she was a young girl, almost falling headfirst over a gallery railing to his feet.

Timothy didn't look to be in danger of falling. In fact, seeing he had an audience, he winked down at Hawk and grinned broadly.

Precocious, bold, and adventurous was Hawk's instinctive assessment: the very qualities that might make a good member of their league.

"I'll be damned," Hawk murmured. A lad like that could be groomed for the Guardians with a good chance of success.

Which meant *he* could be free to follow his own path.

You may have found your way out. You could call off the courtship and still ensure the future of the Guardians.

Hawk waited for fresh regret to strike, but in truth,

this possible solution felt wholly right. The one thing he was not capable of doing was losing Skye.

"I won't be marrying Miss Olwen," he said aloud, as if testing his decision. And with his declaration, he felt as if a great burden had been lifted from his chest.

Ryder slapped his back again. "Very glad you've come to your senses, old fellow. An arranged marriage is a high price to pay for the privilege of commanding the Guardians."

Hawk's mouth twisted in a wry grimace. "Sir Gawain will need to be persuaded."

"I will be happy to help you try."

"No, this is something I must do myself. I shall call on him in the morning and present my idea. Meanwhile, I have a proposition for you to consider regarding young Timothy. . . ."

Sir Gawain's face fell the moment he saw Hawk the next morning. "I can guess why you have come," the baronet said with a heavy sigh. "I realized that Amelia was not the right wife for you when I observed you together last evening. Your union was clearly wishful thinking on my part."

"A laudable wish, sir," Hawk replied sincerely. "Your desire to secure the league's future is supremely admirable. But it would not be fair to your niece to wed only for political reasons, no matter how admirable. Furthermore," he added, venturing to honestly explain his motives, "I have my own personal reasons for wishing to withdraw from my commitment to you. I want to be free to marry for love, and I could never love your niece."

Sir Gawain's gaze turned searching. "If so, it would

be unfair to you as well. In my own defense, I never expected you would love again."

"Nor did I."

The simple fact was, he couldn't marry elsewhere when his heart belonged to Skye. She had carved a place in his heart against his will. "I am truly sorry, Sir Gawain, but I must ask you to release me from our plan."

Recognizing Hawk's resolve, the baronet nodded slowly before sighing again. "I suppose it might be possible to amend the charter so that the league needn't be controlled by a descendant."

"There is another alternative we haven't considered," Hawk replied. "Miss Olwen's younger brother Timothy has the same Guardian blood she does. I met your great-nephew last night, and I believe he has the makings of a Guardian."

Sir Gawain's gaze turned thoughtful. "Tim is only a lad, barely out of shortcoats, and yet . . . You are proposing that he join the order now?"

"Yes. Granted, it may take years to determine if he has the character and skills to qualify as one of us and perhaps even become commander. In the meantime, Ryder could take charge of the league after your retirement. He and Deverill and Thorne can certainly teach Timothy whatever he needs to know."

Trey Deverill and Christopher, Viscount Thorne, were also elite Guardians and two more of Hawk's closest friends along with Ryder. "With proper training, Timothy might eventually become your successor. And if not, Ryder can still act in his place for an indefinite period."

Sir Gawain's mouth curved in a faint smile. "This is

a prime reason you were my first choice, Hawk. Because you are able to see the larger picture and contrive creative solutions. Very well, then. I release you with my blessing."

Sir Gawain's response went a long way toward easing the remaining tension in Hawk's chest. "I greatly regret disappointing you, sir."

The baronet's expression softened further. "No, no, you could never disappoint me. Time and again you have exceeded my wildest expectations. You have given a decade of your life to the order and served faithfully, Hawk. I cannot ask for more. It is time you were allowed to pursue your own life. I took advantage of your grief all those years ago so that you would join us."

"But I was complicit." He had gladly followed the path he'd been offered, Hawk knew. Skye was right. He'd been punishing himself for continuing to live when his family had perished. In the early years he had cheated death frequently, searching for an honorable way to die. And later, he'd filled his days with danger because his life was so empty.

But he had punished himself long enough and no longer needed to continue making himself suffer. It was time to return to the world of the living.

"Do you mean to give up the Guardians altogether?" Sir Gawain asked with concern.

Hawk hesitated. "I haven't decided yet. I believe I want to return to England to live. It depends on other factors."

"Your future bride? Is that the young lady I saw briefly at Hawkhurst Castle? She must be remarkable to have affected you so profoundly."

Hawk smiled wryly, recalling the stormy evening he'd first met Skye. He hadn't realized then that she could be his salvation. She had come into his dark house and dragged him into the light, coercing him to open his heart again. "She is *quite* remarkable. I mean to wed her if she will have me."

"Then I wish you much happiness."

"Thank you, Sir Gawain. I plan to apply for a special license today and return home tonight—after I make my apologies to your niece and her parents."

"There is no need. I will handle my relations. I pushed you into this quandary, and I will make it right for you."

Making it right with Skye was chief on Hawk's mind as he took his leave of the baronet. But he had no misgivings about his decision.

Nothing would be right without Skye. He'd made himself believe he could get through the empty days without her, but he didn't want to face the long lonely years ahead with no one to prod and provoke him to *feel*.

He didn't want a life without Skye in it. He wanted the peace of sleeping with her in his arms. He wanted the joy of being beside her each day, facing whatever the future held together. He wanted laughter to echo in his house again. He wanted children with Skye.

And given the choice between leading the Guardians or marrying her and allowing himself happiness, he chose Skye.

Given the choice between wallowing in her pain and putting on a brave face for her Uncle Cornelius, Skye chose to hide her tears. She didn't want to spoil her beloved uncle's happiness, so she threw herself into preparations for his nuptials.

Rather than traveling to Beauvoir or Tallis Court in Kent, Cornelius and Rachel planned a quiet ceremony at Hawkhurst Castle with only family present, not wanting to undermine her hard-won anonymity or wave a red flag under Edgar Farnwell's nose and needlessly antagonize him by advertising her existence. There would be no public calling of the banns in church for three weeks beforehand either; instead they would be married by special license in a fortnight. If all went as hoped, the delay would allow time to gather the Wilde clan.

The most pressing task for Skye was hunting down her brother. Despite Quinn's cynical views on love and marriage, he would want to be present for the wedding, and his man of business would likely know his location. Ash and Jack had already sent their congratulations and agreed to bring their wives. Katharine had responded with delight, saying she intended to return to the castle at week's end.

It was Hawk's plans that most concerned Skye, however. In truth, she thought of him every waking minute of every day, dreamed of him at night, and dreaded that any moment she might hear the news that he was engaged or—worse—had already married.

Four days after their dismal parting, she was finding it harder and harder to control her dread and maintain a cheerful appearance. The frigid weather didn't help her mood, either. The day had been cold and bleak, just the way she felt. And with a storm brewing as a harbinger of winter, the evening promised to be blustery.

After dinner, the company gathered in the drawing

room, where a roaring fire burned in the hearth and extra lamps had been lit to ward off the gloom. The mantel clock had just struck eight o'clock when the new Hawkhurst butler delivered a letter for Miss Farnwell. As Daphne read the message, her apparent puzzlement turned hopeful.

"This note is from my brother," she announced. "He wishes to apologize to Mrs. Donnelly for his deplorable behavior the other day and requests an audience."

"Lord Farnwell has called here at the castle?" Skye asked the butler.

"Yes, my lady. Additionally, he asks for shelter from the approaching storm. But we were instructed by his lordship to deny him entrance. How should we proceed?"

Skye was inclined to reject the baron's request for an interview, although it would be heartless to refuse him shelter, especially for his servants and horses.

Rachel looked discomfited, but Daphne evidently believed her brother's contrition for she pleaded in his favor. "Please, Skye, this could be our best chance to mend fences."

Just then Skye heard a low rumble of thunder in the distance. The storm decided it for her. She could hardly turn him away when she had faced the same circumstances upon her first visit here. And they had the advantage of numbers—herself, her uncle Cornelius and aunt Bella, and a castle full of servants to protect Daphne and Rachel if necessary.

"Very well," Skye murmured. "Show Lord Farnwell here to the drawing room."

They all rose to their feet when the baron entered. He bowed politely to the ladies and Lord Cornelius but waited to speak until the butler had withdrawn and shut the door behind him.

Farnwell's manner seemed much calmer this time. Indeed, he offered a charming smile. "I would rather speak to Mrs. Donnelly alone, but I can see why you would prefer differently."

"You may speak to all of us, Edgar," Daphne interjected.

"Very well." He inhaled slowly, as if bracing himself for an unpleasant task. "It was unforgivable of me to have threatened you, Mrs. Donnelly," he said then, his tone amazingly repentant. "Pray understand that I was angry and shocked to have my very legitimacy called into question. Now that I have had time to consider, however, I am prepared to make you a lucrative bargain. I will pay you the bulk of my fortune if you will leave the country and disappear again."

Daphne stared at her brother before shaking her head with an expression somewhere between amusement and indignation. "You believe you can bribe her with money?"

Rachel held up a hand. "I must decline, my lord. I hid myself away in near seclusion for a quarter of a century, and before that I was your father's wife and therefore his property, no better than chattel, completely at his mercy. I will never live like that again."

A look of frustration crossed the baron's features, but he visibly struggled to tamp down his anger.

Cornelius stepped forward. "She has suffered more than enough, Farnwell."

"I have no desire to make her suffer further, but consider my position. As long as she is alive, I run the risk of being exposed."

"You will just have to trust her to keep your secret," Cornelius insisted.

"That I cannot do," Farnwell snapped. "She could cause my disinheritance at any moment."

"I told you, my lord," Rachel reassured him, "you have nothing to fear."

He gritted his teeth. "That is not an acceptable answer. You *will* leave England at once, do you hear me?"

His face was flushed red, like a child about to throw a tantrum, but in his eyes there was a lethal rage of a full-grown brute.

Skye felt a twinge of alarm when his hands curled into fists, and profoundly regretted that she had ever permitted him inside the castle, especially when he had been specifically barred.

Her chin raised, Rachel stood her ground, which only angered her nemesis more.

"You will rue defying me," he hissed, raising his fist as if prepared to strike, evidently believing he could physically force her agreement.

For Cornelius, seeing his beloved threatened was too much. With a low growl, he lunged at Farnwell and let loose a blow to his chin, which sent the baron staggering backward.

He recovered quickly, though. With a snarl, Farnwell sprang at Cornelius and threw a powerful punch to his stomach, felling him to the carpet, where he lay curled and gasping for breath. Farnwell then gave a vicious kick to his ribs for good measure.

For an instant, Skye's own shock held her immobile as Rachel cried out and rushed forward to kneel beside Cornelius, followed less swiftly by Isabella.

After that, everything was a blur of motion. Shaking

off her paralysis, Skye leaped at her uncle's attacker, but Daphne beat her to him, evidently not as caught off guard by her brother's actions. She charged at Edgar, arms akimbo, trying to tackle him to the floor. In response, he hunched over and, far more agile than his portly bulk would suggest, threw Daphne off like a rag doll and tossed her onto a side table. The collision was followed by the dull sound of shattering glass as a lamp upended.

Feeling her own rage, Skye used the defensive measures that her brother and cousins had taught her: Raising her skirts, she kicked out hard. Her slippered foot was a flimsy weapon, but she put all her strength into her straightened leg and struck the side of Farnwell's knee.

His scream of pain as he crumpled told her that she had debilitated him, at least temporarily. Breathing hard, Skye looked around, intending to help Daphne, who was sprawled facedown in a daze. Her satisfaction at vanquishing Farnwell turned to fear at the bright, flickering yellow glow she spied.

Evidently the lamp had broken apart when it hit the floor, spewing oil all over the carpet.

Even worse, the largest puddle had caught fire very near Daphne.

Skye watched with horror as the flames licked at Daphne's skirts and began to spread throughout the entire drawing room, burning across the oil-soaked carpet and racing toward the heavy velvet draperies that covered the windows.

Chapter Twenty-three

He was a changed man, Hawk acknowledged as his coach neared home that evening. Because of Skye, the emotion he'd never wanted to feel again had sunk its claws deep in his heart.

Not even the imminent storm could dim the anticipation of seeing Skye soon. There was no rain yet, but thunder rolled and lightning flickered outside his carriage windows, much like the night of their first encounter. Shortly later the wind picked up, buffeting the vehicle as it swept through the pillared entrance gates of Hawkhurst Castle. Despite the jarring ride, a wry smile curved Hawk's mouth at the thought of surprising Skye with a proposal of marriage.

Just before they reached the curve leading to the castle entrance, his pleasant reflections were splintered by a muffled shout of alarm from his coachman. The jarvey's panel slid open and there was panic in the servant's voice when he exclaimed, *"Fire, my lord!"*

From his vantage point inside the coach, Hawk couldn't see a damned thing. Hastily fumbling for the latch, he lowered the glass and thrust his head outside the window. Wind shrieked in his face as he searched the black night. Moments later a jagged white bolt crackled across the night sky, framing the front of the castle in searing light—followed instantly by a shuddering crash of thunder that shook the ground under the carriage wheels. Yet it wasn't the threat of lightning that made dread curl inside Hawk.

It was his nightmare come to life.

Bright flames lit up a front window of his home on the ground floor, although he couldn't tell which room was burning.

"*Faster!*" he commanded over the roar of the wind.

"Aye, my lord!" The coachman whipped up the horses and sent the team galloping along the gravel avenue.

Terrible images tore through Hawk's memory. The coach careened around the curve, then slowed fractionally, but he had the door open before it came to a halt.

He heard his coachman exclaim, "God help you, my lord." Voicing the same prayer, Hawk leaped down and raced toward the front steps. His gaze was fixed on the windows above his head—was that the drawing room? Definitely the ground floor, but the massive castle foundations raised the level nearly twenty feet above the drive—

The fire had spread to a *second* window, Hawk saw.

Panic churned in his gut, spurring his frantic thoughts. The height meant no access from outside, and there was no rain yet to help fight the flames—

The heavens suddenly opened up as he bounded up the entrance steps. Freezing pellets of rain lashed at his face and drenched his greatcoat, but Hawk scarcely noticed as he slammed open the front door.

His heart thundering, he ran through the great hall. Upon reaching the corridor, though, time slowed to a crawl and his nightmare took over. His legs felt like leaden weights as he struggled onward toward the drawing room, his body swimming through a thick sludge, his mind bombarded by searing memories. He could barely move—couldn't breathe at all as he relived the sheer terror of the first tragedy.

An eternity passed before he skidded to a halt outside the drawing room door. Choking smoke obscured his vision as Hawk took stock. The floor was burning at one end, while flames licked the far walls. If Skye was in there, he couldn't see her. Dear God, if he lost her . . . The devastation he would feel would rival any pain he'd felt the first time.

Bone-deep dread gripping him, Hawk roared her name. What bloody irony to have realized his love too late. How blind he'd been. He couldn't live without Skye, couldn't live without her love. . . .

Icy calm replaced fear; grim determination regained control. He couldn't, wouldn't let her die. Sucking in a lungful of air, Hawk covered his mouth and nose with his arm and plunged into the smoke-filled room. In the glow from the flames, he saw figures moving. Then he saw *her* . . . Skye, her pale hair faintly visible through the murk.

She was fighting the fire with every ounce of strength, trying to tear down the burning, floor-length draperies while others struggled to beat out the carpet flames with cushions and pieces of clothing.

When Hawk shouted at Skye again, she responded

with a hoarse cry, "Here, Hawk!" before a coughing fit robbed her of further speech.

Dragging off his greatcoat, he fought his way toward her. Heat singed his skin and acrid smoke stung his eyes as he joined her effort to bring down the draperies, but together they managed it. The velvet fell into a heap much like funeral pyre. Hawk used his greatcoat to smother the worst of the flames while Skye picked up a small cherrywood table and threw it straight at the window, smashing the glass in a loud crash. Comprehending her purpose, Hawk grabbed the table before it could tumble over the jagged rim.

The sudden gust of outside air sent the flames whooshing, but pelting rain instantly followed, blowing into the room in cooling bursts to dampen the fiery pile.

Hoisting the table, Hawk moved to the second window to deal with the slower burning draperies there, duplicating Skye's feat of shattering the glass and letting in the life-saving rain and fresh air. He was stamping on burning cinders when he saw her double over, her body jolted by raw, hacking coughs.

Urgently sweeping away shards of glass with his coat sleeve, Hawk grabbed Skye by the waist and made her kneel by the second window, then pressed her head through the opening. Although she was instantly soaked, she drew great gasping breaths that eventually slowed her spasms.

Behind him Hawk heard more racking coughs as well as sounds of splashing water and the sizzle of dying embers. A quick glance showed scores of servants filing into the drawing room, carrying cans and buckets of water. They formed a line and began passing full buckets to the points of the remaining fire and empty buckets back out again, with Lady Isabella calling out orders. Evidently she had taken charge of the water brigade, aided by the castle caretaker, Thomas Gilpin.

As the smoke cleared, Hawk saw Rachel and Daphne and Lord Cornelius all battling the remnants of the fire. He was more taken aback to see Baron Farnwell among their numbers, limping heavily but striving just as furiously as the others to save the room from incineration.

Just then Skye drew her head inside the window and tried to stand. Hawk carefully helped her up, then held her away so he could assess her. Her face was wet and soot-streaked and her hair was singed, but she had never looked more beautiful.

"Are you injured?" he demanded, his own eyes tearing from the smoke. "Were you burned?"

"Not badly. I wrapped strips of petticoat around my hands to protect them—"

With a shudder of relief, Hawk reached out and hauled her close, embracing her with crushing tightness. Remembering the heat from the fire, the leaping flames, he buried his face in her hair.

"Dear God, I thought I had lost you," he rasped, hearing the haunted note in his voice. "You could have died."

"We *all* could have died," Skye muttered hoarsely against his shoulder between coughs. "Thank God you . . . came when you did. I remembered hearing . . . that you broke . . . the windows to let in the rain during the nursery fire, but the . . . draperies were burning and wouldn't come down. . . ." Cutting off her fearful commentary, she tried to peer over her shoulder. "What of my uncle? Aunt Bella and the others?"

Hawk drew back far enough to assess their condition. The final flames had been extinguished, and Lord Cornelius seemed unharmed, as did the ladies, although they were all coughing intermittently. "They appear uninjured, but we all need fresher air."

The acrid smoke was clearing, due to the rain and wind gusting in through the shattered windows, but a haze still lingered. With an arm clamped possessively around Skye's waist, Hawk urged her away from the elements.

As she took in the smoldering ruins of his formerly elegant drawing room, though, she halted in dismay. "I am so sorry, Hawk. I am to blame."

"*You* started the fire?"

"No, but I allowed Farnwell into the castle after you expressly ordered him to keep away. He hit Uncle Cornelius and assaulted Daphne and caused a lamp to break, which started the blaze."

Skye shot the baron a scathing look where he stood near the others. "At least Farnwell helped fight the flames instead of running away like a coward, but his brutality is inexcusable."

Farnwell must have realized his violence had gone too far, for he started apologizing for his role in the devastation in an imploring voice, "I am sorry, so very sorry, please forgive me. . . ."

Hawk intended to deal with the nobleman shortly, but for now his concern was for Skye and the others. She, however, seemed more fixated on the destruction, for her expression was full of remorse. "Your beautiful house. All those weeks of work gone to waste."

"I don't give a damn about the house. I only care about you. Are you certain you weren't hurt?"

"My hands sting a bit."

"Let me see."

He carefully unwrapped the blackened linen of her makeshift mittens and saw the red welts on her fingers. His jaw hardened. "We need to take care of these burns."

"There are medical supplies in the housekeeper's pantry."

"There should be an ample supply of burn salve among them," he added grimly, steering Skye toward the door, "although how effective it will be after ten years, I don't know."

Before she would leave, however, she had to embrace her uncle and aunt, and then Rachel and Daphne, and make certain they weren't too badly injured.

Only then was Hawk able to usher the ladies and Lord Cornelius from the drawing room, leaving Gilpin to assume command of the cleanup efforts. Farnwell trailed meekly after them but kept his distance, as if bracing himself for some sort of punishment.

When they reached the kitchens, Isabella took charge again, having dealt with many an injury in her long career as a friend and staunch supporter of the Guardians, but Hawk unearthed the burn ointment that had once been kept in ample supply at the castle.

Listening with half an ear as Isabella grimly related the details of how Lord Farnwell had nearly burned down the castle, Hawk personally saw to Skye's injuries, being well versed in burn care after his own excruciating experience.

Skye seemed to realize the significance of his nursing skills, for the sadness on her face spoke volumes each time she glanced down at his hands.

She grew quieter as he completed his task of bandaging her burns and seemed reticent to accept his ministrations. And when he finished, she thanked him in a low voice and edged away, clearly trying to avoid touching him any further.

As he replaced the lid on the jar of salve, Skye finally grit out a question, as if she couldn't help herself. "Why did you return home, Hawk? You are supposed to be in London, courting Miss Olwen."

"I called off my marriage plans," he replied rather casually.

She lifted her head abruptly, searching his face in disbelief. "It would be beyond cruel to jest about such a thing."

"I agree—and I promise you, I am not jesting. One dance with Miss Olwen made me realize that I couldn't bear to be bound to her. And seeing you tonight, surrounded by fire, made me realize that I couldn't bear to lose you."

"I d-don't understand," she stammered. "What are you saying?"

Reaching up, Hawk curved his palm against her soot-smudged cheek. "You look like a chimney sweep, did you know that?"

The rough sound that came from her throat was somewhere between a cough and a growl. "I don't give a fig what I look like! What do you mean—you couldn't bear to lose me?"

"Exactly that. I was terrified that I had recognized my love too late." At her speechlessness, Hawk knew he had to declare himself more plainly. "The truth is that I love you, my darling, lovely Skye."

Chapter Twenty-four

Disbelieving her own ears, Skye stared at Hawk. So many emotions whirled through her—fear, anger, relief, despair, pain . . . not so much from her burns, which truly were minor, but from knowing she didn't have the right to embrace him or even touch him. She had been prepared to break her heart to act nobly and give him up, but simply being this close again was a physical ache in her chest.

However, when Skye saw from Hawk's expression that he was serious, shock flooded her.

Scarcely daring to hope, she pulled him out into the corridor, past several servants who were carrying buckets back to the kitchens. She waited anxiously until they were alone before getting to the crux of the matter.

"But what about the Guardians?" she demanded in a hoarse voice.

"I am free of any obligation to lead the league."

"Free?"

"Yes. I found a replacement for Sir Gawain's role as leader and persuaded him to approve."

Skye scrutinized Hawk's face intently, but all she could see was blatant honesty. His revelation was no cruel hoax, no dream. Ecstatic relief swamping her, she sagged against the wall and brought her bandaged hands up to cover her face.

"I thought I had lost you," she said weakly, repeating his same words.

"You didn't lose me. In fact, you can have me for life if you choose. Will you give me your hand in marriage, my precious Skye?"

She peered up at him. "You truly love me?"

"Truly."

Raw emotion flooded her at the unguarded expression in his eyes. "Of *course* I will marry you. *Gladly* . . ."

Pushing away from the wall, Skye launched herself at Hawk and threw her arms around his neck, catching him off guard and sending him stumbling backward. Laughing in delight, she began pressing enthusiastic kisses over his mouth and face.

When he righted his balance, Hawk returned her ardor, capturing her lips in a totally satisfying manner. When he finally drew back, Skye felt dazed and joyous.

"I gather this means you love me also," Hawk murmured.

"Certainly I love you. There has never been any question. I have been in love with you since I was thirteen years old."

"I am supremely honored, sweetheart. However . . ." Reaching up, he unwound her arms. "We need to discuss wedding plans—in fact, I have a special license burning a hole in my coat pocket. But as loath as I am to postpone this delightful episode, I must deal with Farnwell first."

Skye gave a small sigh of frustration but agreed that the baron took precedence. After his odious actions, he couldn't go unpunished.

She willingly accompanied Hawk to the kitchens, where they found Farnwell sitting slumped on a bench in the servant's dining room, staring at the floor, looking despondent and subdued.

"Pray excuse me a moment," Hawk said to Skye.

Exhibiting a cool, calculated rage, he crossed the room in three strides, grabbed the baron by his coat lapels and hauled him upright, then whirled him around and let loose a punch to his stomach, then jaw.

In quick succession, Farnwell gave a yelp of fright and a grunt of pain, followed by a startled cry as he went flying. He landed heavily on his backside, where he curled into a ball and lay groaning with the wind knocked out of him.

To Skye's mind, it was Hawk's second wholly satisfying gesture in a matter of minutes.

"I warned you once, Farnwell," Hawk ground out, flexing his fist as he moved to stand over the wheezing nobleman.

Still struggling to regain his breath, Farnwell started whimpering and covered his head with his arms, as if fearing another brutal blow.

Hawk gave a growl of disgust. "I should have done that the last time. Only a sniveling coward uses force against weaker beings. But since violence seems to be the only method of persuasion you understand, let me make myself clear. If I hear of you raising a hand to a woman again, I won't just knock your teeth down your throat, you won't live to see another dawn."

Stark silence followed his declaration, except for the baron's mewling. Skye looked around her and found that an audience had crowded into the dining room, watching with varying degrees of satisfaction.

The servants were not overly shocked, considering the destruction that Farnwell had wrought. Not surprisingly, Isabella, Cornelius, and Rachel all looked as if they wholly approved of Hawk's retribution. Rachel particularly. After abandoning her daughter all those years ago, she had been prepared to defend Daphne to the death during the fire, like a mother tiger with her cub. Even Daphne, who was Edgar's closest family, appeared supportive.

"Do you comprehend me, Farnwell?" Hawk barked.

The baron cringed and nodded rather frantically.

Noting the audience, Hawk dismissed the servants, who backed away obediently and shut the door behind themselves.

"We need to settle this issue once and for all," Hawk added, beckoning the other vested observers further into the room.

Daphne, Rachel, Cornelius, Isabella, and Skye gathered around the baron. Skye fully agreed with Hawk. Matters had finally come to a head, and they needed a long-overdue discussion of Farnwell's violence and the disposition of his future relationship with Rachel.

Farnwell was not as eager, obviously.

Seeing her brother cowering on the floor, Daphne knelt beside him and put a gentle hand on his arm to help him up.

Farnwell sniffled and sat up gingerly, then winced at his split lower lip. "Oww! I am bleeding like a stuck pig."

"You know you deserve much worse, Edgar," Daphne said unsympathetically. "You will be fortunate if Lord Hawkhurst doesn't bring criminal charges against you for arson or even attempted murder."

"I told you a dozen times that I am dreadfully sorry."

"That is not good enough. You owe his lordship an abject apology for nearly destroying his home."

"Very well." Wiping the blood from his mouth with his sleeve, Farnwell sent a contrite glance toward Hawk. "I hope you will accept my deepest apologies, my lord. Naturally I will pay for damages incurred to your home."

"Yes, you will," Hawk said curtly. "But I am more interested in how you intend to redeem yourself with your sister."

"I realize I have a temper—" he began.

"A temper?" Cornelius burst out. "You nearly *killed* her."

Skye had never seen her uncle so livid, but Farnwell seemed truly remorseful as he pleaded with his sister. "I pray you will forgive me, Daphne. I vow I never, ever meant to hurt you."

"I suppose I believe you," she replied, relenting a little. "But actions count more than intentions."

"You know I have never done anything so heinous before."

"I also know you had a terrible example in our father. But there is no excuse for your brutality."

Farnwell grimaced. "What must I do to earn your forgiveness?"

Daphne needed no time to consider. "A little groveling toward Mrs. Donnelly would be appropriate. You should tell her how sorry you are for threatening her for refusing to leave the country."

"Yes, of course." Farnwell earnestly repeated his apology to Rachel.

"And you must swear to leave her alone and let her live her own life here in England without fear of reprisal."

"Yes, I swear it."

"Lord Farnwell," Rachel said slowly, "I have a better idea. You will give Daphne half of your fortune."

Farnwell stared at Rachel while Daphne raised an eyebrow. "I don't need his fortune."

"Perhaps not," Rachel replied, "but you deserve it. It is only fair that he be made to share his wealth with you, since none of it belongs to him."

"I would be happy if he will give up control of the settlement my father made me."

Rachel pressed her lips together grimly. "That won't do, my dear. There should be severe consequences for his violence. I was prepared to let Lord Farnwell keep his title and wealth, but I suspect draining his purse will hurt him more than any punishing blows."

Daphne looked thoughtful. "It would be good to be independent and make my own financial decisions, without fear of being at the mercy of my brother's whims."

"I agree, you should have complete independence also." Rachel gazed coolly down at the baron. "I promise you, I will never contest your legitimacy, Lord Farnwell. In exchange for my silence, you will provide amply for Daphne. Allowing you to keep half is rather magnanimous. Without my restraint, you would be disgraced and penniless."

Farnwell again snuck a glance at Hawk and apparently thought better of protesting Rachel's harsh terms. "Yes, whatever you wish."

Skye judged that Rachel was indeed being profoundly generous, considering that she could strip him of his entire inheritance and his very legitimacy. She doubted that Farnwell would go back on his word, knowing that Hawk would enforce their agreement. She also doubted he would be so foolish as to threaten Rachel or Daphne ever again under pain of incurring Hawk's wrath.

With the terms decided, Hawk looked impatient, and Skye felt even more so. She badly wanted to return to the question of his marriage proposal, but for that they needed privacy.

Glancing at Hawk, she cleared her throat. "Now that this matter is settled, may I have a word with you, Hawk?"

Isabella caught the look they exchanged and sensed that something was in the air. "Yes, go, Skye, Hawk. We will supervise cleaning up the horrendous mess. We can cart away the burnt draperies and carpets tonight to diminish the stench. As soon as the rain stops, we can begin airing out the entire house. And tomorrow we will see what can be salvaged."

Skye gave her aunt a grateful look. Picking up a lamp, she preceded Hawk from the servants' dining room through the kitchens. The rain was still coming down in torrents as, careful of her bandaged hands, he took her elbow to guide her upstairs.

To her surprise, he chose the newly renovated master bedroom suite in the family wing. Oddly, the bedchamber looked inhabited. "I didn't realize you had moved into this wing," she observed.

"I began sleeping here last week before I left for London, to get away from the temptation you presented."

The moment she set down the lamp, he pulled her into his arms. "I need to hold you," he murmured into her hair.

Skye was wholly content to oblige. His warmth and hardness were *exactly* the comfort she needed.

They remained that way for some time, her breasts nestled against his chest, her thighs brushing his. When eventually he kissed her again, heat shimmered through her. She felt his fingertips brush her face, her throat, and she pressed closer, wanting the feel of his bare flesh, needing to touch him. Yearning swept over her, suffusing her body with liquid heaviness. . . .

Yet Hawk, evidently deciding it perhaps was not the time or place for passion, drew back.

"I suppose we cannot make love now," she said with a wistful sigh.

Hawk brought the back of his hand softly down the side of her face. "Regrettably we will have to wait. I want complete privacy when I make love to you."

Skye didn't want to wait at all, yet this moment was hardly romantic, what with her burns and grime. The smell of smoke was less prominent here but still pervasive.

Hawk must have come to a similar conclusion, for he led her to the washstand, where he proceeded to gently clean her face of the soot smudges from the fire. "Aren't you fortunate? I am serving as your lady's maid since you cannot manage on your own, given your bandages."

Skye laughed. "I am in great need of a bath also. But Aunt Bella will help me wash my hair and change my gown."

"Later. I'm not letting you out of my sight just now."

Skye felt the same way. "I must look a fright."

He curved his palm against her cheek. "Even scorched and bedraggled, you have never looked more beautiful to me. You are radiant."

"If I am radiant, it is because you said you love me."

"I do, very much."

"And you truly want to marry me?"

"Truly. Tomorrow if I can arrange it."

"So soon?"

"I see no reason to wait, do you?"

Skye couldn't help a small smile. The minor fact that his house had nearly burned down was perhaps a good reason to delay, but she was reassured by his eagerness. "We ought to discuss the particulars, shouldn't we?"

"Yes, I intend to."

When he had washed his own face and hands, he led her to the adjacent sitting room, where he drew her down to sit beside him on the chintz sofa, blatantly disregarding how their smoke-stained clothes might soil the fabric.

Skye didn't care, either, not when Hawk's arm went around her shoulders and tucked her against his body, her head on his shoulder. It was darker here, with only light from the lamp in the bedchamber streaming through the door, and rather chilly with no fire in the hearth, but still strangely cozy with the steady drum of the rain on the windows and the steadier beat of Hawk's heart beneath her cheek.

When she felt a shudder run through him, she suspected he was thinking about the events just past. She raised the back of his hand to her lips and tenderly kissed his burn scars.

"I am sorry you had to relive that terrible time," Skye said quietly.

"As am I." His arm tightened about her. "The terror I felt . . ."

"I felt the same terror." She could hear emotion vibrating in her own voice. "I was never so glad to see anyone in my life."

"Because you needed help battling the fire?"

"No, not only that."

"You were managing well enough on your own. You didn't need me."

Skye gave a muffled laugh at that untruth. "Of course I needed you. I will always need you—rather desperately."

He kissed the crown of her head. "I am an incredibly lucky man."

She lifted her head from his shoulder. The dim lamplight flared against Hawk's molded cheekbones and provided enough illumination for her to see that his beautiful face held unmistakable tenderness.

"Tell me again, Hawk."

He seemed to realize what she wanted to hear. "I love you dearly, my darling Skye. And I want us to be married as soon as possible."

She hesitated. "Would you mind very much if we held the ceremony at Tallis Court?"

"Your home? The Traherne family seat?"

"Yes. I would like all my family in attendance and our vicar to marry us."

When Hawk drew her close again, Skye expounded. "It would mean delaying for a sennight or more, but it may take me that long to locate my brother. Quinn claims his attention is fixed on his latest invention to revolutionize sailing ships, but I suspect he has kept away to avoid becoming Kate's next matchmaking victim. The wedding of his only sister should draw him out of hiding, though."

She heard the smile in Hawk's voice. "Your brother is in hiding to avoid your cousin's matchmaking?"

"I suspect so. Quinn thinks her legendary lovers theory is ludicrous and wants no part of it. I believe his man of business knows where he is, but I need time to run him to ground—and to send out the other invitations. Moreover, the guest list will be rather long. Despite the refurbishments that have been completed, there likely won't be enough habitable bedchambers to accommodate them all here."

"How many guests do you have in mind?"

"Well, Kate, of course, and Ash and Jack and their new wives. You know both my cousins, but you haven't met Maura and Sophie. And then there is Aunt Bella and Uncle Cornelius and Rachel and Daphne. . . ."

"I see your point," Hawk said wryly. "As long as we are having a large wedding then, I would like Sir Gawain and several of my other colleagues and close friends to be present—at least the ones who are already here in England."

"Of course. Fortunately Tallis Court is large enough to house an army of guests." Skye's brow furrowed as a thought occurred to her. "In fact, after we are wed, we could live temporarily at Tallis Court while repairs are being completed here at Hawkhurst Castle. I am certain Quinn won't mind. He hasn't resided at the Court for months."

"I have another idea. What would you say to visiting Cyrene for a wedding trip?"

Skye did not have to think twice. "I would love that. I could see where you have lived for the last ten years."

"A journey there would also allow me to resolve the status of my breeding stables. I want to bring some of my prize stock to England."

"What do you mean?" she asked, puzzled.

"I plan to return to England to live permanently."

Easing away, Skye gazed up at Hawk in consternation. "But you cannot give up the Guardians. They mean too much to you."

"I needn't give them up completely. I can continue my work here in England. This is my home, where I want to be. I am ready to move on with my life . . . with you, my love."

It was Skye's turn to shudder. "Thank God you didn't go through with wooing Sir Gawain's niece."

"I agree."

"You should be thanking me as well. I saved you from making a terrible mistake."

"I am willing to concede that you changed my fate much for the better. You made me believe in love again."

Skye widened her eyes innocently. "Did I? How very inspired of me."

He chuckled softly. "Indeed. I don't want to live without your love."

"You have my love, Hawk. Always and forever."

She clasped his hand and drew it against her breast where her heart thrummed with love for him. This was the feeling she had always dreamed of: caring, yearning, needing until it hurt.

The hurt was physical as well. She wanted badly to consummate their love, to show Hawk how very much he meant to her. Her need to feel possessed was as fierce as her longing to possess him. When heat flared in his gaze, she knew he felt the same longing.

She was willing to wait, though, Skye decided as she raised her mouth for another long, tremendously satisfying kiss. Very soon she would be his bride, and nothing would ever part them again.

Epilogue

Kent, England, November 1816

Hawk's impatience with delaying the marriage ceremony grew when Lord Cornelius proposed holding a double wedding at Tallis Court. But between preparing for both weddings, procuring another special license from London, repairing damages from the latest fire, advancing current renovations to Hawkhurst Castle, and planning for the voyage to Cyrene, the next week flew by.

Hawk felt content with his decision to make his home in England with Skye. Although the Isle of Cyrene was a Mediterranean paradise, and the island and its people had provided him a place of refuge, he had exiled himself long enough.

As for the Guardians of the Sword, he was still obliged to keep their secrets. However, once he and Skye were wed, he could reveal the legend of the order's creation and show her the magnificent sword that had once belonged to England's most valiant king.

Exactly one week later, Hawk and Skye traveled to Tallis Court, where most of her family, the second bridal party, and other guests would soon join them. There had been no word from Traherne, although Skye professed faith that her brother would arrive in time for the wedding ceremonies.

Skye was gladly welcomed home by the large staff at the Court, where she had been mistress since the death of her parents at the tender age of ten. Clearly her servants adored her and were excited for her marriage. But Hawk would have preferred them much less underfoot and effusive in their eagerness to please.

That night he dined with Skye and then spent the evening discussing final plans for the wedding. Hawk bided his time, watching her for the sheer joy of it, aware of the warm affection in his chest and the lightness in his heart. But once the household retired to bed, he came to her bedchamber. He had almost lost her, and he would not wait one minute more to claim her as his wife, even if the actual ceremony wouldn't occur for two more days.

Seized by the need to hold her, which occurred with great regularity of late, Hawk wrapped his arms tightly about Skye.

"Privacy at last," she murmured with a pleasurable sigh.

They undressed each other with barely restrained haste, craving the feel of skin to skin. When they were both nude, Hawk's hands rose to caress her bare breasts, arousing her easily, while she stroked his chest and loins. Her bandages had come off recently, with no lasting effects or scars, so she was able to reciprocate in inflaming his passion.

After a time, he led her to the bed and followed her down. Aching hunger drove his fingers deeper into her pale tresses as he devoured her lush mouth. When he parted her thighs, she was wet and eager for him. His own body hard with need, Hawk sank inside her, groaning as her tight sheath clenched around his cock.

Soon her hips were rising and falling in a timeless rhythm, matching his urgency. A heartbeat later, when Skye shuddered and cried out in ecstasy, the fierce need of his body engulfed him. Hawk poured himself into her in a violent climax, a confirmation of love and life.

In the aftermath, he felt shaken as he lay there, absorbing the healing warmth of her body against his. He'd fully believed he would never again love, but thankfully he was wrong. His first love had been youthful and ideal, but this felt deeper, more intense. His love for Skye had been forged in fire, quite literally.

He would forever be grateful to her. Skye had helped free him from his dark past and banished the great emptiness inside him. Because of her, he now had the fortitude to face the nuptial bed at Hawkhurst Castle that he had once shared with Elizabeth. Sorrow and loss would always be a part of him, of course, but the pain and grief were nearly gone because he had Skye.

He had no thought of sorrow when he shifted his head on the pillow to gaze down at her. In the flush following lovemaking, she looked more radiant than ever. The drowsy, contented smile curving her mouth warmed him, as did the life pulsing through her.

She was as life-giving and vital as sunlight, Hawk

thought. Indeed, he felt as though the sun was shining on his face for the first time in many years.

Easing closer, he kissed her softly, his lips lingering. "This is forever," he murmured, a promise, a vow.

Her eyelids fluttering open, Skye regarded him steadily. The love shining in her eyes was so fierce, it took his breath away, as did her quiet words:

"I will cherish you all the days of my life," Skye vowed in return.

Naturally, he had to respond. Gathering her to him, he tilted her face up for an ardent kiss—the beginning of a magical night together.

He left her bed early the following morning, before the servants rose. Skye dozed and when she woke, she lay there pinching herself. She had realized her dream of true love, and the knowledge filled her with joy. Hawk had let her into his heart, *finally,* and shown her with his body how much she meant to him.

More crucially, they had made a pact to treasure each moment of their time left together on earth. They both knew how precious and fleeting life could be, how priceless love was, and that they couldn't live life in fear, afraid to lose loved ones, afraid to love.

The contingent from Hawkhurst Castle—Uncle Cornelius, Rachel, Daphne, and Aunt Isabella—arrived late that morning as expected. Quite unexpectedly, however, Daphne had guessed the secret of her parentage.

"After seeing Lord Cornelius's tenderness for my mother," she confessed to Skye, "their love for each other seemed too powerful to have occurred in so short a time, and they confirmed my suspicions. To be honest, I am quite glad. Strangely, I never felt wholly part of our family, nor could I explain my differences with Edgar, both physical and otherwise. As for the man I always believed to be my father . . . given his cruelty, my having no real blood relation to William Farnwell is actually a relief. I am elated that I now have a new, loving family whom I never would have discovered without you."

Skye was elated as well. She had hoped Cornelius and Daphne could come to know each other as father and daughter, and now they would have the chance.

Cornelius was eager to provide for Daphne financially and had offered to fund her research and travels to investigate new species of roses, but if Edgar kept his word, she would soon have her own significant funds to use as she chose.

Without a doubt, Daphne had Wilde blood running in her veins. Her determined independence, her lively charm and intelligence, her brazen disregard for the limits society placed on females in particular, and her scholarly bent and interest in exploration, were all indicative of how well she would fit into their clan.

Kate said as much when she arrived that afternoon, accompanied by Ash and Maura and Jack and Sophia.

Skye was most grateful when her family heartily welcomed her soon-to-be husband into their ranks. Although Kate had reassured both Ash and Jack about Hawk, Skye had a nervous moment when her male cousins interrogated him at length, yet she couldn't fault them. The Wildes were overly protective but fiercely loyal and loving, just as families should be. And apparently they were convinced of Hawk's love for her by the time the other wedding guests arrived at the Court.

Skye truly enjoyed meeting some of Hawk's closest friends and colleagues. The elderly Sir Gawain Olwen seemed world-weary—understandable given the weight he had carried on his shoulders for so many years as leader of the Guardians—and deserving of retirement, as well as profoundly relieved that Hawk would not be giving up the Guardians for good.

Sir Alex Ryder and his beautiful wife, Eve, were fascinating additions to the guest list, as were Christopher, Viscount Thorne, and his stunning wife, Diana. Daphne and Diana were both skilled artists, so immediately had common interests to discuss.

When the company dined that evening, what began as a formal gathering soon became much lighter with lively conversation and laughter. She and Hawk planned to sail for Cyrene in a week, so Skye was pleased to spend several hours after dinner learning about what she could expect from the island, and hearing tales from Isabella about some of their adventures.

By late that evening, Skye grew concerned Quinn might not arrive in time to give her away at her wedding. And when she woke the following morning, she considered postponing the ceremony but decided against disappointing the others.

After breakfast, Kate and Aunt Bella helped her dress in a rose-colored silk gown, covered by a cream brocade pelisse, since the morning was chilly, despite a watery sun. The wedding parties met at the chapel toward the rear of the estate, where the vicar awaited inside.

They were about to enter the building when the

morning quiet was broken by the sound of galloping hooves. Pausing, Skye soon recognized the horseman as her brother. Gladness filled her heart as Quinn leaped down with an athleticism she was certain that even Hawk admired.

Quinn looked as if he had ridden through the night to reach the Court in time, Skye decided as she hurried down the chapel steps to meet him. His fair hair—a darker gold than hers—was tousled beneath his tall beaver hat, and his jaw was stubbled with several days' growth. Yet even unkempt, he had an unmistakable aristocratic elegance. Quinn was also far taller and much more muscular than she, and his vivid blue eyes were a deeper shade. Even as his sister, she realized his appeal. That masculine allure, combined with his daredevil aura and extreme cynicism, made him an irresistible challenge to the opposite sex. Despite the scandals that seemed to mark his amorous affairs, Quinn was the target of countless marriage-minded females.

Skye embraced him ardently even as she scolded him. "Where the devil have you been, Quinn? I almost despaired of your arriving in time."

"How was I to know you would go and get yourself engaged?"

Skye noted that he hadn't specifically answered her question, but just now, where he had been hiding himself wasn't important, for Hawk had followed her down the steps.

"I believe you know my wayward brother," she said when Hawk reached them.

The two noblemen clasped hands like old acquaintances, but Quinn's piercing gaze was highly judgmental as he scrutinized Hawk.

"You needn't worry," Skye told her brother. "Jack and Ash have already interrogated Hawk thoroughly and approved my choice of husbands."

"I am under no allusions that you would have heeded my opinion had I disapproved," Quinn retorted dryly.

"Certainly I would have heeded your opinion," she protested. "I would simply have twisted your arm to convince you otherwise."

Quinn chuckled. "Vintage Skye. In fact, I understand *you* were the one who pursued *him*, minx."

"Who told you that?"

"I have my sources. But I could have guessed your scheme on my own. I know you too well."

Hawk slipped an arm around her waist. "I never stood a chance once she set her sights on me." When he locked gazes with her, she could see the smile deep in his gray eyes.

Smiling in return, Skye turned her attention back to her brother. "Why did you disappear?"

"You know very well why. When I last saw you in September, you and Kate were set on finding me a bride. Remaining within reach would have been lethal to my bachelorhood."

Katharine joined them in time to hear his complaint. She gave Quinn a quick hug, then tucked her arm in his. "This is three cousins down, plus our uncle. Only two more to go—you and I, Quinn."

His grimace held exasperation and disgust. "You should work on your own tale and leave me be. I am happy as I am."

As the most romantic Wilde cousin, Kate was not

about to abandon her search for true love for either Quinn or herself. Kate was severely disappointed that her own legendary lovers tale wasn't evident yet, but she planned for Quinn's romance, Skye knew, to follow the Greek myth of Pygmalion, a sculptor who had fallen so deeply in love with the statue he'd created, the gods took pity on him and brought her to life.

"I have the perfect bride picked out for you, Quinn," Kate informed him. "You need a young lady of birth and breeding but malleable enough that you can mold her to your exact specifications."

He gave a mock shudder. "God forbid."

"I have won Ash and Jack over to my theory. With your scientific bent, you ought to be able to see the proof right under your nose."

Skye chimed in to tease her brother. "Tallis Court will need a mistress now that I am leaving."

"I will muddle through without a wife somehow."

Skye suddenly realized the lateness of the hour. "There will be time to argue about your bride later. You are delaying my wedding."

"How wicked of me."

"Perhaps you should go inside and greet Aunt Bella? I will be there in a moment."

When he and Kate obliged, Skye slid her arms around Hawk's neck. "Are you sorry that I pursued you?"

"On the contrary. I am immensely thankful for your stubbornness."

Skye smiled victoriously. "I almost feel sorry for Miss Olwen."

"And why is that?"

"She won't have you for her husband. I am claiming you forever. But I am certain Kate could find her an eligible suitor—and Daphne as well, for that matter."

Hawk shook his head. "I can see why your brother made himself scarce."

"He still believes he can withstand our combined efforts, but we are plotting a new strategy for Quinn, and Kate is a matchmaker extraordinaire. She helped me find you."

"But Isabella deserves more credit for bringing us together."

"Not all the credit," Skye objected. "Aunt Bella might have advised me about techniques for enticing a man, but it was no small feat, seducing a beast, let me tell you. Although you *are* changing. You haven't growled at me in quite some time."

A lazy, heated smile gleamed in his gray eyes. "You are still a beauty."

Skye met his gaze and laughed. "Beauty or not, I am confident I am your ideal match."

"You are my match in every way. I can't imagine living without you now."

Bending his head, Hawk gave her a tender, reassuring kiss that made her heart swell. "You taste like hope, a new beginning. . . ." he murmured against her lips.

"That is a beautiful thought, my love."

"Shall we proceed with the wedding ceremony?"

Skye felt filled with life and joy as he took her arm. "Most definitely."

Of one accord, they turned toward the chapel. Upon entering, they moved together down the narrow aisle to stand at the altar before the vicar, with

Rachel and Cornelius on one side, Skye and Hawk on the other.

The elderly vicar looked out benevolently over the company, then cleared his throat and began: "Dearly beloved, we are gathered together here . . ."

Read on for a look at Nicole Jordan's next
book in her sizzling Legendary Lovers series

THE ART OF TAMING A RAKE

Chapter One

London, April 1817

"*Take care, Venetia.* Traherne has a magical touch with the fair sex. If you tangle with him, even *you* may find him impossible to resist."

Her friend's recent warning echoing in her head, Venetia Stratham watched the tableaux across the crowded gaming room. She had run her quarry to ground at London's most notorious sin club and found him surrounded by fawning beauties.

Well, perhaps not *surrounded*, Venetia corrected herself in a fit of honesty. But he certainly wasn't lacking for adoring female companionship just now.

Quinn Wilde, Earl of Traherne, was reportedly a splendid lover, and Venetia had no doubt the gossip was true. In all likelihood, his expertise in boudoirs and bedchambers was a chief reason women vied for his favor and tripped over themselves to earn his patronage. Whatever his sensual attributes, though, he was indisputably a rake of the first order. She had come here tonight seeking proof of his transgressions to show her sister—and here it was, right before her eyes.

Beware of what you wish for. The cautionary adage came to mind, and oddly, her feeling of triumph was trumped by keen disappointment.

She had hoped she was wrong about Lord Traherne.

An inexplicable, exasperating reaction if she had ever felt one.

Traherne was lounging carelessly in his seat at the Faro table, but she had easily located him among the gamesters upon her arrival some twenty minutes ago. With the striking features and form of a Grecian sculpture—tall, sleek, muscular—he stood out in the company. She could not miss his aristocratic elegance either, or his gleaming fair hair—dark gold streaked with lighter threads of silver.

The two lightskirts hovering at his shoulder, showering him with attention, were also an identifying clue and put to rest any lingering questions Venetia might have had about his predilection for debauchery.

Her lips pressed in a frown of self-reproach. She should be extremely pleased to find the confirmation she'd sought. To think she had once held Lord Traherne in high esteem. In her defense, her admiration had developed before she'd known the kind of heartbreaker he was. Before she had lost her hopeless naïveté to another sinfully seductive nobleman.

For her, "Beware of blue-blooded Lotharios" was a more appropriate admonition than careful wishing. She had learned that particular lesson quite painfully.

And most definitely, she didn't want her younger sister falling prey to Traherne's spellbinding temptation.

Oh, his other vices such as gambling for high stakes did not overly concern her. With his enormous fortune, he could well afford to risk large sums on the turn of a card, especially since he regularly won. It was the carousing and womanizing that gravely troubled Venetia. Clearly Traherne was no better than her former betrothed, intent on only carnal pleasure, no matter who suffered hurt and heartbreak.

Just then another curvaceous Cyprian brought the earl a glass of port and remained to observe the play at his table. When the painted beauty draped herself over his arm, trailing suggestive fingers along the sleeve of his superbly tailored coat, Venetia stifled a sound of disgust in her throat.

Now Traherne had not two but *three* clinging demireps eager to serve his every need.

But then, women of all ages tended to tumble at his feet. She herself was not immune to his lethal charm, much to her dismay. His smile was captivating, piercing female hearts with deadly accuracy. And when those clever blue eyes glimmered with amusement . . . well, her pulse quickened each and every time, as if she had sprinted a great distance.

In fact, Traherne's entire family possessed the same formidable charm in extraordinary abundance. The five Wilde cousins of the current generation were the darlings of the ton—

Suddenly his lordship's blue gaze shifted in her direction to scan the company. Quickly Venetia adjusted her face mask and tried to blend into the throng of gamblers and *filles de joie*. She had attended a sin club once before, in Paris with her widowed friend Cleo, and this one was similarly genteel. The gaming room boasted a large gathering, as did the adjacent drawing room, where dancing and refreshments and a lavish buffet supper were offered for the guests' enjoyment. She could hear music and laughter and gay conversation drifting through the connecting doorway.

Except for the risqué apparel of the women present, this could have been an elite artist's salon—the sort of sophisticated assemblies she had frequented during her past two years of exile in France. Yet she ought not have come here tonight. If she was caught in this den of iniquity, it would only cement her scandalous reputation, which could further wound her family. But she had needed proof of Traherne's sins to show her sister just how dangerous he was to any gullible young lady's heart.

As if to prove her point, the earl glanced up at his adoring companion and smiled his brilliant smile. A pang of jealousy hit Venetia with astonishing force.

How absurd—how *infuriating*—to be so foolishly affected, even if her reaction could be blamed on elementary human nature. She well knew that masculine breeding, charm, virility, and stunning good looks were potent weapons against the fair sex. In her case, Traherne's keen wit and sharp mind had impressed her far more.

It was a grave pity that he was such a rake, squandering his exceptional intelligence and talents on dissipation and libertine ways. Ordinarily she wouldn't care how many women he seduced or how many mistresses he kept, but her sister was very dear to her,

even if they *had* been estranged these past two inter-
minable years.

And if *she* could not conquer her attraction to him,
what chance did her highly susceptible sister have?

Despite the rumors about his budding courtship of
the younger Miss Stratham, Venetia could not credit
that a nobleman of his stamp actually wished to wed
a green girl barely out of the schoolroom. But whether
he had marriage—or worse, seduction—in mind, it
could not end well for starry-eyed Ophelia.

As if sensing Venetia's scrutiny, Traherne refocused
his penetrating gaze through the crowd to stare directly at her. The spark that flared in his vivid eyes at
her immodest attire made her breath catch. She had
borrowed her evening gown of scarlet velvet from
Cleo in order to fit in with the other ladies of the evening. The décolletage dipped much lower than her
usual wont, leaving her shoulders and the upper
swells of her breasts bare.

The shock of Traherne's admiring masculine pe-
rusal caught her off guard. Instinctively, Venetia took
a step backward, swearing to herself. A mere glance
should not have impacted her so powerfully, no matter how lascivious. He was simply being a *man,* after
all.

She was also concerned that he would see through
her disguise. Lord Traherne had witnessed firsthand
the most humiliating, painful event of her life. Not
only witnessed but actively *participated.* She was to
blame for her own downfall, of course. But his actions had triggered the rash, prideful decision that
had changed her fate forever. Moreover, she did not
wish to give him the satisfaction of seeing her at such

a disadvantage—forced to sneak around clandestinely, an outcast of decent society.

"May-yi have the honor of a dansh, my lovely?"

Venetia gave a start at the interruption. With her thoughts so fixed on the earl's sinful character, she'd been unaware of another gentleman approaching, this one much shorter and somewhat younger than Traherne, with darker hair and more flamboyant garb. The dandy's slurred words suggested that he was already half foxed.

Venetia hid a grimace at the unexpected annoyance. She needed no complications to divert her attention from her goal of saving her sister from the Earl of Traherne's romantic pursuit.

With effort, she pasted an apologetic smile on her lips before answering sweetly. "Thank you, kind sir, but I will not be staying much longer this evening."

Rather than accept her rebuff, the drunkard slipped an arm around her shoulders and drew her close.

With an inward sigh, Venetia set about the task of extricating herself from this unwanted predicament. She was not afraid of being assaulted in so public an arena. Even a notorious hell had rules of accepted behavior to follow, certainly one that catered to high-class clientele such as this. Any number of nobles and gentlemen of the ton were present tonight, as well as a few wellborn ladies attending incognito.

But this was simply one more damning demonstration that men were often led by their lustful urges rather than honor or common sense, and she was growing exceedingly weary of having to deal with their peccadilloes.

* * *

Distracted from his fruitless Faro game, Quinn narrowed his gaze on the masked beauty across the room. She had endeavored to remain unobtrusive, but she was far too noticeable.

Puzzled and curious as to why she was watching him so intently, Quinn absently played another card. Her familiarity nagged at him. She wore a demi-mask and feathered silk turban to hide her hair, but her feminine attractions were quite apparent. The graceful carriage, the ripe breasts, the lush mouth—

Quinn abruptly gave a mental start as his gaze shot back to her. She was indeed familiar. Miss Venetia Stratham.

What the devil?

He would have recognized her anywhere. She was the kind of woman a man never forgot. Not least because she had been engaged to marry a friend and peer.

She was one of the loveliest women he had ever encountered—luminous dark eyes, rich brown hair, creamy skin, with the most kissable mouth imaginable. Pure temptation even to a man of his jaded appetites. More than once he had fantasized about kissing those luscious lips. In truth, he'd wanted her from the first moment they met some four years ago during her coming-out Season. But he had carefully controlled his lust. Miss Stratham was strictly forbidden to him. A gentleman did not poach, particularly from a friend.

Quinn was taken aback—no, startled—to see her here at an elite gaming hell known more for its sexual sport than high stakes gambling. She was still every inch an elegant lady, despite being gowned in brazen red velvet that complemented her shapely figure and almost regal bearing.

His attention now riveted, Quinn watched as an obviously inebriated gamester tightened an arm around her bare shoulders.

The sight troubled him enough that he barely heard the silken voice whispering in his ear:

"How else may I serve you, m'lord?"

"I want for nothing, thank you," Quinn replied, dismissing the high-flyer at his side with much less finesse than usual.

His mind was fixed solely on Venetia Stratham. Had she fallen so low that she was now offering her body for sale? The possibility fiercely disturbed him. Remorse sent his thoughts winging back two years ago, when he'd last laid eyes on her.

She had shocked the ton by jilting her noble fiancé on the church steps, creating a spectacle by boxing his ears and aborting the wedding ceremony in front of over two hundred guests. She'd then flung Quinn a scathing glance as she passed him on the way to her waiting carriage, no doubt despising him for the role he'd played in her bridegroom's dissipation.

The very public denunciation of her betrothed had been the talk of London for weeks, until another titillating scandal had come along to supplant hers.

Quinn badly wanted to know what the devil she was doing in a high-class brothel. And why was she observing him so surreptitiously?

Her unexpected presence was enough to distract him from the task he'd set for himself—gaining leverage over his current opponent, Edmund Lisle, by winning overwhelmingly at Faro tonight.

And watching a young fop proposition her was downright unsettling.

Quinn voiced an oath under his breath as he recognized the young blade. Lord Knowlsbridge was in his cups, swaying as he embraced her. Evidently Miss Stratham was not welcoming his attention, though, for she had pasted a pained smile on her lips while trying to extricate herself from his grasp.

She was ill-equipped to fend off a drunken lecher, Quinn suspected, his protective instincts keenly aroused. And seeing the young lord attempt to kiss her was the last straw.

Experiencing a quiet swell of fury, Quinn tossed down his cards and surged to his feet, scattering the lightskirts surrounding him and surprising the pretty Faro dealer. It was poor-mannered of him to treat the pleasure club's attendants so thoughtlessly, and supremely bad form to leave a game in mid-play. But even had his concentration not been shattered, he couldn't sit still while a soused coxcomb pawed at Venetia Stratham.

With a faint smile of apology to the others, Quinn addressed his opponent. "Pray forgive me, Lisle, but I willingly concede. We must resume our game at some other time."

He could feel Lisle shooting daggers in his back as he walked away. There was no love lost between them, with their contentious past involving a jealous mistress, and now the question of how Lisle had come to possess a distinctive piece of jewelry that might once have belonged to Quinn's French mother. But solving the mystery of a missing family heirloom would have to wait.

As he weaved his way through the crowd, intent on rescuing Miss Stratham, he saw Knowlsbridge endeavoring to remove her mask while she strove to keep it in place. Quinn doubted she wished her identity revealed, for even if she had joined the muslin company—willingly or not—her family's reputation could still suffer from a fresh scandal. And with a younger sister of prime marriageable age, Venetia would be wise to keep her affairs discreet.

He had nearly reached her when, despite her predicament, she saw him approaching and visibly flinched, whether in surprise or dismay, he couldn't tell. For an instant, she started to retreat, then stood her ground, her chin raised, as if bracing herself for the encounter.

"There you are, my dove," Quinn said easily as he came up to her. "I have been eagerly awaiting your company."

When Knowlsbridge took advantage of her temporary distraction to cup her breast, another sharp wave of anger flooded Quinn.

"I'll thank you to leave the lady alone," he warned an instant before she managed to drive the point of her elbow into the sot's flaccid belly and make him grunt.

"Sheesh not . . . a lady," the young lord complained, wheezing for breath.

"Regardless, she is mine."

Quinn slipped an arm around Miss Stratham's waist and drew her close. "I have missed you, darling. Have you missed me?"

She possessed huge, lustrous dark eyes, which were mostly hidden behind her mask, but even obscured, her gaze held startlement. She was clearly wondering what he was about.

But Quinn knew the jackanapes beside her understood the situation quite well: A more powerful male marking his territory, showing possession.

"Are you not pleased to see me, love?" he prodded Venetia.

"I . . . why, yes, my lord," she stammered, reminding Quinn how pleasantly musical her voice was.

"Perhaps you should show me how much."

Bending his head, he captured that full, kissable mouth the way he had longed to do for years.

She gave a faint gasp at the contact and stiffened in response. Quinn could feel shock ripple through the graceful curves of her body, while his own breath quickened at the enticing taste of her.

Her lips were just as delectable as he'd imagined, he thought, relishing their softness. Lush, resilient, the texture of silk, ripe and warm as her body.

When she tensed further, he increased the pressure, parting the seam of her mouth and slipping his tongue inside to tangle with hers.

Her lips trembled under his. Encouraged, he changed the slant of his head and took her mouth more thoroughly, coaxing her to participate in her own seduction, parting her lips wider with his thrusting tongue.

When finally she opened completely to him, Quinn felt the unexpected impact like a jolt of lightning: Heat, pleasure, excitement, sheer satisfaction.

Her taste was keenly arousing and infinitely sweet. Sliding one hand behind her nape, he pulled her closer so that he could drink more deeply of her.

The crowd fell away so there was only the two of

them, man and woman, enjoying an embrace powerful enough to shake them both. Her scent wrapped
around him as he savored her mouth.

It was a slow, devastating, spellbinding kiss. When
her entire body softened instinctively against him,
her surrender only increased his craving for her. Painfully aroused now, Quinn felt a primal male urge to
take what he wanted—and an even stronger need to
heighten her desire.

When his tongue delved insistently inside her mouth,
exploring, she gave a helpless moan and leaned into
him. The sharp pleasure of it stabbed him in his loins,
a pleasure that only heightened when her hand crept
up to twine about his neck.

He felt another measure of triumph when her
tongue met his willingly this time. Raising a hand to
cradle her jaw, he angled his head even further, the
better to devour her mouth.

Her breath faded to a sigh as their tongues mated.
The tantalizing promise of her response stirred a searing need in Quinn. It had been a very long while since
he'd experienced such a sizzling sexual attraction.
Perhaps never.

Stark lust turned him hard and renewed his fierce
feeling of possessiveness. The sensation rocked him—
and Venetia, too, he had no doubt, aware of her
shiver of aroused excitement.

When at last he broke off, he kept hold of her waist
to support her as she swayed weakly.

Her eyes fluttering open, she raised her face to stare
at him. Despite her demi-mask, he could see those
lovely eyes were dazed. Her hand rose to touch her
lips in wonder, as if feeling the burn there.

She was profoundly shaken, he knew. He felt her trembling as she returned his gaze speechlessly.

Quinn was at a loss for words himself. He couldn't recall ever feeling such tangible desire . . . .

The sound of nearby laughter served to break the spell.

Venetia visibly shook herself and pressed her hands against his chest. Reluctantly, Quinn released her and cleared his throat, quelling the urge to adjust his satin breeches in public. He couldn't remember a time when he'd lost control of his urges so blatantly.

When he heard another nearby sound, this one an admiring male scoff, he realized the cawker was watching with resentment and envy.

"You have all the damnable luck, Traherne," the young lord mumbled almost soberly. "'Tis a pity."

"Pray take yourself off, Knowlsbridge," Quinn ordered in dismissal. "You can see we are occupied."

His voice was husky with passion but held enough authority that the drunken gamester did as he was bid and ambled away, leaving Quinn in sole possession of Venetia.

She was still flustered from his kiss, yet she recovered her tongue readily enough. "I should have expected you to act so outrageously, Lord Traherne."

He raised an eyebrow. "What was so outrageous?"

"You did not have to kiss me."

"It seemed the easiest way to prevent that fribble from pulling off your mask. I presumed you would not want to be recognized. Was I wrong?"

"No," she answered reluctantly. "But I am not your *dove*."

"You and I know that, but for his benefit, I needed to stake my claim to you."

When her mouth curved in frustration, Quinn quizzed her. "I thought you would be grateful to me for saving you."

"I did not require *saving*, my lord—"

Her voice had risen noticeably, and she cut off her exclamation upon realizing that they were the object of numerous curious pairs of eyes.

"Shall we take this discussion elsewhere, darling?" he suggested. "Unless you prefer to cause a scene?"

She clearly didn't like his endearment, yet knew he couldn't use her name if she was to preserve her anonymity. And she must have comprehended the wisdom of his proposal, for she nodded briefly.

When Quinn gestured toward the staircase at the rear of the gaming hall, however, she hesitated. "Upstairs, do you mean?"

On the floors above, carnal amusement was the prime entertainment.

"The pleasure rooms are the most appropriate choice if I am to command your services for the evening."

Her lovely mouth fell open, but when he added in explanation, "It will give the appearance of your being my chosen inamorata," she stifled her protest.

Before she could change her mind, Quinn swept out his hand, indicating for her to precede him. After another long study, she turned toward the stairs, the delicate line of her jaw set in a stubborn grimace.

Hiding a wry smile, he followed Miss Stratham. Anticipation lightened his previously sour mood and eased the physical pain of kissing an irresistible but resistant beauty, leaving him with a sense of unfulfilled promise.

His frustrating evening thus far was becoming more intriguing by the moment.

For updates, bonus content,
and sneak peeks at upcoming titles:

Visit the author's website
nicolejordanauthor.com

Find the author on Facebook
Facebook.com/nicolejordanauthor